UNLEASHED

A DARK ENEMIES TO LOVERS BRATVA ROMANCE

BRATVA KINGS

JANE HENRY

BRATVA KINGS

Unleashed: A Dark Enemies to Lovers Bratva Romance

This is a literary work of fiction. Any names, places or incidents are the product of the author's imagination. Similarities or resemblance to actual persons, living or dead, events or establishments, are solely coincidental.

ISBN: 978-1-961866-25-6

ISBN: 978-1-961866-42-3 (Alternate Cover Print Edition)

ACKNOWLEDGMENTS

A special thank you to the following individuals for their assistance during the production of this book:

- Wander Aguiar for providing cover model photography
- Sylvia Frost at *The Book Brander* for creating the cover design for *Unleashed*
- Haya in Designs for creating the cover design for the *Alternate Cover Print Edition* of *Unleashed*
- Dharma Kelleher for providing essential sensitivity reader services
- Steph White at *Kat's Literary Service* for editing the book through multiple drafts
- And finally, to Jessica & Michael at *J Henry Publishing Inc.* for always doing the things I can't so I can focus on writing the best book possible

Playlist

Scan QR Code to listen to the playlist for 'Unleashed: A Dark Enemies to Lovers Bratva Romance" on Spotify ©

A huge thank you to Noa Shalev for putting together this stunning playlist that captures Rafail + Polina's story so perfectly!

~Jane Henry

Follow Noa here:

https://www.instagram.com/solariaroyalblue/

SYNOPSIS

I wake up chained to the bed of a stranger.

He says I'm his wife.

I have nothing—no money. No friends.

No escape.

He's everything I never imagined: ruthless, calculating, feared. A beautiful monster with a face like a god's, cold and untouchable. A mafia kingpin whose wealth could buy empires and whose power makes the world tremble.

My captor.

My husband.

He vows to protect me at all cost, and in return demands... everything.

My body. My obedience. My submission.

Every touch, every brutal kiss stirs a dangerous desire neither of us can control. His words may be laced with venom, but his touch is fire, and every time he's near, I burn.

As days bleed into weeks, the fog of my past refuses to lift. The more I fight it, the harder I'm pulled into his orbit.

But as my memories start to unravel, I wonder—what if the past I can't remember holds the key to our destruction?

And when the truth finally comes out... will either of us survive?

CHAPTER 1

RAFAIL

I STARE AT THE COLD, empty altar in front of me. I demanded simplicity, fitting for nuptials in a godless church and a loveless union.

A vase of fading white roses, their petals curling at the edges, sits on the marble altar, the cloying scent nearly nauseating. Shadows cling to the high, vaulted ceilings, cast by candles that flicker in iron sconces. Above, darkened stained glass depicts saints and martyrs in muted colors, their hollow eyes staring down through fractured light.

A faint trace of incense lingers from Sunday mass, mixing with the damp smell of old stone and earth. Here, walls seem to absorb sound, muting every breath, every heartbeat.

Every secret.

The priest my uncle summoned stands before me, his face pale in the half-light, almost skeletal in the shadows. His fingers tremble around the ancient leather-bound book he holds to his chest; its gilded edges tarnished with age. His eyes dart between me and the altar as though he expects some divine wrath to strike at any moment.

He looks as if he's about to faint. Coward. They should have appointed someone more powerful to be in charge of a place named The Cathedral of the Eternal Martyrs, nestled in the heart of my family's hometown of Zalivka, a stone's throw from Moscow. I can almost feel the reproachful looks from their images in stained glass windows of forest green and blood red.

"Relax, Father," I say, my voice resonating in the cavernous church. I look away. "It's not your fault she pulled this stunt. I won't blame you." He blows out a breath as if I granted him a boon. Hell, maybe I did.

I can't help that my reputation precedes me. Sometimes I wish it didn't. It would make shit easier.

Eh, maybe not.

I can see the whites of his eyes and don't miss the way he's cleared his throat seventeen times in the past five minutes while I waited for my bride. She isn't coming. Not now, not ever.

The small crew of loyal friends and family who showed up to witness the ceremony sit still. No one dares to move. It looks like they're hardly breathing. Makes sense. They don't know if I'll burn this church to the fucking ground or call a mob to go after her.

Even I don't know how to react to being stood up by my future bride.

Mocked. Humiliated.

Disobeyed.

My hands clench into fists. When I find her... when I track down my bride and drag her back to me, I won't unleash my rage on her. No. I'll demand *penance* from her. Absolute surrender, body and soul, until she's broken and bound to me.

Out of nowhere, the raucous sound of someone pressing down on an organ breaks the silence. I turn abruptly, my gaze fixed on the choir loft, where a red-faced, flustered organist shakes her head.

"I'm so sorry, Mr. Kopolov. I stumbled. I'm sorry, sir. It won't happen again."

I shift away from her, dismissing her with a flick of my wrist. My fingers trace the edge of my cufflinks, an old family heirloom that once belonged to my father, and his father before him, and his father before him. I barely notice Semyon until he's already there, a quiet shadow moving into my peripheral vision.

Semyon stands just a few feet away, his lean frame blending into the dim lighting near the altar. I see the faint gleam of his glasses as he watches the room, his gaze sharp and calculating, missing nothing. He waits, a small shift of his gaze the only sign that he's asking permission to approach. Always the strategist, his mind whirs with the next step, cold and watchful. I jerk my chin in his direction, a signal. He ascends the three steps soundlessly, his calmness a stark contrast to the silent storm brewing inside me.

His footsteps echo on the marble floors as he walks up the three steps to where I stand by the altar. Younger than I am by a few years, he resembles me but with a leaner build.

"She isn't coming," I confirm in a low whisper. His eyes, ever unreadable, flicker toward me, then back to the entrance. I gave explicit instructions for her father to send her alone. I didn't want a ceremony, a big to-do. This was a transactional agreement, no more, no less.

Anissa fucking jilted me.

"Predictable," he murmurs, a faint edge of disinterest in his tone. He's always had a gift for neutrality I envied, a calmness that can unsettle even the most seasoned. His icy glare a promise of retribution. The Kopolov family will always stand as one.

I look away from him and stifle a curse. The air in the church is cold, musty, reminiscent of the catacombs I visited when I was a child. It was my favorite place to go, away from the hustle and bustle of family life. Away from my father's cruel, relentless oppression and my mother's quiet dignity.

The church seemed bigger then. Hell, everything did, even my father.

I wonder what it would feel like standing before him now if he were still here.

I look at Semyon and hold his frigid glare. My jaw locks, every muscle in my body conditioned to control, but underneath the calm, rage claws at me like a beast ready to break free. *No one* fucks with the Kopolov family, and the fact that Anissa made a mockery of us will not go unpunished.

My jaw tightens, my gaze calculating, but underneath it all, turmoil churns. I stare at the empty pews in the back of the church and watch as my brothers give each other quick, anxious glances, uncertain of what to do next.

I'll make her wish she hadn't. I'll make her wish she'd come like the obedient little girl she'll learn to be.

I'll make her regret the day she disobeyed me.

Why did she run?

How did she get away?

Only the sound of distant whispers and the faint rustle of clothing breaks the silence.

"If I can assist in any way..." the priest begins. One look from me, and the words die on his lips.

A low, dark, irreverent chuckle comes from the pews. I glance at my youngest brother. Where Semyon embodies cold precision, Rodion is the unpredictable wildfire none of us can fully control—to be honest, nor do I want to. It helps to have someone like him on my side. Leaning back with his arms spread along the back of the pew, that ever-present smirk on his lips and glint in his eyes promise me that one word is all it would take from me and he'd happily burn this church to the ground—and roast our enemies in the flames with glee—if I asked him. His loyalty borders on madness. He left his motorcycle parked outside and probably has more weapons on him than he has tats, and that's fucking saying something.

I shake my head, give Rodion a meaningful look, and turn back to the priest. "That won't be necessary, thank you."

The only people who will "assist" in what I have to do next are already here before me. Armed and ready.

My bride was here earlier. I saw her from a distance. I'm not supposed to see the bride before the ceremony, and even I'm not going to fuck with tradition. As my grandfather says, "Superstitions may be for children, but adults are old enough to follow them."

So I did my duty when I came here. I wouldn't tempt fate and look at my bride before the ceremony. I turned away when I saw the flurry of white fabric and a gauzy veil, when I heard the click of heels on the marble floor in the foyer. There were only two strangers here—my fiancée and her bodyguard.

She was here though. And now she's gone.

"Did anyone see her leave?" I say in a low voice to Semyon. I narrow my eyes on the doorway. "Is it possible that she was taken?"

Would somebody dare to take the bride I was about to marry? If anyone touched her, if anyone touched one hair on her fucking head—

"She wasn't taken," Semyon says. "We just found video surveillance from the basement. She left on her own. Paid off her guard, ripped her dress off, and ran."

Jesus.

I look to the priest. "You didn't tell us there was video surveillance in the basement, Father."

His heavy book falls to the floor with a clatter. He stammers as he tries to make an excuse. "I didn't know there was," he says. "That's not what I handle here. I'm sorry. If I knew, I would've told you—"

I shake my head. "Even I won't bring down the fury of hell by harming a hair on a man of the cloth in front of an altar, Father," I say quietly. "But don't test my patience. Or God's."

He clamps his mouth shut, his thin lips forming a perfect O before he swallows hard. Good. A wise man knows that sometimes silence speaks much louder than words.

I turn to face my family, my voice booming. "I'm calling an end."

My youngest sister, Zoya, jumps in her chair, though my sister Yana sits ramrod straight and doesn't move. She holds my gaze and gives me a slight nod of encouragement. Steadfast and loyal with sharp eyes that seem to take in everything around her, Yana has an aura of calm and stillness, though underneath, she is always thinking. Resilience is her middle name.

Zoya, however, is delicate and sensitive, and I feel like a dick for making her jump. Her kind, wide eyes are fixed on me. Shit. She's the only one who can make me feel guilty for raising my voice.

When she gives me her small, little smile, I swallow hard and nod, asking her forgiveness. She inclines her head, and her eyes grow soft—granting it.

One family, one fight—never apart.

I don't miss the way her fingers tighten on the small matte-black purse she carries, her own family heirloom. If I don't marry, I'll have no choice but to marry *her* off since Yana's already married. The thought fucking kills me. She's seventeen years old and still a child in my eyes. I can't do that to her. I fucking *won't*.

It is for her—it is for *all* of them—that I'm even here.

Beside her, my grandfather sits, his back ramrod straight, but his eyes warm with reassurance. One gnarled hand rests atop his cane, the other on Zoya's shoulder. His gaze tells me everything I need to know—he has total confidence that I'll handle this.

I stare out the stained-glass window, a brutal yet somehow beautiful depiction of the beheading of St. John the Baptist, and past it to the graveyard where my life changed forever.

It was there that I witnessed the burial of my parents. There that I buried my youth. There that I became the guardian of my siblings, inherited my family's wealth and every one of their enemies.

I made a vow that day that I would be buried alongside my parents before I would allow anyone to break our family apart.

And now Anissa has done that very thing. What would cause her to run from me, knowing my wrath was inevitable?

My knuckles whiten where I clench my fist, aching for the chance at retribution. I blow the breath out through my nose when footsteps approach me, and a heavy hand comes to my shoulder.

"We'll find her, Rafail."

I know it's my uncle based on the smell of his cologne before I even turn to see. His wife loves to doll him up like he's her personal plaything. Fuck, maybe he is. "We will. No one can hide from us in this city."

I turn and face the priest, pinning him to the spot, determined to maintain civility and control. "Tell me what I owe you for this farce, Father."

"No, no," he says magnanimously. "No charge, Mr. Kopolov. I didn't perform the duty that you hired me for."

I shake my head. "I appreciate that, Father, but it is exceptionally bad luck not to pay for services rendered by the Church. Even debts to God have to be paid, or we know the repercussions."

When he begins to protest, I hold my hand up, palm facing him, and his words die on his lips. "And you don't have to give me that whole thing about not performing any services yet. I won't bring down superstition on my house." I give him a humorless smile, reach into my pocket, and take out my wallet. I peel off a thick stack of bills and hand them to him. "I'll be making a donation to the food pantry as well."

Good luck comes from donations to the Church. I don't tempt fate.

"Thank you, Mr. Kopolov," the priest says, his voice trembling. The bastard probably expected the roof to cave in—or maybe expected me to hit him. He doesn't have to worry about that. I don't touch a man of the cloth unless he proves himself to deserve it.

"Thank you, thank you. And when you find your bride," he says, unnecessarily cheerful, "let me know right away, and I will perform the ceremony you came here for. I promise," he adds with a smile.

I nod and turn abruptly.

"Everyone back to the house," I unbutton my cufflinks and roll up my sleeves.

It's time to get to work.

My enemies circle like predators, sniffing for blood. And as soon as word gets out that I was jilted at the altar, they'll close in.

Our plan was to go back to my home and have dinner in the dining room. Now, instead of a celebratory dinner, we'll plan our next move. Not an attack but a strategy.

"We'll go back to my house. The food is ready. We'll discuss our options, scan through footage, and call in our allies. I want everyone to assemble within the hour."

My uncle bows his head to me. "Wise move. I would do the same," he says as if that should somehow console me. Right.

I snap my fingers, and my brothers rise, their movements swift, ready for war.

"Let's move."

CHAPTER 2

POLINA

"Polina," my mother says softly. Even though her soft gray eyes twinkle at me, she can't hide the fear that lies beneath layers of concern. She reaches across the table and holds my hand in hers, giving it a gentle squeeze before she lets it go. "You remember I told you as a child you could be anything, right?"

I groan. I know exactly what she's talking about and where she's going with this.

"I didn't mean that you should *actually try* everything before you settle down," she finishes, her voice with barely contained laughter.

"I know," I say with a sigh. I should laugh along with her. I remind myself that she loves me and wants what's best, but it stings being the butt of my family's jokes. Sucks being the only daughter in a family of men. I mean, knowing that no one, literally *no one,* will ever harm a hair on my head without bringing down the wrath of the entire Romanov brotherhood is... *kind of* nice, but...

But I know my mother's real fear. If my father were still alive, he'd be hard at work planning my arranged marriage. My eldest brother Mikhail, the head of our family, hasn't taken those steps... *yet.* But changing plans to a fourth college major isn't helping my case.

"I just don't know... what I want to do next. None of it has felt *right* yet. I feel like I'm trying beds like Goldilocks, and none of them fit yet. Do you know what I mean?"

My mother's eyes are soft but sad when she nods. With a sigh, she tucks a wisp of my platinum-blonde hair behind my ear. "I do know. But I also know that we don't have all the time in the world, my love. You know that too."

My mother was married at nineteen and knew her future before my parents even exchanged vows. She was destined to be the matriarch of the Romanov family, with no hope for a college education, a career, or anything more than being the wife of a Romanov. I know this, and I believe it's probably more for her sake than even mine that I feel such a strong need to find my place.

In the past years, since my brother took over as the head of my family, I've tried midwifery, criminology—yes, the irony was not lost on me—and even women's studies. None of them suited me or felt appropriate for the youngest daughter in a family of powerful, old-fashioned Russian men.

Maybe I should've studied finance.

"You do you, babe," my sister-in-law Harper says, winking at me from across the room. She lifts a decanter of amber liquid and pours some over a glass full of ice.

"Drink?" she says with a smile. I shake my head. I don't like to drink. Since so much of my life whirls out of my grasp, I clutch at whatever modicum of control I can maintain.

"I'm good, thanks."

"Are you sure this one is really Russian?" Harper says, winking at my mother. "She doesn't even drink vodka."

"Are you sure this one's really Italian?" I quip, rolling my eyes. "She doesn't even eat cheese."

"You know that I love cheese," Harper whines. "It just doesn't like *me*," she adds sadly.

"I like you just fine," my brother Aleksandr says as he enters the room and walks up to his wife. He slides an arm around her waist, tugs her to his chest, and plants a soft kiss on her forehead.

"Ugh," I say sarcastically. "Get a room."

"Jealous much?" Aleks says with a sly smile. Like my other brothers, he looks nothing like me. Unable to have children but determined to build a family legacy, my parents adopted. Whereas I'm fair and so blonde my hair is nearly white, my brother Aleks is classically tall, dark, and handsome. His gorgeous Italian bride, Harper, stares at him as if he hung the moon.

"I'm not jealous of you lovebirds," I lie. I am totally jealous of those two lovebirds. "I just think that sometimes—"

The study door opens with a bang. Harper startles, and her glass crashes to the floor, but nobody moves. Mikhail, my oldest brother, stands in the doorway, and we all know instantly that something is terribly wrong.

My mother is on her feet, but her voice doesn't waver. Ekaterina Romanova is never ruffled. I swallow and rethink my decision on the vodka.

"Misha," Mom says softly, the one word holding a world of questions. She only calls him his pet name—*Misha*—when she's afraid. We all know it could be anything. Over the past few years, as my family has risen to power, we've encountered formidable rivals and formed dangerous alliances.

We've also practiced self-defense when we were attacked.

I make a quick mental tally of the weapons I have on me.

But Mikhail doesn't look at my mother. He doesn't look at my brother Aleksandr or Harper. His eyes bore straight into mine.

Shit.

"Polina, you're in danger. You have to go."

The skin at the back of my neck crawls, and a shiver runs down my spine. It's obviously not the first time my family's been in danger. Hell, we've been in so many dangerous situations, I'm damn used to it by now. But it's the first time I've ever seen fear in Mikhail's eyes, and I've seen the man go through a lot. And it's definitely the first time his fear was for... me.

"What is it, Mikhail?" I ask, thankful that my voice doesn't waver either. I will face whatever this is head-on. I will not cower.

"You have to go away. Aria's discovered something, and you're not safe here anymore." Mikhail's wife Aria, a world-class hacker, misses nothing.

"Be more specific, please," I say. Outside the window, storm clouds rush in. The gray of early evening has turned dark, and a half-moon illuminates the garden outside my mother's family home. I almost expect a werewolf to howl. I shiver, clutching the ratty hoodie I've strewn over my shoulders closer around me.

"Manuel Soloto, head of the cartel in Colombia. He's after you. Remember that Isabella said you weren't safe here anymore?"

"Yes, but I thought she said—"

Mikhail shakes his head. "You thought he changed his mind? That he got married and forgot about you? It was a lie. A ploy. He's not forgotten about you. He's coming after you."

I try to laugh it off, but I fail. "But you guys... You always protect me. We have a whole team of bodyguards. This house is practically a fortress. And you're telling me—"

"Polina," Aleksandr snaps. He never raises his voice to me, but now he almost sounds like our father. I turn and stare at him. "Don't you know that if Mikhail is telling you you're not safe, you can trust him? You know that he would do everything in his power to protect you. If he's telling you you're not safe, you have to go... quickly. This isn't the time to talk back."

Jesus. I wrap an arm around my chest and squeeze my shoulder absently.

"I'm supposed to start my classes tomorrow."

"Who cares about your classes?" Mikhail snaps. "This is what, the tenth time you've picked up a different study anyway?"

Tears burn at the back of my eyes, but I blink them away. It's unlike him to be harsh with me like this. I know he's afraid, but he doesn't have to be a dick.

"You heard me," he says. "We have a bunker in Manhattan."

"A bunker?" I stare, and my mouth falls open. "Are you serious right now?"

I close my mouth because my mother is giving me that *look*. It's very rare for her to put her foot down, but I can tell by the narrowness of her eyes and the tightness of her lips that she's on the cusp of it.

And right then, I hate my life. I hate it so hard. Yes, I have a family that loves me. Brothers, sisters-in-law, nieces, and nephews. I live in a beautiful, luxurious home. I belong here; I'm one of them, and still… I can't… be myself. I can't be *normal*.

I'd give anything to escape my brothers' overbearing protection and the strict control of my family. I dream of finding freedom and love on my own terms, without being passed around and forced into something I don't want. I want independence, a life where I can make my own choices. And yes, they might tease me for studying one thing after another, but I am *so tired* of being treated like a fragile object and kept in this gilded cage. I want to break free from the oppression so badly it hurts.

"No, Mikhail," my mother says quietly. She and Mikhail share a look. She never contradicts him. Nobody does. "She'll be safer in Moscow. You know she will. I have contacts there. We both do."

I expect him to refuse her, but instead, he runs a hand through his hair. Moscow is better than a *bunker*.

"How long do we have?" she asks.

"An hour," Mikhail says. "He's already on his way."

I stare, my belly churning. I close my eyes and kiss my hopes and dreams goodbye. I'm not going to school tomorrow, that's for sure.

"Polina Romanova, did you hear me?" Mikhail snaps at me.

Oh, for *fuck's* sake. "You're not my father!" I yell at him.

My mother gasps. "Polina..."

"No," I say, holding my ground. "He doesn't get to talk to me that way."

"This is not the time for you to pull this bullshit," Mikhail growls, his golden skin turning a faint shade of red. He's barely holding onto his anger.

God, I love my brothers, but you can absolutely hate and love somebody at the same time.

I clench my teeth. "Don't *talk* to me that way."

He throws his hands up in the air. "I'm going to secure the border. I'm going to make sure that we're safe. Talk some damn sense into her," he snaps at my mother before he storms away.

Harper stares at me, her eyes wide. "What will Soloto do if he gets you?" she says in a small voice. She was married to my brother in an arranged marriage, sight unseen. And that worked out... well. Eventually. Maybe this man...

"We won't talk about that," Aleksandr says quietly. "He has no interest in marrying her, Harper." His voice lowers. "He has no interest in doing anything that we would ever allow anybody to do to her."

The chilling sound of his voice sobers me. I have to escape, whether I want to or not. Today is not the day I will break free from my brothers' domineering ways.

"Mikhail told me to get you ready," my mother says quietly as she lays a hand on my arm. "I already had a bag packed in case something like this happened." She knew. My mother knew. "On the floor of my closet is an ivory bag. There's a silver luggage tag on it. That's yours." She draws in a breath. "The one next to it is mine. Go get both of them."

"You are going with me?" I ask, my heart pounding. "Yes," she says softly. "But I have some phone calls I need to make. Go, Polina. Get the bags. We're going to Moscow."

CHAPTER 3

RAFAIL

"Is she alone?"

"Of course she isn't," Semyon says with an eye roll and icy glare. "She's got an old lady with her and two guards."

"Old lady?" It's illogical, frankly, unless she's employing the classic tactic of hiding in plain sight, exactly where she's least expected. Right in the heart of Moscow, within walking distance of Zalivka.

"Are you *sure* this is the right person?" I finger the cufflinks in my pocket, my good luck charms. I don't go anywhere without them.

Semyon's eyes narrow at me as he slowly pushes his glasses further up his nose. He *never* makes mistakes. His precision is perfect in damn near everything he does. My right-hand man, Semyon is calm and pragmatic, a master of calculated methods and, when he executes, foolproof. We're identical when it comes to brute force and fear as an effective tactic, but Semyon is the strategist, always seeing several moves ahead.

"Of course I'm right. Do I make mistakes?"

Arrogant, yeah, but he knows his shit. I give him a sharp look as he scrolls through footage and notes on his phone.

Tall and muscular with sharp, angular features, Semyon's demeanor is cold but composed. He's protective of our younger siblings, prone to showing his care through actions and not words. The cool technician behind our empire's most successful operations. I know what he's put on the line for our family. I know what I have. I know that both of us prioritize our family's stability above all else, and even though I am the eldest and was technically guardian of the rest, he's always pulled his own weight.

"Remember why we're here," Semyon reminds me, always the foil to my intensity. He checks his watch, a force of habit, before he glances at the specs of our location on his phone. "And remember who's watching. Tempting as it may be, you can't punish her on the streets of Moscow, Rafail, no matter how badly you want to." His voice drops, and his eyes grow ice-cold. "No matter how much she deserves it. Save that for when you get her back to your house."

I breathe in through my nose, and I know he's right. I didn't get to where I am by being hardheaded and impulsive. That would be Rodion, who is standing behind me now, casually flipping a switchblade open and closed.

"Put that away," I snap. "Jesus." Always the reckless one, though he'd call it courageous, and always the one to land on his two fucking feet like a cat. But thankfully, he has some respect for me.

I narrow my eyes at him. "*Rodion*." He blows out a breath and, with great reluctance, tucks his knife away. He loves his fucking weapons. Some assholes jerk off to pinups or porn, but I swear to fuck, Rodion would stroke one off with his handgun if he could.

"What's your plan?" he says, not bothering to hide a note of jealousy in his tone. "Take her back. Tie her up." He wriggles his brows. "Punish her before you do dirty things to her?"

My vision blurs as rage thrums through my veins. "She fucked over our family," I say with cold deliberation. "I *will* bring her back. I *will* tie her up. And I *will* punish her."

"Fuck, stop bragging," Rodion groans. Kinky bastard.

"And keep in mind she'll be your wife," Semyon says quietly. "It might be in your best interest to keep it... *mildly* cordial."

"And it might be in my best interest to teach her who is the man of this fucking house," I say with chilling decision.

I'll show her in vivid detail why no one escapes me. I'll make her beg for mercy. I'll strip her of every last defense, every vestige of defiance, until she doesn't know where pain ends and pleasure begins. She'll learn her place—beneath me, pleading, desperate, begging. And when I finally claim her, I'll take my sweet time, every stroke a reminder of the vows she tried to escape.

Semyon holds a hand up, his gaze razor-sharp and focused ahead of us. "There she is," he murmurs. "Look."

The air is tense but chilly. Winter comes to Moscow and neighboring cities with a vengeance. I turn toward the icy cold and look for her.

What is she doing here? When my uncle got word that she'd been spotted, we left dinner immediately. My stomach growls with hunger.

Dressed in all black, we hide in the alleyway bordering an empty square. A bird crows overhead, and behind closed doors, someone plays the violin.

Her shadow passes by a first-floor window. I've stared at those pictures in my file so many times she's begun to haunt my dreams. The Siberian princess, she's called. A delicate, precious jewel that I'm going to break.

Yeah. That's her.

Originally from Siberia, she's in her early twenties, so a little older than my sister Zoya. Slender and graceful, she has delicate, aristocratic features and a pale, snow-like complexion. Her long, almost white-blonde hair spills down her back like moonlight, and the pictures I've seen show ethereal blue eyes that reveal a deep well of emotion. Just by looking at her picture, you wouldn't think she was the type to run away from someone at the altar. She seems far too clever for such a reckless, desperate move.

I wonder what she thinks about me.

She appears fragile, almost delicate, but I sense a fiery spirit. A fiery spirit I'm going to fucking tame.

And then something nearly miraculous happens. We step back when she steps onto the pavilion alone. No old lady, no guards, just my beautiful, willful bride. She stands and looks out, not even turning in our direction, and then she turns back and faces her room. Her voice carries in the cold, dark night.

"I'm going for a walk," she says quietly. No one objects. The older woman is talking with the guards as she looks from side to side. Maybe it's a stroke of luck, or maybe fate is playing its hand and uniting us, but I watch in surprise as she walks down the staircase alone.

The guards are talking with the lady as she quickly slips out.

She's *mine.* I haven't seen her this close before, but now that I am, I note the pale canvas of her skin, her thick, nearly white hair, the delicate bones in her wrists, and the slender breadth of her shoulders. The need to claim her claws at me with inhuman strength.

I want to take her. Punish her for betrayal, for putting my family and my entire empire at risk. At the same time, I want to grab her by her delicate shoulders and shake her. How careless—putting herself on display like this, bathed in moonlight—she's a vulnerable target, ripe for the picking.

Doesn't she know I'm looking for her? Does she have no sense of self-preservation? I watch as she turns away, her delicate hand brushing against her cheek.

Is she... *crying*? Does she have any remorse?

Or does she know any semblance of freedom she has is about to be snatched away?

"Surround the perimeter," I snap. "I want every exit secured."

But it's unnecessary. She seems completely oblivious to the fact that I'm here.

"Are you *sure* this is her?" I ask Semyon. "She doesn't look like she's afraid."

Maybe she hasn't quite registered the danger she's in.

"How could it not be her? She's identical to the pictures we have."

"She is." She looks exactly like the woman in the picture. The one I've been watching. I've memorized the slender curve of her neck and imagined my face between her breasts. I've fantasized about that long, silky hair wrapped around my thick fingers before I pull it. The woman is grace personified. Her skin is as pale as the roses she left fading on our altar. *Our* altar. The one that she abandoned. And now she's mine. She is the one I will lay sacrifices upon in atonement.

The older woman comes onto the porch. They speak rapidly in Russian, and my bride laughs. Anger flares in my chest. How could she be so unconcerned? How can she be so blasé about what she's done?

The older woman turns sharply when someone calls her. "No, no, not that one," she says in English. She rushes away, and my bride follows. I know before she makes her decision what she's going to do, and I can't believe my luck. The glances, the way she grabs her little bag, the way she looks from side to side tell me all I need to know.

She tips her head into the air, pulls her shoulders back, and breathes in deeply as if, finally, she has some freedom.

"Enjoy that last taste of freedom," I say under my breath. "It's the last you'll ever have."

If she were mine—no, she *is* mine—she's going to learn that a little jaunt in the woods is out of the question.

I run my thumb along the silk strands in my pocket, ready to bind my bride's wrists and ankles. I'm hard as fuck just imagining that... that, and so much more.

I'll bring her back where she belongs—home, with me. I'll teach her that her place is by my side, where she can't run or hide again. I can see it now—that pale, porcelain skin tinged pink as she blushes, her lips parted, gasping for breath when my hands wrapped around her neck, just enough to remind her who I am, just enough so she knows she's at my mercy. I can already feel the heat of her punished ass against me when I fuck her, her face pressed into the sheets, and my hand on her back, holding her down. She'll think she's on the brink of insanity, begging for release, but I'll keep her right there as long as I need to make sure she feels her punishment.

I'll claim every inch of her perfect, sweet body. I'll make her shudder beneath me, scream my name while she claws my back and begs for mercy I won't grant until she knows she's *mine*. She'll feel it in her bones and crave my control. When I'm done, she'll never again question who owns her.

Without warning, six enormous Russian men step outside. They speak into their walkie-talkies, their voices hard. They fucked up, letting her out of their sight. I would punish the shit out of them for that.

"Jesus. *Go*. I don't know why you're waiting," Rodion says.

He's the fucking wild card of the family. Charming, reckless, impulsive—he's been in trouble since I've known him, and he made my job as his guardian that much harder. But for him, his natural charisma allows him to get out of damn near everything. His insatiable thirst for thrills and aversion to responsibility keep me on my toes.

I ponder what he says for half a minute. I could rush in, claim her for my own, fight them. Drag her back by her fucking hair and put a bullet between the eyes of any man who tried to stop us...

"Because I understand the blowback to the rest of us. I like to have self-control, Rodion."

He narrows his eyes at me. "If that were me, I wouldn't show weakness. I'm not the kid you think I am anymore, Rafail."

I grit my teeth and go to respond, but Semyon gets to him first.

"Rafail is the leader in the underworld and our family, Rodi," Semyon says coldly. "He knows better than to act recklessly."

I watch as her guards bring her back inside. She's a feisty one, snapping at them in Russian. I hear a door slam. I run my fingers over the silky threads of the bonds in my pocket once more, and I make my plan.

CHAPTER 4

POLINA

It's beautiful here in Moscow, but I don't feel like I belong. I want to be back home, in The Cove, where I was raised. I long for the salty sea air, the simpler world that was black and white and so familiar. Even though my family, most notably my oldest brother, is driving me crazy, I like it there. My brothers have all married, and I adore their wives. We're a tight-knit group, and I love all of my sisters-in-law. I miss them.

And it's interesting to see my mother in Moscow. She has history here—friends and some family, and everybody wants to see her. She wants to keep our presence quiet, though, so this time, our visit is almost secretive. We are in a small apartment on the outskirts of Moscow, which is admittedly a nice change. I'm used to living in a large home, with lots of people who work for us, and it's strangely nice to do things like prepare my own meals and know that the only people working for us are our bodyguards.

It's impossible to ask for freedom from our vigilant guards. I couldn't escape their watchful eyes if I tried. They're here to keep me safe.

It's not often that I see fear in my brother's eyes. But he wasn't just afraid—he was terrified. The entire way here, I kept looking over my shoulder.

Here in Moscow, I'm unfamiliar with the guards—older men, friends of my mother's. She says they worked with my father back in the day. I'm a little surprised by these other people my mother has chosen because they're not as agile and young as the guards back at home. But there's a brutal efficiency I haven't seen before.

One of them only speaks Russian, which pleases my mother. She loves her native tongue, and we rarely speak it at home. He's taller than I am, with a large frame, but when you look closely, there are liver spots on his hands, and his skin looks like well-worn leather. Still, there's a cold calculation in his eyes that tells me he will stop at nothing to do his job. And I suppose that's what my brothers want the most. The other is taller, his gray hair slicked back from a broad forehead. Scars run along his cheek, down his neck, and under the shirt that he wears close to his skin. He's a soldier who's proved himself in battle, though the war he fought was probably decades ago. Both men don't speak to us. Both stand guard. Both are like shadows that never quite go away.

And both of them need to sleep, which works well for me.

I'm not foolish or impulsive, but I do like some space, and I can't be blamed if I want to go for a little walk.

So early on a Friday morning, two days after we arrive in Moscow, I get out of bed and into a pair of running pants and a tank top. It's beautiful here in Moscow in the early morning, especially in the secluded part where we are. Early mornings feel magical, as though the world holds its breath for daybreak.

When I was a little girl, I used to pretend that the fairies danced at dawn, sprinkling fairy dust on dew. Aleksandr, the pragmatic brother of mine, would explain in brutally scientific terms what really happened, but I just told myself that he was ignorant of the ways of the fae. And even now, as an adult, I like to imagine the way my breath becomes vapor, the early morning fog swallows my footsteps, and the way even my thoughts seem to tiptoe from one to the other signifies that there is something magical about early morning.

So I slip out the door and lace up the running shoes I left in the entryway.

Of course, it shouldn't surprise me that I don't get too far.

"Where do you think you're going?" a raspy voice says in Russian behind me. I grit my teeth.

"Out for a run. Care to join me?"

"I don't run, so neither do you."

Oh no, he does not. "I do, so I guess you better get your shit together."

He curses behind me when I start to warm up. And thankfully, he's right. He doesn't run. He sucks at it.

Finally, a little taste of freedom. I can outrun this bastard.

Even if he does catch me, I have defense training that my sister-in-law Isabella taught me, thank you very much.

The first mile always makes me feel like I am suffocating, but I lean into it, sucking wind and waiting for that moment to hit—and then it does. I hit my stride. Adrenaline courses through me. I breathe more freely, sweat knits my brow, and an early morning wind kisses my skin. *This.* Freedom. There's something about pushing my body, the wind in my hair, the way my skin feels, that makes me feel alive.

My guard calls out after me, but I toss over my shoulder, "If you want to stay close to me, pick up the fucking pace."

I turn the corner, and sunlight nearly blinds me. The sun has begun to rise, orange fingers of light kissing the ground around me. It's beautiful. Pregnant with possibility, but at the same time, as the sunrise paints the sky in vivid orange and yellow, I become aware of the fact that I'm not alone, and it's definitely not my bodyguard who's following me.

A second pair of footsteps matches mine. No, not matches.

The person behind me is running faster than I am.

My heart kicks up because now I have a dilemma. I have to run slower for my guard to catch up, but whoever's behind me will catch up first.

I've made a mistake. A grave, grave mistake.

Ahead of me lies a patch of green, a tiny park nestled in a secluded area of Moscow, flanked on either side by brick buildings. I could rent one of the buildings, but every residence is closed right now. Running to the park would at least give me a view of whoever's following me. I take a sharp left, the smell of flowers filling my senses. An older woman with a cane in her right hand holds a dog leash in her left. Her tiny dog looks at us in surprise and yaps. I run right past, glancing behind me.

Shit. I wasn't wrong. My pulse spikes. A man runs behind me, wearing a sleeveless white tank T-shirt, baggy faded blue Adidas track pants and running shoes. I don't take the time to look too closely, but from here, I can tell he's built—muscled and covered in ink. *Fuck.*

He's chasing me.

Even as I run, I notice how every passerby looks right past me, their attention fixed on the man pursuing me. Do they have no idea what he's doing? One young woman flicks her hair over her shoulder as if trying to catch his attention, and another pair of women stop talking mid-sentence. One makes a low growl of approval, and the other covers her mouth, giggling, her eyes fixated on the paragon of masculine perfection who's chasing... *me.*

My god, don't they see how dangerous he is? Or is that what makes them blind to the peril I'm in?

I duck under a vine-covered trellis, my mind racing. At first, when I heard those footsteps, I went through the usual doubts. Maybe it's just somebody going for a run. Maybe he doesn't know who I am. But one look at that man and I knew that all of my fears were right—he knows me, and he's after me, and he's nothing but raw, alpha male with a mission.

Fuck. I didn't bring a weapon with me. But I know how to get away if he catches me. What else can I do? One more glance over my shoulder, and this time, I realize he's close enough to meet my eyes. Close enough that his gaze locks onto mine—dark, menacing... swallowing me whole.

Raw fear lances through my chest the moment his dark eyes connect with mine. I'm too far to make out the color, but it doesn't matter. They're dark and bottomless, an abyss ready to pull me under. Something about his gaze reaches deep inside me, an invisible noose around my throat. It isn't just the threat but the raw power, the absolute control that burns in his eyes, daring me to defy him. My pulse races, and heat rises to the surface of my skin. He's not just watching me. He's *after* me with a marksman's laser focus. Nothing about that look tells me I have a chance of escape. It's a promise that he'll catch me—and when he does, I'll be wholly at his mercy.

My adrenaline spikes, and I try to run faster. But it's not fast enough. He isn't even winded, and I feel as if my lungs are going to burst. It looks like he's jogging.

A busy street. I look over my shoulder again, and he's so close to me now, I can see the broad expanse of his shoulders, slicked with sweat, the corded muscles of his arms and chest. To my right, two women in workout clothes jog at a slow pace. One smiles at the other and murmurs something, and the two women look appreciatively at the man behind me. There's something about him that says *raw, attractive male—preen yourselves, ladies.* Do they not see the menace in his face?

Oh god... What does he have wrapped around his hand? A rope? Is that a *chain*?

"Stop!" he commands, his voice a deep, low growl. Another woman nearby watches him in wide-eyed wonder, awe written in her features. Yes, yes, he's sexy, masculine perfection, but don't they realize he's dangerous?

I keep running. "I know who you are. You know what you did. Stop."

What?

There's nowhere else to go. Ahead of me are the red-brick walls of the Kremlin, the symbol of Russian power and authority. The sight of guards patrolling in front of me enhances my desperate need for help.

Why did I protest my brothers' oppressive protection so much? I'd give anything for one of them right now.

In front of me I see a busy street, early morning commuters already racing to get to the office.

I decide to make a run for it when the unthinkable happens—he catches me. I scream when he grabs me by the waist from behind and pulls me against the rock-hard wall of his chest. I scream again, fighting against him, when a heavy, rough hand crashes against my mouth. A man ahead of me turns and starts our way. "Hey—" he begins, but he takes one look at my captor's face and *runs*.

Oh my god.

His breath is hot on my neck as he whispers to me, "Did you really think you'd be able to get away from me?"

Within seconds, he's ducked us both in a darkened alley near a brick building. I'm struggling, but it's useless. He's too strong for me, and everything I've learned about self-defense flies straight out of my head.

I struggle in his grip when he pins my wrist about my head, pressing me to the cold, rough brick. Our faces come dangerously close. It's strange because he looks as if he... as if he knows me. This is no random attack. But I've never seen this man in my life—I would remember someone so devastatingly masculine, handsome, and *terrifying*.

I squirm when I feel heat radiating off him. "You fucked up," he says, shaking his head at me with dark eyes that promise wicked retribution. "You'll pay for what you've done."

"Me?" I gasp. "I don't even know who you are."

He takes a moment to snarl in fury at me, but it's all that I need—that one split second. I aim for his groin but barely land the blow. *Shit*. He fumbles, grasping for me, but I'm already sprinting toward the street.

People. Cars. Crowds.

I have to cross the street and hope that he gets caught behind in traffic. I can make it. I can make it if I push with the last bit of energy I have, and then once I get into the street, I can melt into the crowds milling around Red Square. I know I can. I dash into the street and hear the blast of a horn. A crash. Blistering, searing pain, a deep bellow of rage behind me... then darkness.

CHAPTER 5

POLINA

I DON'T EVER REMEMBER FEELING so much pain—it's carved into my bones, relentless and unforgiving. Crushing. My head feels three times its normal size, and my shoulder and arm throb relentlessly. The skin on my face stings, and something is very, very wrong with my leg.

What happened? Where am I? I try to recall something that will bring reassurance but can't.

But there's one question that troubles me far more than the pain does: *Who am I?*

I hear voices talking over me but not to me because they think I'm still asleep. Am I still asleep? My stomach roils with something like hunger, and my mouth waters. I feel as if I'm going to be sick. I try to open my eyes, but they feel too heavy. One thing is clear—at least I'm not dead. It doesn't seem possible that death and pain this intense can coexist. Or maybe that's all there is—maybe there's nothing but pain after death.

I try to sleep. It's minutes, hours, maybe days later when I try to open my eyes again. I need answers. Who am I, and why does it feel like everything I knew has slipped away?

This time, I'm able to open my eyes a bit, even though it seems to take every single ounce of my energy. I see someone sitting in front of me, with long, auburn hair that I don't recognize, and the inside of a well-appointed room that's equally unfamiliar. I look down at my body, hoping that I will recognize something. I stare at my hands. The fingers are long, the nails trimmed, painted with a tip of white. What's that called? I can't remember. There's a white sheet over me, and on the left side, something bulges underneath the sheet. Why is my left side so much bigger than my right? I'm aware of deep voices and high-pitched voices, but none are familiar. It terrifies me because *nothing* is familiar.

"I think she's waking."

I blink and open my eyes again and realize what I thought I was seeing was just in my imagination, my half-conscious awareness. Because my hands are *not* in front of me. They are tied to the bed, shackled with metal handcuffs. I gasp and try to move my legs and realize they are cuffed too.

I open my mouth to speak, but nothing comes out.

"Don't fight it." The voice belongs to the small woman at my bedside. I don't even know if I can call her a woman. Girl? She's definitely younger than I am, but I couldn't tell you my age, no matter what you offered me. "Don't speak right now. You're in recovery."

Recovery from... what? Did I have surgery? That must be it. I had surgery, and they gave me medicine that made my brain forget everything for a little bit. I breathe through my nose and exhale. In a little while, it will come back. I'll remember why I'm here.

What is my name? I never knew how important it was to remember my name until I couldn't.

I yank my wrist, but the metal is unyielding. I pull my ankles, and it's the same thing. I need help. I ignore her advice because I have something to say.

"Why am I like this?" My voice wobbles.

The young woman looks concerned.

"You really don't know?"

I shake my head, but it hurts. It feels like my brain is going to explode out of my skull.

"Never mind that. We'll have time to get to that. Tell me, are you in pain?"

Finally, something I can answer. "Yes. So much pain." The words come out in Russian.

I speak Russian. I understand Russian. Something I can hold onto.

"She needs morphine," the young girl says quietly. I didn't notice the other person in the room, dressed in white.

"No," I say, my voice shaky. I know that morphine will make me disoriented, and I don't need to be more disoriented.

The young woman, who stands in the shadows—I don't

know who she is, stares at a man beside her. I blink. I didn't realize anyone else was in the room. "Sir?"

She's asking him for permission? Wait. Do I know that man? He's tall and broad and towers over the two women.

"No morphine," he says in a low growl of a voice. "No painkillers at all."

No painkillers? I'm bound to this bed and not allowed anything for the pain. A moment ago, I contemplated not having them at all, but being disallowed them is another level of cruel. I stare at the man, trying to place him, but he's shadowed and unfamiliar.

The girl's voice trembles as she protests. "Rafail, that's too cruel."

I don't know the name Rafail. But I don't even know *my* name.

"Since when do I give a shit about that?" he snarls, turning away from the deprecating look she gives him.

"Please," I say, my voice trembling. "Someone tell me how I got here. Who I am. What happened?"

The man steps out of the shadows. I note the sharp angle of his jaw, the utter coldness in his cruel eyes. For some reason, he's vibrating with barely controlled rage, directed straight at *me*.

"Wait," the woman says with concern. "She doesn't know who she is."

His unconcerned shrug troubles me. "Not out of the ordinary." Turning back to the woman in white, he orders, "Give her water and food so she can keep her energy up. *No* morphine."

I watch as she prepares a cocktail of sorts for me with deft fingers.

Questions spin through my mind. I open my mouth to speak to the woman, but he's watching me. I don't trust anyone in this room. My instincts tell me I can at least trust the gentle one, but I don't even know who I am. Can I even trust my instincts?

While they talk in low voices among themselves, I note everything I can. First, I am shackled to a bed. The woman next to me is friendly enough, but she obeys the big, muscled man.

That guy is hot. Devastatingly, dangerously handsome, if cruel. Decidedly used to getting his way it seems, and for some reason, which is wildly confusing to me, he hates me. He's obviously powerful, so I can only assume I've done something to offend him. Too bad I have no idea what that is.

But because this young woman next to me seems like an ally, I can maybe use her kindness to my advantage.

I push through the discomfort and use my voice. It hurts. Who knew that it could actually hurt to speak? But my chest tightens, and my throat is dry. "How long have I been here?" I begin with an easy question. Something that should be simple enough for her to answer without fearing the wrath of the man.

She leans in, her voice kind. "You came here last night, and you've slept all day."

Not long, then. How did I get here?

When he stalks toward me, the young girl sits up straighter, her eyes wide in fear. "Rafail," she says, pleading.

"You know what she did. I'm not going to be gentle," he says in a growl. "Do I need to excuse you from her care?"

"No," she whispers, her face pained as she turns away.

"I promise. I won't hurt her in front of you."

I blink in shock. In front of her? What will he do when he has me alone?

He looms over me like a fire-breathing dragon, and I shrink back on the sheets. *I'm not going to be gentle.* Who is he? Who am *I*? What did I do that's infuriated him?

He's tall and unyielding, his large frame filling the space between us. I'm dwarfed by him. His face is all sharp angles and hard edges—dark-brown eyes glaring at me, a chiseled jaw clenched in barely contained rage, a full mouth pressed into a cruel line as if he's holding back a thousand things he wants to hurl at me. Dark stubble graces his sharp jawline, adding a raw, dangerous, masculine edge to his flawless appearance.

His eyes are dark and intense, a deep, bottomless black that seems to drink everything in, pinning me in place. They're cold, and yet, something like fire burns in their depths. Broad shoulders fill out a pressed white dress shirt, his muscles straining against the fabric. A man built for dominance. Strength. A man made for *War*.

I stare at his arms corded with muscle, large, capable hands, one clenched at his side while the other rests on the edge of the bed, trapping me as if the handcuffs aren't enough. Leaning over, he inspects my injuries in silence, as if... as if I belong to him. It's disconcerting. No, it's terrifying.

"Who are you?" I whisper when he brushes his fingers along my jaw, his thumb grazing my lips. Fear spikes my pulse, and I try to turn away but can't. The touch is so... intimate. Possessive. And he's a stranger to me.

A shadow crosses his features. Frowning, he asks me, "You really don't know?"

I shake my head. Pain explodes in my skull and along the back of my neck. I wince.

Moving his hand to cup my cheek, he whispers to me, "All you need to know is that you're mine, and you're not going anywhere now."

I shiver at his touch, consumed with an odd mixture of fear and curiosity. Before he releases me, he brushes a kiss to my forehead, but it doesn't feel tender. It's like he's showing me that he *can*. A searing touch that feels more like a statement than a caress, more like a claim than affection.

Turning, he stalks to the door, leaving me with the young woman. Girl?

"I'm in so much pain," I say in a low voice to the young woman. "Do you really think it necessary for me to be shackled to this bed?"

"I think it's necessary to do whatever my brother tells me to do," she says in a little voice. "And soon you'll learn that's true for you too."

Her brother. Now we're getting somewhere.

I press on. "It's uncomfortable being chained like this."

With a look of chagrin, she wrings her hand for a fraction of a second before she nods. "Yes, I know. I'm sorry. I really can't let you go."

Tears blind my eyes. I don't ever recall feeling this helpless, but then again, I don't recall much of anything. It's like waking from a nightmare only to realize you're still dreaming.

I take a shaky breath and let it out.

"What's your name?" I ask quietly. Can she answer that? Her brown eyes are as soft as a doe's, her thin face pinched.

"Zoya," she whispers.

I ask her the question that plagues me, my voice trembling. "What's mine?"

CHAPTER 6

RAFAIL

I WALK the halls outside the guest room where I have my bride imprisoned.

Zoya thanked me for allowing her to take care of her, so maybe it was the right choice. When we brought her home, she begged me. My youngest sister gets away with everything. I can't help it. She was just a child when our parents died, and she's always looked to me for guidance. She's the only innocent one in our family.

Unlike the others, Zoya was too young to remember our parents' deaths and grew up insulated from the darker dealings of our family life. She's sweet, naïve, shielded from the underworld, and sometimes I wonder if she knows more than she lets on. Zoya has a heart and is deeply empathetic —somebody needs to be.

My brothers tell me that I baby her, that I hold them to standards I don't hold her or my sister Yana to. Maybe they're right. Perhaps I do, and I am protective of her. So when she asked me to take care of my bride, I let her. Somebody needs to keep a thread of humanity around here. Fuck knows I'm not the one who will. I think they're particularly angry that I'm softer on Yana, but I have good reason. She's fought an uphill battle most her life, and for her, more so than the rest of us, my father's demise was at least in part a stroke of luck.

My phone buzzes with a text. I open it

Zoya
Rafail, she really doesn't know who she is.
What do I do?

She doesn't know who she is? What?

I text her back.

"Wait. I want to test that theory."

She doesn't respond. She doesn't know who she is? I need to get outside and get some fresh air. This is the first time I've left her bedside since I brought her home last night. I needed to update my brothers.

I look out the large windows near the foyer. Each floor has a balcony that overlooks the lush green grass below. I like to be on a balcony when I need to think, when I need to plan. The secluded cottage, the family estate passed onto me and left in my care, is located on the outskirts of Moscow in Zalivka, far enough from the public eye to give us privacy and security but close enough to the city for me to manage everything. It's surrounded by acres of private land and forests—a natural barrier that gives it a fortress-like atmosphere. And I love it.

I've done what I could to make this place a fortress, a stronghold, but still a family home despite the imposing walls, thick, wrought-iron gates, and maze-like hallways.

I push open the balcony door to find my grandfather sitting with Vadim—Vadka, for short. My best friend and most loyal lieutenant.

Rugged and solidly built, with a perpetual five o'clock shadow, Vadka is tough but has a friendly smile when he's around people he trusts. Like my grandfather. Like me.

Next to Vadka, my grandfather is small and frail, with warm eyes and a soft voice. He walks with a cane, hunched over, but still maintains an air of dignity. My mother's father, he's the only living grandparent we have left. These two are my most trusted advisors, and while I rarely ask for advice, there's a time and a place.

"My son," my grandfather says in his shaky, rasping voice. "You look as if you've seen a ghost."

Vadka sits back in his chair and takes a swig from a bottle. "I don't know if I'd describe him that way. Looks like he's angry." He tips his head to the side. "Somebody key your car again, boss?"

He's the only one I let get away with bullshit like this. "Got another one?" I ask him. Of course he does. He takes the cold drink from the ground beside him, pops the top off, and hands it to me.

I gulp half of it before I speak. I swallow and sigh, looking over the balcony. "She has no memory of who she is."

"No shit," Vadka says, his eyes wide. My grandfather doesn't respond at first, though his bushy gray eyebrows knit together.

"Are you positive about that?" he says quietly.

"That's what Zoya tells me. I have to test it."

My grandfather nods thoughtfully, stroking the gray on his chin. "You definitely do. What does she gain from pretending she doesn't know who she is?"

"Everything," I snap.

He holds up a hand before I continue. "Easy, son. Think. What does she gain if she's your bride? Your wrath. Her lack of freedom. Punishment."

I talk over him. "Yes. Of course. She earned that by putting our entire family at risk." He shakes his head and raises a palm.

"You don't need to explain to me what's at stake or why you're angry." He doesn't approve of our criminal empire but understands that his grandchildren were thrust into a life we couldn't escape. He's the calming presence in our family, offering wisdom in a world filled with brutality.

"If she doesn't know who she is, does she escape any of that?"

I shake my head. "No."

"Then it stands to reason that she has nothing to gain by lying, correct?"

I swallow hard. "Correct."

"But think of what *you* gain if she doesn't remember who she is."

I think, turning over the possibilities in my mind as if holding jewels in my palm, each facet reflecting sunlight. "A new story."

Grandfather smiles. He may despise organized crime and eschew the Bratva, but he fits right in.

My thoughts race.

"If she doesn't know who she is," I continue, "maybe she never jilted me. We're already married. Her family doesn't know she escaped; nobody does. I spread the news of a secret ceremony so news gets out.

"You'll make her wear your ring," Vadka supplies. "The one she lost in the accident." He chuckles. "I do love how your wicked mind works."

Grandfather watches us both with interest. "Of course, everyone needs to be in on this. Are you confident that deception is the way to continue?"

I face him, my temper rearing its ugly head. "She stood me up. She put everything I've worked for at risk. I'm doing her a favor if we skip straight to wedlock, and she's now married to me."

My grandfather nods thoughtfully, his fingertips pressed together. "Fair enough. And what if her memory comes back?"

"By then, it will be too late." I scowl. "She'll belong to *me*."

Grandfather continues nodding, his bushy white brows knit. "We need details about how her memory might work."

Even while I'm consumed by uncertainty, I have to maintain control. So I call Dr. Zuta, a trusted associate. The noonday sun is high on the horizon when he finally answers. My voice is low but forceful, the weight of my concern bearing down on me. I need to know if her memory loss is genuine. I need to discern whether or not she's lying.

"Mr. Kopolov, to what do I owe this pleasure?" the doctor asks.

I explain quickly what happened. "So you need to determine if you're dealing with amnesia," the doctor summarizes. "In this case, if she truly has suffered trauma, it's not uncommon for memories to become fragmented or temporarily inaccessible. She may be confused or have gaps in memory, and there's no real way to test if she is lying. What you'll have to do is watch for inconsistencies. But be careful, do not push too hard, or you could cause further damage."

My jaw tightens. I am not someone who suffers uncertainty, and I despise the ambiguity of the doctor's words. My mind flashes back to Anissa—those fragile, hauntingly familiar eyes. Or were her eyes perhaps *too* wide? Is there anything I can trust about her?

"And if she is lying?" I ask, my hand clenched into a fist, my voice colder now. I'm trying to hide the desperation in my words. I've gone from chasing down the bride who stood me up to having one who may be deceiving me.

"There's no real medical way to prove it," the doctor replies. "But as her memories return—and they very well may—there might be behavioral shifts. Maybe she'll react to you differently. Just treat her carefully for now. Her mind needs time to heal."

I stifle a growl, holding my anger back with difficulty. This might not be the chance I'd hoped for. "Give me examples of inconsistencies to watch out for."

"Names, relationships," he says. "See if she remembers if she has any brothers or sisters. You might watch how she behaves in familiar surroundings."

I don't know much about her. That will have to change.

"In severe cases of amnesia, she would struggle with basic daily tasks, like finding her way around a kitchen. But if she navigates her area easily, she might be remembering more than she lets on. Ask her about her favorite food, her opinions on things. See if her memory is intact."

Right.

"She may have some emotional responses, involuntary habits, muscle memory—things like that. The sense of smell can be powerful. Just keep in mind a triggered memory doesn't necessarily indicate she's lying."

I see. My mind reels with possibilities, eager to use this knowledge to further tighten my control over my... bride. "Thank you for your time."

I send a text to my entire family and everyone in my trusted circle.

Anissa has no memory of who she is. From this moment on, you all will treat her as my wife. That is what she is now. I want it announced wide, loud and clear that my wife and I have taken our vows. Let her family know. Let everyone know. Anissa is mine.

My decision made, I head back to Zoya and Anissa.

Rodion texts back.

Got it. Do you love her in this scenario? 😈

I scowl at the screen and shake my head. Will he ever learn?

Of course not.

CHAPTER 7

"ANISSA"

I'm lying in the bed, staring at the wall. Trying to remember who I am or why I'm here. It's strange having a vague sense of self, of purpose, and yet realizing I can't quite grasp any of it. I think our identity is something we take for granted, the natural order of things, and when it's gone, it's as if the sun's been turned off, and you no longer recognize the playing field anymore.

Zoya, the sweet girl that she is, has told me almost nothing.

I watched as she opened her mouth, then looked at her phone and promptly shut it again. She stood, pacing at the foot of the bed, and though she looked perplexed, she didn't respond when I asked her what was going on.

She says my name's Anissa. I expect it should sound familiar, if that's my name, but it's completely unnatural, like a shoe that doesn't quite fit.

Zoya stands and flits toward me, wringing her hands, though her voice is steady and calm.

"Rafail is coming back to see you. He will answer your questions," she says, a new hardness to her voice as if she's angry with him.

"Did he give you permission to unfasten me?"

I imagine that I am a captured princess, with people out there who love me, coming to save me from whatever lies ahead.

I feel fragile and dependent, and I hate it.

"You can ask Rafail," she says quietly. "He's your..." She shakes her head. "No, I'm going to let him tell you that."

She comes to my side and presses something cold and small in my hand—a tiny silver charm of a bird in flight. "For luck," she murmurs, glancing nervously at the door as if we're going to be discovered at any moment. "This is yours. Or it... was." The delicate bird feels strangely familiar, like a piece of a lost dream.

Her voice trembles. "Anissa, I *know* he can be scary. I know he's dangerous. They all are, really, though I think you'll like Yana, and I think she'll understand..." Her gaze trails off as her voice does. "But you're going to be okay." Giving my hand a gentle squeeze, her tone is vehement. "You're *strong*."

"So are you," I whisper, even though I hardly know this woman. She's small and fragile, and I know that whatever she's been through has made her stronger. I can see it in her eyes.

A ghost of a smile crosses her face as the door opens.

The air grows icy, sending a shiver down my spine. It's utterly still.

My captor's back.

Now that I'm a little more awake, I decide to assess the situation. He's maybe in his mid-thirties, tall and commanding, rugged and dangerous. His dark, intense eyes seem to pierce right through me. Right through anyone, I'd imagine, with that laser focus. He has a sharp jawline and high cheekbones, and something tells me he is not a stranger to violence. Everything about him embodies raw power, but there's something more, something familiar... He's a man used to being obeyed.

Dressed in a white T-shirt, faded jeans, and leather boots, he feels oddly familiar, and even in casual dress, he exudes unbridled physical strength. His dark-brown hair is a touch too long, with a hint of curl that would seem playful if not for his cold expression and mask of control. The stubble on his chin is somewhere between rugged and five o'clock shadow, enough to give him an edge of dominance I crave. I shiver. He's harsh and ruthless, there's no doubt.

Zoya would tell me nothing, nothing of substance.

He walks over to me and folds his huge frame into the small chair at my side. "Feeling any better?" The rough, angry tone of his voice sets me on edge.

I shake my head. It feels like my brain rattles against my skull.

"No," I say. "I'm not. I have no memory of anything. I don't even know the name *Anissa*; it's foreign to me. Don't know why I'm in this bed. And Zoya, as nice as she is," I amend because she is kind, "won't tell me anything."

"That's because I ordered her not to," he says sharply. He nods to her as if silently thanking her for her obedience.

"So you're the boss around here?" I don't bother to hide my disdain.

"I am." His cold, calculating gaze defies me to challenge him.

I swallow hard. "I have questions."

Narrowed eyes meet mine, and he speaks in a half growl. "I'm sure you do."

Frowning at him, I try to sit up, but it proves impossible with my wrists restrained. I do, however, manage to keep my voice strong and sure. I don't know who this arrestingly handsome asshole is, but I'd like to find that out as soon as possible.

"You act as if you hate me, and I don't even know who you are. So do me a favor and fill me in so I know if I should hate you back and decide if your lack of hospitality is warranted."

"Lack of hospitality?" he snarls. "You're warm and fed, and that's more than you deserve."

I purse my lips. "I don't know much, but I can say with confidence you and I have very different concepts of *hospitality*. So why don't you tell me what I supposedly did since it's an obvious point of contention between us."

Despite his stoic expression, mild surprise registers in his eyes before he leans forward. Rising to his full height, I half expect him to do something drastic, but he only stares down at me as if assessing me.

That's when I notice he has a small silver metal key in his hand. Thank god.

But he's in no hurry. He takes his time unlocking me, his hands brushing mine. Rough fingers graze the tender skin at my wrists as he reaches for my hands above my head and slips the key in. With a soft click, my wrists swing free. God, it feels good to be able to move them again, even though it hurts.

Silently, still scowling, he takes my wrists in his large, rough hands and massages the chafed skin with his thumbs. I try to push away, to sit up, only to have him push me back down with a firm hand on my shoulder.

I swallow and stare up at him. I'm nothing close to free, even if I'm unshackled. I release a shuddering breath.

Leaning over, his voice is a low, dangerous murmur, each word a promise and a threat. "You say you don't know who I am. We'll cover that. I'll explain in vivid detail what I expect of you. You've been brought here because you ran from me, and I had to make sure that never happened again."

I blink up at him. "Excuse me?"

He says all this as if it's just a matter of fact. With narrowed eyes, he shakes his head. "You think this is cruel, you being chained to a bed? Disobey me again, run from me again, and you'll see firsthand what cruel really feels like."

My jaw drops open as his hand drifts to my neck, his thumb pressing against my pulse, just enough to make it a little harder to breathe. I'm caught in his gaze, pinned into place by his oppressive, all-consuming presence.

I eye him suspiciously. I may not know much about my current situation, but I know this—nobody restrains anyone this securely, this uncomfortably, just to keep them *safe*.

What the hell did I do to this stranger?

"My ankles too," I remind him quietly. He moves the sheet at the bottom of the bed, and my cheeks immediately heat when I realize I'm wearing nothing but a short tee and a pair of panties. My instincts tell me to cover myself.

"Evacuate this room," he snaps to everyone else as he pulls the sheet back over me. Everyone leaps to obey, even little Zoya.

We're alone. I'm staring up at my captor, his angry eyes riveted on mine. "I know you say you don't remember who you are, but I don't buy it. It's hard to imagine someone forgets her own husband that easily."

My brain can barely catch up to the words. *Husband*?

"I can't be your wife," I whisper, trying to return an excuse. "I have no... I have no ring," I say wildly. Doesn't a wife wear a wedding band? "And you had me *tied* to this bed. Who *does* that to his wife?"

"A man afraid that she'll run away again when given the chance."

I stare at him, aghast.

"I ran?"

He reaches into his pocket with the sort of smile that doesn't reach his eyes, but one that looks almost calculating. "You lost your ring in the accident. But I have it right here. And I told you, I had you restrained so you wouldn't run again."

Husband... I'm still reeling from the news. This apparently wealthy, powerful, dangerous man is my... *husband*? *What*?

I'm supposedly in one of the most intimate relationships two people can share, yet he's a total stranger.

Zoya said my name is Anissa.

Anissa.

"Say my name," I whisper, hoping that if he says it—if my husband speaks my name—it might trigger a memory, a hint of familiarity.

I don't anticipate the note of pride in his voice when he responds. "Anissa Kopolova."

Nothing.

I shake my head. "Why does that sound so foreign to me?"

I hate how small and vulnerable my voice sounds. I turn away from him. "Why did you look at me like you hated me? If I'm your wife... this doesn't make any sense."

He doesn't answer for long moments, his gaze trailing over me like... like he's imagining the ways he could hurt me. I grip the sheets tighter. There's no tenderness in his eyes, only cold hunger, a craving I don't understand but feel deep in my bones.

And when he finally speaks, his voice is low and dark. "You don't understand yet, do you?" I flinch when he reaches for me and he drags a thumb across my lower lip. Rough. Possessive. "You will."

How is it that I remember nothing about who I am, much less who *he* is, but I remember everything about human behavior?

For example, that muscle ticking in his jaw tells me he's having a hard time being patient. The tentative way his thumb rubs along my wrist, unaccustomed to being gentle. But when I saw him with his sister, he was gentle with her.

Why not me if I'm his wife?

And why was she afraid of him?

"We've had a... rocky relationship," he says. "Just because we're married doesn't mean we've gotten along."

Hmm.

"Well, why not?" I ask him. It seems stupid to me that people would get married because they supposedly loved each other or whatever, and then they fight.

"Why don't we get along?" he repeats.

Buying time? Looking for clarity. Or as baffled as I am?

I lick my lips. My voice is husky. Shaking. "Remind me why I hate you."

Something that comes close to humor ghosts his face. "It's actually not very complicated," he begins. "I like to be in charge, and you don't like to be told what to do."

"How's that working out for you?" I snap. Once again, his features register something close to humor. The way the corners of his lips twitch tells me he's not accustomed to smiling either. Why? Why is he so sober? So angry?

"Not very well. I have a wife who ran away from me because she was angry with me. She didn't want to be with me anymore."

"I ran from you," I repeat, as if stating this out loud would make it more comprehensible. For the first time since I woke up, something that rings with the smallest touch of familiarity hits my consciousness.

I *do* remember running. Yes. Yes, that part is true. "So I'm a runner, then?" I ask.

He lets out a sigh. "You could say that."

What does he mean? I look down at my body. I'm fit, I know that. It's not like I woke up in a body that's wholly unfamiliar to me.

I flex my toes and make a decision. I may not be able to run now, but I *will* run again. From him, too, if I have to.

"So here's a question for you," I say. Goddamn, it hurts to talk. "Why did you tell Zoya I'm not allowed to have morphine if I'm your wife?" My voice trembles, and to my horror, when I blink, a tear slips down my cheek.

"You misunderstood," he says quietly, releasing his hold on me. I shiver at his icy tone and the loss of his touch. I have the distinct feeling if wolves could talk, they'd sound just like this. "You've been disoriented, confused. I want you to have pain relief, but the sort that will allow you to talk and function. Like this, so you're not confused anymore."

"So I can have pain medication," I repeat, just to be clear. Is this guy gaslighting me?

Is that why I hate him?

I'm so tired of having all these questions, and it feels like I've just begun.

I try to sit up in bed, but the pain is killing me.

"So I ran from you, and I was hit by... what, exactly?"

At his murderous look, I clutch the warm fabric of the duvet cover in my fist for protection. I'm doing my best to feign bravery, but something tells me that even if I could remember who he was, I would *still* be terrified. Maybe even more than I am now.

"You were hit by a car. That's one of the problems, Anissa. You're impetuous and disobedient and ran wildly into oncoming traffic."

Impetuous? *Disobedient*? I feel my brows lift in surprise. "One of the problems you have with *me*? I'm not a child. I know that much. I'm sorry, I know I was in an accident, but did I somehow go back in *time*?"

He growls and doesn't speak for a moment as if he's trying to compose himself. "You're definitely no fucking child."

His gaze grows hungry as he licks his lips, and I'm once more reminded of a wolf, but this time, he looks ready to eat me alive. I blink and stare, trying to compose my thoughts and my expression all at once and failing at both.

I chatter on, trying to regain some control. "So far, we've established that I'm your wife. I ran from you heedlessly and was hit by a car. My reason for running from you had something to do with your high-handed ways? And I'm guessing you must have a ring that I lost in the accident."

"Yes," he says, and something like regret crosses his face. There's a vague familiarity about all of this, but just enough off-kilter to make it feel like I'm staring into the mirror at a funhouse. The truth is distorted. His ragged voice utters a low, harsh command. "Give me your hand."

When he takes my hand in his much larger, much rougher one, I note the golden ring that glints in the overhead light. "Your ring," he says, slipping it back onto my finger. It's heavy and cold. I notice a small engraving inside—a twisted line that looks as sharp as barbed wire. *In hardship and loyalty,* it reads.

I stare in wonder as he slides it onto my finger. It feels vaguely like Prince Charming sliding the glass slipper on Cinderella's foot because it fits perfectly.

I rub my thumb along the ring, waiting for it to feel foreign, but it doesn't. It's a perfect fit. At the same time, though, it's reminiscent of the cuff he just took off. A teeny, tiny perfect handcuff. I can't remember the ceremony, but the words resonate. I note the matching ring of gold that glints on his finger.

"How long have we been married?" My voice feels detached and hollowed like I'm speaking in a tunnel. I'll ask questions until I know who I am.

"One week."

My jaw drops. My *god*. "One week, and we already hate each other?"

A ghost of a smile crosses his features again. "We never liked each other, Anissa. You were given to me by your father. He owed me a debt, and he paid it with you."

I blink in shock. "Jesus," I mutter. "What a dick move."

This time, he actually does laugh. I start at the sound.

"Some men value their lives more than their virtue," he finishes.

"I see." I'm quiet for a moment before I continue. "So I was angry with you or... something," I begin.

"Or something," he finishes with a nod. "Yes."

"And I ran from you, and I got hit by a car. Wow. I suppose I'm lucky to be alive."

His gaze grows murderous, his tone chilling and laced with danger. "Lucky for the person driving that car that you're alive."

I lick my lips and swallow hard. "So... what happened to the person who hit me?"

He sits up straighter, and his eyes darken. His muscles tense. "What do you think? I did exactly what a husband is supposed to do when someone hurts his wife."

I stare at him. Again there's a twinge of familiarity, but I'm not sure if it's *him* that triggers it. There's something about his undeniable protection, cloaked in danger... Something about his violent, unbridled strength that makes me feel like I'm protected in a gilded cage. It's all so familiar to me, and yet it makes my heart race. I lay my head on the pillow because the effort of talking is exhausting.

"I'm tired." I rest my head back and sigh. "And I'm sorry that we didn't get along before. Maybe you'll remind me why I don't like you. But for now, I'm glad you've given me some answers."

Something tells me we're going to have a lot more questions before this is through, I think, as sleep beckons.

"Those pain meds... okay, can you hook me up?" I'm guessing he doesn't really know that much about me. I was given to him in marriage, which doesn't actually surprise me. The arranged marriage idea is strangely familiar. Maybe it's because I was married to him, or maybe it's for another reason altogether. "I think I need a pair of crutches," I tell him. "I can't walk like this. And I really need to get out of this bed."

His phone rings. With a scowl and a curse, he shuts it off and shoves it into his pocket so hard I'm surprised it doesn't crack.

"What'd your phone ever do to you?" I mutter, but he only grunts in response.

"I'll get you whatever you need," he says. "For now, I'll carry you."

Panic flits across my chest. I don't know him at all, but if what he tells me is true, I know we've already shared... *something*. I bear his last name and his ring. This stranger of a man knows more about me than I do.

What else does he know about me?

"You'll carry me," I repeat, licking my lips. That's going to mean me coming in much closer contact with him than I'm comfortable with. But I can't walk. I'm completely consumed with pain. Something has to give.

"Do you want me to get your wheelchair?" he asks with a hint of a sneer and narrowed eyes. I can tell he's testing me.

"Absolutely not," I insist. "Fine. I suppose you can carry me, then."

"I wasn't asking for permission."

Argh. Of course not.

"So where are you taking me, then?"

I feel like a child... as if everything is out of my control and I'm completely dependent on someone I don't know. But what's most disturbing of all is that *I'm* someone I don't know.

"To our bedroom. You obviously need some help. You need rest."

I nod, not trusting my voice enough to say anything else.

Our bedroom.

Our bedroom.

It feels oddly intimate, and I can't reconcile intimacy with a stranger. I'll be alone with him, a thought that both terrifies and exhilarates me.

I stifle a scream when he scoops me into his arms, cradling me like I'm weightless. But there's nothing even remotely gentle with the way he grips me, his fingers pressing into my skin as if branding me. I feel his strength, his power, and for one terrifying second, one wild thought arrests me: is this how it will feel when he claims me? No softness. No tenderness. Just raw power?

As his fingers brush my skin, I notice a thin, worn leather bracelet on his wrist. A charm dangles from it—a tiny wolf's tooth. Something tells me this bracelet has significance and has witnessed things, dark secrets held by men like him.

I'm momentarily dazzled by his strong, calming, masculine scent. They say that smell is one of the strongest triggers, but I still can't remember a thing. I'm only aware that he smells clean and strong and utterly masculine.

His arms are warm, his grip certain as he straightens with effortless ease. My leg aches, but I bite my lip and bear it. I want to get out of here.

Maybe if we don't get along, we can bury the hatchet. Maybe there's hope—*no*. I can't trust him. I can't trust him.

"Do I have family?" I ask him.

Am I all alone in this world?

For some reason that I can't put my finger on, I believe that I do.

I remember being... loved. I remember laughter. I remember feeling like I belong. But I also remember being oppressed. Wanting to escape...

Is that what I did?

"I told you about your father, who sold you to get out of debt. You have no mother and no siblings."

Right. Wow. Okay, then. Just a father. I'm like Beauty from

Beauty and the Beast; only her father actually cared about her. Lucky me.

"Just so we're clear, I will not have my wife communicating with someone who would sell her off like that."

I turn this over in my mind. I don't know how to mourn the loss of someone I don't even remember, but it still hits my heart. People should have mothers and fathers. And some people maybe should have siblings too.

"I don't know why I would want to be in touch with someone I don't know, much less someone who thought so little of me, but okay then."

We are approaching a doorway at the end of a hall, and my heart beats frantically faster. I don't know what's coming.

"You haven't answered all the questions." I'm buying time, terrified about what he'll do when we're alone in our *bedroom*.

His brow furrows as if he's puzzled or he's confused. "I've answered everything you asked me."

"Not quite. I asked you what happened to the people who hit me with the car."

I watch as his jaw firms and his shoulders seem to expand. I've stoked his anger. "I'll admit, I may have lost my temper."

Oh god. Somehow, I knew he'd respond like this, but I'm still unprepared for the way my heart races in fear. I don't know what it would look like if a man like him lost his temper. Even when he's on his best behavior, he's terrifying.

"Oh?" I ask. I wince when he steps over the threshold.

"I'm sorry," he says softly. "I'm trying not to jostle you."

"It's fine," I lie. It's not fine. It hurts so badly I'm crying. I turn my face away from his so he doesn't see it. I know intuitively that he wouldn't like that. And I want to hear him answer the questions I asked.

"They were reckless. You could've been killed." His voice is choked, his anger palpable. I look down to note the veins in his arms, strong muscles, tan skin, and black marks of ink that are vaguely familiar but not identifiable, like markings out of focus.

"I told you I took care of it. Someone was reckless enough to hurt my wife, and I handled it the way I had to. Trust me—no one will make that mistake again."

His voice is as dark as a whispered threat. "When someone hurts what's mine, they live to regret it. If the streets of St. Petersburg could talk..." His gaze is distant for a moment, as if he's remembering past deeds. What has he done?

I bite my lip, unsure if I want details and uncertain if I want to stay ignorant.

"Right," I whisper.

"You're mine," he growls, his voice a low, dangerous whisper without a hint of comfort or love, nothing but stark obsession. It seems as if this assurance should bring me a measure of comfort, but the latent warning in his tone makes me tremble.

He continues in a low rumble. "I made an example of the person who hurt you," he says. "It wasn't pretty, and you don't need the details. Do you know who I am, Anissa?"

I shake my head. "My husband," I say, my voice wobbling. The medication he gave me has made me sleepy, and I want to go to bed, but I have to push through. "All I know is that you're my husband."

"Yes, but since you don't remember who you are, I'm going to assume you don't know what my job is." He blows out a breath. "We'll get there."

We're walking down a long hallway. The rubber soles of his boots are practically silent on the gleaming hardwood floors. It's simple, sophisticated. The home smells like old wood, reminiscent of a library. Large blossoms in a rust-colored glass vase sit on a side table. Everywhere I look, there's bright light. I have the strange thought that someone like him needs a lot of light to give him something to hope for. To shine light in the darkness. If he lived in a cavern or a place with closed blinds, the abyss would swallow him. It hurts to turn my head, so I only take in what's in my immediate surroundings.

If he's my husband... "Is it just the two of us? In a house like this? It looks enormous."

He shakes his head gently, careful not to disturb me, careful not to jostle my cast.

"No," he says quietly. "Definitely not just us." When he doesn't offer any more information, I push a little more.

"Zoya? Your sister?" And then a horrible thought strikes me. "Not your parents," I add, unable to imagine being married to a man like him in the presence of his parents.

"I suppose we're jumping right into the middle, aren't we?" he says with a thoughtful look. His face deepens into a frown, and he doesn't speak for long minutes, as if he's trying to condense a lifetime into just a few sentences

He continues to walk with purpose, taking large strides, but careful not to jostle me too much.

"My name is Rafail Kopolov," he says. "Does that mean anything to you?"

His name stirs something faint but nothing familiar, an echo bouncing in a vast, empty room. I remember a chill in the air, distant city lights blinking like stars. I remember the shout of a voice... anger. A chase.

But no, his name is unfamiliar.

I shake my head. Nothing.

"My *own* name doesn't mean anything when you say it," I tell him. "I'd like to talk to a doctor. I need to know when my memory will come back."

"Your father is involved in various aspects of organized crime," he continues quietly. "And I am the head of the Kopolov Moscow branch. My father died young, like his father before him. A curse, some say, though I don't believe in superstition the way most here do. But the Kopolov name carries with it a legacy." His voice sharpens. "One I intend to protect."

I swallow and nod.

"We're Bratva, Anissa."

I blink.

Bratva. Familiarity rings with fear and awe. I know the Bratva. Russian organized crime. Lethal. Powerful.

Familiar.

"Eleven years ago, my parents were killed. As the eldest, I became the legal guardian of my family and *pakhan*."

Wait. *Legal guardian of his family*?

"Oh. Oh, wow. How many of you are there?"

His jaw firms. "I have two brothers and two sisters under my care. They came into my care as minors. My brothers work but sometimes stay here as well."

"I see. So you're the legal guardian of Zoya, that sweet girl I met earlier?"

He nods. "And a few other not-so-sweet siblings you'll meet eventually."

Alright then.

My mind wanders. It's beautiful, in a strange way, this concept that maybe it's just the two of us. I can still hear him, though, and it would be foolish to ignore what he's saying.

"Say that again." I wonder what his expectations are. "How long have you been your siblings' guardian? Eleven years?"

"Yes."

Yikes. I always thought it was kind of sweet, even poignant, when a brother stepped up to guard his siblings in the role of father figure. Maybe my primal instincts tell me he'd do well as a father to my own children. Maybe it shows he's dependable and trustworthy.

But I don't know anything about him, not really. Perhaps he's incredibly permissive, letting them get away with murder. I give him a second look. No, that definitely wouldn't be his downfall. He's probably the opposite—overbearing and authoritarian.

God. Maybe I should just wait and see and not make any rash judgments. I should probably stop trying to figure it all out right this minute.

"I have an uncle and aunt who live nearby," he says, "but they don't live here. I have staff as well. You did, too, Anissa."

That triggers a faint memory. I can't give him names or places, but I remember someone cooking in the kitchen, mopping the floors, folding laundry.

"Mmm. Yes. So what will you expect of *me*?" I ask, suddenly unsure. Am I supposed to be cooking? Cleaning? Taking care of the younger ones? Would that be strange? No, they're probably old enough not to need anyone like a mother.

"I've told you," he says, his voice soft but firm. "You're expected to do what you're told."

Right. I blow out a breath, unimpressed with the platitude or threat. "For someone who's trying to improve his first impression on me, you could do a lot better, you know." I roll my eyes. "I just meant, do you expect me to cook? Clean? Things like that. Do I even know what I'm doing in the kitchen?"

"If you want to." He shrugs like it's no big deal. "Of course, for now, you're going to have to get better. Heal from your injuries. And you haven't been in the kitchen yet, so time will tell." He raises a brow to underscore his words. "*After* your leg is better."

Great. I'm handicapped in more ways than one. I frown. "What exactly was my prognosis?"

"You'll have the cast for a minimum of eight weeks. I'm watching you for signs of a concussion. You have no internal bleeding or bleeding on your brain, but I'm insisting you get a second scan in two days. You have lacerations on your back and arms and a sprained elbow."

"My god!" I gasp.

"You're lucky you're alive," he says, his voice low. "They said if you had been standing still and not running at the speed you were, you wouldn't have made it."

I need to know the answers to the questions that haunt me. Why was I running? Why was I running from *him*?

"No running for a while, Anissa." It's far from the first concern on my mind.

He stands in the doorway of a bedroom. The open door reveals a large primary suite. The room is grand, with high ceilings and soft, elegant lighting. A plush, deep indigo-colored rug covers the hardwood floor, and tall windows flood the space with light. The furniture is dark wood, rich and commanding, and there's a fireplace in the corner, unlit and cold. But what I notice most, of course, is the imposing bed in the center of the room. It dominates the space, draped in luxurious fabrics and surrounded by tall, intricately carved posts.

Again, this room looks somewhat familiar—and I wonder if

I've seen it before. Or is it just that I've been in a place like this before?

No, no... he said that we were married. Not for long, but I have definitely been in this room before. Then why does it all look so new? I close my eyes because a headache is forming behind my temples, throbbing. I try to take in the details, but it's overwhelming. It feels as if someone's holding a metal pot in front of me and clanging it with a wooden spoon, the noise reverberating in my skull.

"Remember what I told you," Rafail says.

"You told me a lot of things," I say, trying to hide the petulant tone of my voice and failing. I'm tired. Overwhelmed.

"The doctor said too many questions or pushing too hard will impede your recovery. No more questions, Anissa. The doctor's coming in to check on you. I want you to rest. Are you hungry?"

I shake my head and resist the urge to lay it on his chest. It feels nice being carried like this, as if I'm weightless, by a strong man like him. I'd have to be immune to every female instinct in my body to not enjoy the way he holds me, nestled in his arms. I can feel the strength of his muscles and how he's not even struggling to carry me.

There's a couch in the bedroom with an array of pillows on it. Beside it is a small table and a few books. I look around the room, but there's not much to see. It's well-appointed but simple, not unlike a luxury hotel room. I half expect to see small bottles of body lotion and shampoo in the bathroom when I go, maybe white hand towels twisted into the shape of a dove.

"So this is my new prison," I say dryly. Silk sheets as soft as a lover's touch brush my skin, and yet I feel caged. Gilded chains in the form of rare paintings line the walls, and fresh-cut roses—too perfect, staged—sit on every surface. It's beautiful but as suffocating as iron bars.

He looks at me sharply and doesn't reply.

When his phone vibrates, he answers it and turns away from me, speaking in Russian. I realize it's easier for me to understand Russian than English. Russian must be my first language, then. How strange to need to remember that.

He told me to rest. He told me that if I push it, I will impede my recovery. Rest it is, then, but it's a lot easier said than done with my brain.

It's human nature to want to sift truth from lies, but how does one do so without a foundation of memory? I try to piece together what he's said without taxing my brain. He says he's my husband and that we didn't like each other. That I was hit by a car after running away from him and lost my memory.

I have two choices then: believe what he tells me or don't and seek the truth.

Overcome with exhaustion, the pain becomes too much. I close my eyes, thankful for the clean sheet beneath my chin and the soft mattress. I like the sound of his voice, I think, as I start to drift off to sleep. He's confident. Commanding. And somehow, that brings me no small measure of solace.

As I drift into darkness, faint images glimmer at the recesses of my mind. Laughter. A shadowy figure. A whisper in Russian.

Maybe when I wake up, I'll remember who I am. Maybe when I wake up, I'll remember everything. Maybe when I wake up, I'll be able to distinguish truth from lies.

Or will I?

CHAPTER 8

RAFAIL

While she sleeps, I make a few phone calls. My mind races. She's curious and bright, and even though, so far, her memory is spotty, there's no question with a mind as sharp as hers that it *will* come back.

And fuck me, she's *gorgeous.* I wasn't prepared for this. For her. Every inch of her challenges my self-control. Those wide, almost innocent eyes that glint with defiance, the gentle part of her full lips when she's surprised, almost like she's tempting without even trying. Her skin is pale and flawless, and when she shifts, the curve of her neck beckons to me. Her hair falls in soft waves around her shoulders, as brilliant as a Snow Queen's.

I clench my fists, willing myself to focus, to remember that she's here because she ran from me, but every inch of her soft skin, every delectable curve, only makes it harder to concentrate. The sooner I truly claim her, the sooner I truly make her *mine*...

When I held her, the scent of her skin, soft and slightly sweet, hit me like a drug, raw and intoxicating, making my pulse race. When she looked up at me with wide eyes, her pretty lips just inches from my own, I could hardly keep myself from tracing the line of her jaw, from pressing my lips to the place where her pulse beats just beneath her delicate skin.

I want to bury my hands in her hair and my cock in her tight, hot pussy until she arches beneath me, helpless and *mine.* I've fought, controlled, dominated, and conquered so many before her, yet nothing prepared me for *this.* For *her.*

The woman who brought near devastation to everything I've ever built, who put my entire family at risk.

I'll claim that sweet, hot cunt of hers until the memory of my touch is seared into her.

I look out the window at our estate. I poured blood, sweat, and tears into keeping this house in my family's name. In *my* name. When I was still barely over the threshold of adulthood, it was a much harder task than I'd anticipated.

People have always called it "The Cottage," but it's anything but small and simple—more like a fortress. Our large, sprawling home just outside of Moscow blends with the old-fashioned style of old Russia with modern touches—tall stone walls, large windows, and intricate iron gates that almost make it feel like a citadel. Inside, I've kept it simple and functional—my office and command center on the first floor are the only places I've focused any of my attention. My sisters, however, have brought warmth and comfort.

Yana begged me to let her decorate, insisting that every room needed a touch of "her unique charm," as she put it, her playful grin challenging anyone. I gave my sister what she wanted. I had to. It gave me no small pleasure to know my father would turn over in his grave in disapproval.

I look toward my bedroom.

When I'm confident Anissa's resting, the medication keeping her in a light state of sedation for now, but the effort she expended exhausting her, I step into the hallway and meet up with my brothers, who hover nearby. They're eager to back me up as always, but there's a hint of fear in their eyes over what happens next. I peer in at her, the door slightly ajar.

No one's come into this home since our parents' death. My marriage—however unofficial it is—changes everything.

"How'd she take the news?" Rodion asks me.

I shrug and sigh. "She has a lot of questions, but so far, so good." I shake my head and keep my voice low, even though I know she can't hear me. "I tried to tell her as much of the truth as I could."

"Now, brother, there's no need to lie," Rodion smirks, obviously delighting in my predicament. "You definitely didn't tell her as much of the truth as you could. You may have told her as much of the truth as you could *get away* with." He snorts. "I ought to know. That's my specialty."

I grunt. He's not lying.

"I believe what you meant to say is that creative truth-telling is my *only* tactic." Semyon says, smacking Rodion's shoulder.

I love these assholes, even if I want to throttle them sometimes.

"How much time do you have?" Semyon asks. "Like, what if she wakes up tomorrow and remembers who she is?"

"I don't know how much time I have. I could have months, weeks, or days." I shove my hands in my pockets. "But it sounds like it's very rare that one's memory returns rapidly."

"So, you must focus on making that woman of yours like you," Rodion says with a lopsided grin that makes him look like a cat with a mouse's tail trapped under it's paw.

I give him a withering look. "She doesn't have to *like* me," I say with disgust. "I wouldn't know the first thing about that anyway."

My brothers share a look.

"What?" Frustration mounts in my chest. I scowl. "What the hell are you looking at each other like that for?"

Semyon sighs. "He's not wrong, brother. It might help, you know."

I think about this for a moment without responding. Help with *what*?

Rodion leans forward, holding my gaze. "You look genuinely perplexed. Do you mean to tell me that for once in my life, I actually have an opportunity to fill my big brother in on something? Imagine, after all these years, after everything you've taught me, I actually know something you don't?" He shakes his head and curses.

I grunt at him and look back through the open door to where my bride rests. She was pretty wrecked. And she was definitely concerned about what I did to the people who hit her.

That's none of her concern. It won't ever be. He was reckless, careless. He could've killed her. The asshole was playing on his phone instead of watching the road. And yes, she shouldn't have run into traffic the way she did, but if he had been paying attention, it would've been easy to swerve.

From here, I can see the gold-framed mirrors Yana put up, the soft silk curtains drawn tight, and the roses Zoya placed beside the bed. My bride rests in a room as finely appointed as a queen's—but with every lock and guard in place to keep her mine.

What if she wakes up and she's disoriented? What if she wakes up and looks for me? Or worse, what if she wakes up and remembers who she is?

Will she try to run again? When I join her, the door to our bedroom will be locked, as is every other exit to the house, secured with my men. I would think that if she woke up and remembered who she was, she wouldn't make the mistake of running again, especially with her leg in a cast and her other injuries to account for.

Rodion leans in, clearly delighted that he gets to tell me what to do for once.

"You have two choices here, Rafail. The carrot or the stick. And trust me, when it comes to a beautiful woman like her, you want to at least *start* with the carrot." His eyes gleam with a hint of challenge. Behind him, Semyon raises an eyebrow, silently daring me to show restraint.

I clench my fists and narrow my eyes at Rodion. "Don't you ever fucking make a comment about my wife's looks again."

"Whoa, sorry," he says, holding his hands up. "I didn't mean anything." He looks at Semyon, who meets his gaze.

Yeah, I called her my wife. By all intents and purposes, that's exactly who she is, whether that's official on paper or not.

I growl at him but keep my eyes trained on him. Maybe he does have something to teach me.

"The stick worked fine for *you*."

Semyon chuckles. "He's got a point, brother."

My younger brother was a wild card, and some like to think he still is. He needed a firm hand. Discipline. He tried my patience like a motherfucker, but I stayed the course, and he finally grew the hell up.

Now, he's a dependable, full-fledged member of our Bratva, but I haven't forgotten who he was. Maybe all of us carry a thread of who we were, no matter how we evolve or age.

"You should at least consider what he says," Semyon suggests. "You don't know how long you have. What if she remembers within a week? If she still hates you, you're going to have a woman who knows she's not actually married to you," he says in a whisper, "who *still* hates you, who escaped you once and would no doubt try to escape you again."

"I have at least eight weeks," I respond, staring at her, prone in the bed. "She's wearing a cast."

Semyon's brows shoot up, and he shakes his head. "You're telling me a woman bold enough to run away from the most powerful man in Zalivka is going to let a little thing like a cast hold her back?"

I grunt again. "You don't have to fall in love with a woman to get her to respect and obey you. I have rules. She'll follow them." I give them both a meaningful look. They learned. Why complicate shit?

"Jesus," Semyon says, rolling his eyes. "I feel like the candlestick or the clock or whatever the fuck in *Beauty and the Beast* trying to tell the Beast to mind his *fucking manners*."

Rodion snorts. "You are definitely the clock. He's the high-strung one."

What the fuck are they talking about? I shake my head and text Vadka.

What have you found?

A lot. Briefing coming to your inbox in ten minutes. Look it over, then we'll chat.

I nod and shove my phone in my pocket, glance back at the room, and my heart leaps into my throat. The bed's empty.

"What the fuck?"

Semyon places a hand on my arm. "She got out of bed two minutes ago when you were texting Vadka. She hobbled off to the bathroom. Relax."

Relax. Jesus. I'll relax when they lay my body in a grave. I have too much at stake to *relax*.

I knew I should've stayed right there. Jesus. What if she falls? She doesn't have any crutches.

“Dinner at six,” I snap. “Don’t be late.”

As I reach the door to our bedroom, I can still hear Semyon grumbling from down the hall. "Dinner at six, as if we haven't had it at six every single night for years. Does he think we'll forget?"

I flip him off without turning around, catching Rodion muttering something I don’t quite hear. So what if I like routine? Structure. So what if I feel like everything is slipping through my fingers, and I’m holding on to whatever scraps of control I have left?

I stop just outside the door, taking a moment to steady myself. The late afternoon sun filters through the hallway windows, casting long shadows. Outside, the landscapers finish the lawn, and from downstairs, the quiet clink of dishes tells me Zoya’s busy in the kitchen. She begged to cook, and it keeps her busy. I’d hire someone in a heartbeat, but knowing Zoya’s occupied calms me.

Inside, my bride waits.

My bride.

The woman who betrayed me. It doesn’t matter that she doesn’t recall what she did—her choices put my family and my family’s legacy at risk, and for that, she’ll pay. Semyon can say whatever the hell he wants about how I handle this. But I know exactly what I’m going to do. She’ll know who I am and who she’s married to. That’s all that matters.

I glance at the two guards stationed outside her door. They straighten immediately as I approach.

"How is she?" I ask, my voice colder than I intended. I don’t want them to see the instinct of panic when I saw she was out of bed.

"She's awake, sir," one of them answers.

I square my shoulders, pushing the door open, my mind filled with the warnings of my brothers. I won't fall into the trap they think I will. This woman may be my wife, but she must understand what happens if she crosses me. When she remembers what she did—when she recalls running from me—will she realize the damage she caused?

Will it matter if she does?

Before I step inside, I catch sight of Zoya at the end of the hallway. Hesitating at the top of the stairs, when she meets my gaze, she flinches and backs away.

She knew how I handled the others—harsh when necessary. I had to, there was too much at stake, too much at risk. I've never laid a hand on her, yet she still shrinks from me like a frightened kitten—and I fucking hate it.

I've always held this family together, with no choice but to control the chaos, especially with my brothers. The girls were easier, but all of them needed me. I had my grandfather as my guiding light and, to a lesser extent, my uncle. Vadka was my sounding board and my backup. There were hard lessons. I had to be the bad guy. I wouldn't say I ever liked it, but if I had it to do over again, I wouldn't change a thing.

We're here. Safe. Together. And I'll do damn near anything to keep it that way.

"What is it?" I bite out, watching her wring her hands,

patience hanging by a thread. I try to keep my temper back, but I want to see my wife.

"Why are you angry, Rafail?" she asks, her voice barely above a whisper. Even the way she says my name feels like a gentle reproach.

"I'm not angry." But it's a lie, and I never lie to Zoya. So I blow out a breath and shake my head. "Maybe I am. I just don't like these circumstances."

She swallows and absentmindedly tugs on the hem of her top, a habit she's had since she was a child. It makes her look younger. Vulnerable. "I don't either. How long do you think this will last?"

What does she mean by "this"?

I look over my shoulder to see that Anissa is still in the bathroom. Still, I don't want her to hear any of our conversation.

"I don't know," I tell her, trying to answer all the questions at once and answering none. I exhale in frustration.

I don't like the way she flinches when I scowl. My anger isn't directed at her. I would do *anything* for my brothers and sisters. Anything.

Including playing the role of husband to an absolute stranger.

"You came here to talk to me. Was that your question?"

Zoya shakes her head and stutters, "No, no, I-I made some food. I cooked a bunch of different things because I don't know what she likes." Her brow furrows adorably. "Do you?"

Of course I don't. I know hardly anything about the woman on the other side of that door who shares my future.

"No." I don't even know if *she* knows what she likes. This is frustrating. "Thank you," I grind out. Forcing my voice soft feels like pulling teeth—unnatural, like a rottweiler rolling over to show his belly. I draw in a breath. "Thank you for that. I'm not going to make her come downstairs. She's in too much pain."

"No, no, of course not," Zoya says. "I'll bring up a tray."

I shake my head. "No, Zoya," I reply firmly. "Prepare it, and I'll bring it up."

"All right," she says softly. "Thank you."

She does a clumsy little head nod before she flees, and it makes me feel like a dick. She's my sister, not my servant. *Jesus*. I turn back and face the room. And *she's* my prisoner, not my wife.

What the fuck have I gotten myself into?

Right now, all of Zalivka is talking about my bride. Everyone knows that I'm married. And everyone knows there was an accident, but nobody knows what happened. I aim to keep it that way.

Certain the guards are in place, I decide to go downstairs now and get the food myself. If Zoya decides to disobey me and carry the damn thing, I'll have to scold her, and I fucking hate doing that. So I go downstairs and try the food as she plates it.

"Delicious." I don't even taste it, but I'm trying. Goddamn, I'm trying.

"Just a few simple things," she says quietly. "I really hope she likes them. And you, too, of course," she stammers, shaking her head. "But you like everything I make, Rafail." She gives me a shy smile. On impulse, I reach for her and give her a quick hug. No matter how much I scold her to eat, she only pecks at her food like a little bird, small and fragile.

"I do love everything you make. Thank you for this. She's going to be very glad to have you as a sister, Zoya."

I take the platter, turn, and head upstairs. The smell of roasted potatoes and savory meat pie makes my mouth water and my stomach growl. I like a good meal, but I don't remember the last time I ate one. It's been a bullshit couple of days with one thing after another.

But now I need to slow down, something I don't do very well. I need to get to know my new wife. How the fuck do I do that?

I've never had to make small talk or be personable. *God.*

The idea makes me sick.

I don't know what the fuck those guys were talking about with the "beast," but I feel for the guy if this is what he had to go through.

I take the stairs two at a time, and when I step into the room, she startles awake. I didn't realize she'd fallen back asleep.

Her wide eyes dart to me, and she shrinks into the couch like prey sensing the predator's approach. When I see the bruise on her cheek and the cast on her leg, the rage surfaces again. She ran from me. She ran from *all* of us. The car, her pain—it's all part of a game she tried to play. In the life I lead, you either run toward danger, or it *finds* you.

I haven't forgotten that *I* was the one she was running away from. *I* was the one she was trying to escape. It's *my fault* she was hit by a car.

And for the first time, I wonder, why did she run from me to begin with? We hadn't even met. What drove her to do that?

"I brought you some food." She jumps at the sound of my voice. I guess it's louder than I expected. It booms in the interior of the room. Terrifying everyone around me seems like the order of the fucking day. Why does that not bring the satisfaction it once did?

"Thanks," she says in a quiet voice. "Do you know if I'm due for pain meds? I'm in a lot of pain."

I lay the tray down. "Let me check." It's taking every ounce of self-control I have to keep my voice quiet and gentle. Between her and Zoya, I practically have to reinvent myself every time I turn around.

I glance at the little timetable to see when she's due for meds next. It's just about time, but she isn't due yet. She still needs a heavy dose, then.

"Yeah," I say, looking at the orange bottles in front of us. "You could definitely use some more." I shake some into my palm and hand her a glass of water. She picks it up without a word, and it hits me hard. She has no choice but to take what I hand her—the meds, the food... the truth. What I hand to her is all she knows, all she can swallow. Having someone's life in your hands is heavy enough. But this? This is something else.

I drag a hand through my hair, surprised to find it damp. It isn't even warm in here—what the hell is this? Nerves? I don't get nervous. I sit down beside her.

"That was a pretty deep sigh," she murmurs, shifting as she tries to push herself up. I hadn't even realized I sighed. Leaning forward, I take her by the elbows, lifting her so I can adjust the pillows behind her back.

"Better?"

"Much. That smells *so* good. I didn't realize how starving I was."

"Me neither. My sister is quite a cook."

She frowns, looking down at the food. "Zoya?"

I nod. "You don't like it?"

Zoya has given us such a variety that I'd be surprised if there wasn't something here she liked. There's a generous bowl of borscht with sour cream drizzled on top, golden pelmeni stuffed with savory meat, and a platter of pirozhki, the smell of freshly baked dough making my mouth water. Even blini, thin and delicate, with bowls of honey, sit beside the plates. In the corner sits a small crock filled with cookies Zoya's recently baked. A carafe of wine completes the ensemble.

"No, sorry," she says softly. "This looks amazing. I was just trying to remember if I know how to cook. Do you know? *Can* I?"

I try to answer as many things honestly as I can. "I don't. Remember, we haven't gotten along before."

"Yes, that's right," she says.

I reach to take a napkin off one of the dishes, and she flinches back—something I should be used to by now. Everyone I know fears me, even Zoya and Yana, my own flesh and blood. But when Anissa shrinks back, it's different.

But maybe this time, it *has* to be different.

"You should eat food with that medication. You should not take it on an empty stomach." She nods wordlessly. Reaching for a fork, she takes the food I give her.

"Think of it this way," I tell her with a pretty lame attempt at humor. "*Everything* is a new experience."

She doesn't smile. My god, but she's beautiful. Porcelain skin, wide blue eyes framed with thick, blonde lashes, her hair so light it's almost white, cascading down the side of her shoulder, hiding the lacerations on her arm.

"That is one way I could look at it," she says with a little smile. "I don't know much about what happened to me, but it doesn't make sense that I have no memory at all, Rafail. I shouldn't say that," she says, shaking her head. "I remember a few faces. And I know some of them are familiar." Frowning, she looks down at her tray. "But *you* are wholly unfamiliar to me. So is this room. Your sisters, your brothers... I feel as if I've never met any of you before."

I ignore the wave of guilt that twists in my gut.

"You would think that I would remember *some* of you. Why don't I remember you?"

"I don't know," I lie. She eats rapidly as if she just wants to give herself something to do. Goddamn, I don't blame her.

I'm glad to see her packing it away, though, one bite after the other. Zoya will be pleased.

I live for control. I would absolutely hate being in her position, not knowing who I am, and having to rely on other people to tell me.

"I don't know exactly how amnesia works, but I do know the doctor said not to tax your memory. Just take things as they come," I say, "and I know that's a lot easier said than done." I shake my head. "I would hate being in this position." I frown and admit, "I don't think I would handle it very well."

Her beautiful face breaks into a little bit of a smile. "I feel like I've just met you, and I can already say with certainty that you absolutely would *not* handle a loss of control very well."

I grunt in reply, which seems to amuse her.

"Well, I can say one thing," she says, changing the subject. "This food's delicious. *Pelmeni*. Incredible. I can't say I've never had better, but it seems like the truth. And I definitely enjoy sweets." She eyes me as she takes a mini chocolate cookie in her hand and bites into it as if I'm going to scold her for eating her dessert before finishing her meal. I just care that she's eating.

When she reaches for another cookie, her sleeve shifts, and I see it—a faint, dark mark on her wrist. A tattoo. Curled lines form an intricate symbol, almost like a chain, no... a snake twisted around a flower? It's delicate, nearly hidden

Why was this not in my notes?

"I know what this is," she says, her face breaking out in a smile. "And I know it has something to do with my family."

She smiles, pleased with herself. "There. It *will* come back. I just have to be patient."

She pops another cookie in her mouth. "I like chocolate."

Why didn't I know about the tattoo?

"Is there anything else you can remember about me, Rafail?"

Time stands still for a fraction of a second. Fuck, but I love when she says my name. Just hearing it in her pretty, musical voice makes my dick hard. I shift uncomfortably. I want this woman... broken stranger that she is. "Anything at all?"

"You were brave," I say, surprising even myself.

"Brave?" She tips her head to the side.

"Yes, you did what I've never been capable of doing." I look away. I didn't mean to say that. Something about being in the presence of this woman who's supposedly my *wife* does strange, unexpected things to me.

She swallows, absentmindedly running her finger over her tattoo. "And what's that?"

I hold her gaze and take a sip of wine before I continue. "Surrendering control to somebody else."

"Well," she says thoughtfully, her gaze fixed on my wine. "You haven't given me much of a choice."

"Not much of a choice, no. But it *was* a choice."

She stares at my wine. "Can I have some of that?"

"Just a minute." I pull out my phone and type in the names of the meds she's taking. I read the contraindications and shake my head. "No, not with those medications you're on." I put my own glass down. "I won't have any if you can't."

She gives me a thoughtful look but doesn't respond. We eat in an almost amiable silence for long minutes until she pushes the tray away and leans back against her pillows, spent. I glance down at the tray. She's only really nibbled.

"You said I was a runner, but I have a hard time believing that. How is it that I was a runner and actually tried to outrun the likes of *you*, but I've exhausted myself by eating only enough food for a child?" She frowns as if disgusted with her lack of energy and stamina.

I stifle a growl. "You're correct. You barely ate a child's portion of food. Eat more, Anissa. You have to get your energy up." I push the tray back over to her.

She folds her arms across her chest and frowns at me. "I'm not hungry," she says with a note of defiance in her tone.

"You haven't eaten enough to gain any strength," I insist.

"Fine," she snaps at me, reaching for a second cookie. "Another cookie. How is that? You'll have a nice, sedentary, fat wife with a big butt."

I frown at her. "Keep it up, and you'll be a wife with a *sore* butt."

She opens her mouth to protest before she slams it shut again. With flushed cheeks, she pops another cookie in her mouth, another blini, and a few more bites of soup.

"Good girl." The words feel natural, right. She pleases me when she does what I tell her.

Her cheeks flush, and she looks away from me. "Now are you going to be satisfied?" She sighs. "Other than that, I think all I've *done* is behave myself. Jesus."

Her gaze lingers on the large bed, sitting flanked against the wall. Housekeeping has tucked in every corner of the duvet and sheets, the bed impeccably smooth. I imagine her hand fisted in the sheets, the way I'll wrap them around her body. I can see myself kneeling on the floor and her legs wrapped around my neck...

"Well, at least *that's* big enough," she says as if she doesn't know what to say.

I almost laugh. "I'm a big man."

She gives me a slow, lazy once-over that makes my cock stir. "I've noticed."

I swallow hard and push the tray away before she frowns and turns her head away from me. "Um. So. Question. Have we...? You know."

Fuck. This is where shit gets complicated. I haven't thought this through. If I tell her no, that I haven't taken her yet, she'll wonder why we've been together a week without me claiming what's mine and consummating our marriage. Any man in my position would make damn sure his wife knew who she belonged to.

She better be a fucking virgin. The very idea of another man's hands on her drives a dark fury through me. I'd hunt down any bastard who touched her. She's mine, whether she remembers it or not.

I decide to take a risk. "You disappoint me, Anissa. I didn't expect *that* type of blow to my pride. I would've thought at least our wedding night was memorable."

She's achingly beautiful when she smiles at me. Her voice drops, and she gives me a sheepish little smile. "Well, maybe when I'm better... you'll have to refresh my memory."

My pulse races. I *want* this woman. All of her. I hate that she ran from me, but goddamn, I'll make it my mission to make sure she never does—never *wants* to—again.

She's mine.

"Count on it. But for now, let's get you situated. You still have a ways to go." I stand and gather up the tray of food. As I turn to place it on my desk, she asks me another question.

"Do I have a job? How am I supposed to entertain myself? I don't know who I am, what my role is here... what do I do?"

This isn't too complicated. "I made you leave your job when you got married to me."

I turn to see a shadow cross her features as she narrows her gaze on me. "What did I do?"

"Lots of things, nothing of consequence." Jesus, I'm a dick, but based on what I read about her, she didn't have a career but dabbled in a few tame areas of the family business her father probably thought wouldn't put her at risk.

"We'll find something for you to do. Maybe for now, since we don't want to tax your brain, you can watch a TV show or read books."

She frowns and looks perplexed. "May I have a cell phone?"

Shit. If she gets her hands on a cell phone, she'll start looking shit up. Asking questions. Maybe she'll trigger a memory... I have to think fast.

"The doctor said not to tax your brain, and staring at a screen will definitely do that. Of course you can have a phone," I bluff, "just not right this minute. Let's wait until your healing's coming along."

Frowning, she nods. "I want to look up my name. I want to remember who I was."

At least she isn't lying.

I sit up straighter, my gaze sharp. "That doesn't matter anymore. You're mine now. Your name is Anissa Kopolova, and you're married to *me.* Whatever we were before the accident, it's done. We're starting fresh." I lean in, my voice low and unyielding. "On *my* terms. Your memory will come back in time, but until then, all you need to know is that you belong to me. And from this point on, you do what I say."

She stares at me and purses her lips but doesn't respond.

Maybe my brothers were right.

I make it sound as if we have all the time in the world when, in reality, every second we're together is a ticking time bomb.

CHAPTER 9

"ANISSA"

I GLANCE at the large bed in the center of the room. Questions swirl in my mind, but the most pressing one is—how do I share a bed with a stranger?

And how am I supposed to accept this man as my *husband*? There's an implied intimacy that makes no sense to me. How can I be close with a man I hardly know... a man who honestly scares me?

"I'd like to talk to the doctor tomorrow," I say thoughtfully. "I want to know more about this amnesia. About how I can bring my memory back."

Frowning before he answers, he finally nods. "I'll see what I can do."

Wordlessly, I watch him walk over to the chest of drawers made of dark maple, worn but obviously well-made. It matches the bed and the bedside table, all of it solid wood.

I wonder if this was his parents' room.

"You said your brothers are adults?"

Something flickers across his face before he answers without looking at me. "Only Zoya's still a minor."

I watch him, trying to stay focused but unable to hide my unbridled curiosity. He is my husband, after all. Those muscles? That tanned skin? Those corded forearms with visible veins, a smattering of dark, coarse hair, and strong, powerful hands I can almost feel all over my body—*mine*.

I swallow hard. Opening the top drawer, he pulls out a white T-shirt and a pair of boxers. But then, his hands shift to an ivory tank top and matching shorts—women's clothes. I don't recognize them, but I wonder if they're mine.

"Are those... mine?"

Not bothering to turn, he throws them aside. "No. My sisters thought you'd need those." I see a corner of his lips quirk up when he gives me a sidelong look, his eyes burning a hole straight through me. "Cute."

I stare, my mouth open. "What do you mean?" I finally manage to ask.

"You're my wife, Anissa." His tone is tight, clipped, and laced with authority. "I'll give you leeway, knowing you can't remember many things, so allow me to remind you." When he turns fully to look at me, I nearly swallow my tongue. Sweet Jesus, it's like looking at the body of a vengeful god—beautiful and terrible, capable of utter destruction and relentless protection. When he continues, there isn't a hint of hesitation.

He studies me and steps closer. I feel the weight of his glare, the heat of his gaze, his masculine scent overwhelming me as he draws near. His fingers trail down my neck, lingering with a possessive, almost punishing slowness that makes my pulse race.

"You'll obey me, Anissa," he murmurs, his voice a low rumble. "And in turn, I'll give you everything. Safety. Devotion. A life where no harm will ever come to you. All you have to do is submit to me. Learn your place as my wife."

That's it, eh?

Still, a thrill—unsettling yet undeniable—weaves through me, wrapping around me like a spell, an unbreakable vow, something ancient and powerful binding us together. I feel half hypnotized in his presence. I open my mouth to protest, to resist, to claim a part of my identity, but my resistance falters when his thumb sweeps against my jaw, tipping my face up to meet his dark, stern gaze.

"You're asking me to surrender to a man I don't remember," I whisper, my voice shaky, even as a part of me knows, somehow, that this was always my destiny. Somehow, I can't remember my own name, but I know the law of the Bratva.

"I'm not asking, Anissa," he corrects, his grip both firm and reverent. "I'm demanding it. In return, I vow my utter protection. I'll shield you from anything that tries to hurt you. But I am not a man who shares or who gives up an ounce of control."

Something inside me stirs like a forgotten memory, a whisper that somehow, this is a familiar dance—a test of wills, an exchange of power I both hate and somehow crave.

"Do you understand me, beautiful?"

I nod. "I do," I whisper, unable to fight the need to say yes, to see him actually make good on his promises. "Yes."

Bending toward me, he claims my mouth in a punishing kiss, his fingers anchored in my hair. His tongue licks mine, and my insides melt into liquid fire before he pulls away.

Our foreheads meet. "That's my girl," he says in a heated whisper. "Good girl." His hand strokes down my back in a gentle, possessive sweep, and I shiver under his touch.

Then his voice drops, a rough edge slipping into his tone as he whispers, "*Moya dyevochka... moya kharoshaya dyevochka.*"

My girl... my good girl.

My heart skips at the words—low and intimate. I close my eyes as his praise washes over me, threading through me, bringing life to my tired body and awakening a primal need as he traces the outline of my jaw. His gaze darkens. "*Ty prinadlezhish mnyeh.*"

You belong to me.

His fingers tilt my chin up, forcing me to hold his gaze. "And that means no one gets a piece of you. Not your heart. Not your loyalty."

I can barely breathe, caught in the intensity of his stare and the raw promise of his words.

I nod, the barest hint of agreeing, but it's enough. His thumb brushes my cheek, and I see the satisfaction flicker in his eyes as he repeats, softer this time, "*Moya kharoshaya dyevochka.*"

I watch, almost hypnotized, as he removes his shirt. His arms lift, the fabric sliding up to reveal his bare back, every bit as powerful as I'd imagined. My first impression was spot on. He's built like a warrior, with silver scars crisscrossing dark ink on his shoulders, back, and torso—his past etched onto his skin. My heart aches.

Those marks. I know them. Every muscle, every scar, tells a story of battles fought and won, of violence barely kept in check. And I realize with brutal, heart-stopping clarity—that *I'm* his next challenge.

The sign of Bratva… like mine.

He's honed his body to perfection, unsurprisingly. He's a man who values firm authority—over his environment, and over those under his care. It shouldn't surprise me, then, that he exercises rigid control over his own body.

I am not complaining. If I have to share a bed and take vows with a man I hardly know, it might as well be a man who looks like *that*. *Vavoom*.

He tosses his shirt toward the bathroom, and it lands in the wicker hamper.

I swallow and lick my lips. I had the distinct impression under those clothes of his, he hid a powerful, sexy body, and I am *not* disappointed.

Next, he unfastens his jeans. The moment feels too intimate, too private for two strangers. Yes, on paper, we're married. At least that gold ring on my finger says so, and so does he, but it feels like just today, I learned his name.

We need weeks, maybe months, before we can even begin to understand what it means to get to know each other, but my thoughts quickly jumble together like soup when he steps out of his faded jeans.

Oh. *My.*

I stare, unashamed, at how his broad shoulders taper into defined abs, accentuated with a smattering of coarse, dark hair and powerful hips that—okay, *alright.*

Phew. I swallow and lick my lips again. His legs are thick, muscular, solid, and so utterly masculine my breath catches. I glance down at my own body—trim and pale in comparison. Fit, yes, but much smaller. Daintier. We couldn't be more different physically.

My body reacts instinctively, drawn to the sight of him. I wait for him to pull on pajamas, but instead, he walks over to me, nearly naked, except for that tiny strip of fabric he calls boxers. It seems wildly inappropriate, but logic tells me it really isn't.

"You don't need to wear anything to bed." Is it my imagination, or has his voice gotten deeper? Huskier? More masculine?

Oh god. There is no damn way I'm letting this stranger undress me. "I'm fine," I say, panicking. "I'll just sleep in this." We both look down at my running shorts and rumpled tee.

His scowl sends a jolt through me, hardening my nipples under his intense gaze.

So maybe we *don't* need weeks or months. My body already knows what to do.

"The hell you are. I'm your husband, Anissa. You'll do what I say. And I've explained disobedience will earn consequences."

I open my mouth to protest, but no words come out.

"I'm losing patience," he says in a low growl. A small part of me is curious what happens when he loses his patience, but the logical part of me realizes that wouldn't be very fun. "You don't want that to happen."

Or would I?

"I don't remember you. I don't even remember *me*. I feel strange being undressed by you."

His voice is low, raspy, commanding. "I don't give a fuck if it's strange. I gave you an order, and I expect to be obeyed."

Again, my jaw drops in shock, unable to respond. What the hell am I going to do about it?

My libido gives me a hint of false bravado. "What if I don't want to obey you?" I can tell by the sharp set of his jaw and the cut of his eyes that he doesn't like my response. He opens his mouth as if to snap at me and then thinks twice about it.

"So you want to undress yourself," he says quietly. His jaw firms as his gaze meets mine. I want to take a step back; I want to turn away, but I make myself meet his stare.

I try to hold my ground. "I need time to feel comfortable getting naked in front of you."

His eyes flash. "I'm your husband." The words hang in the air between us as if he's staking his claim.

"Exactly. I'm not one of your siblings that you're in charge of. I'm your *wife*."

His brows rise in mild surprise. Surprise at my words or my pushing back at his commands? Maybe both.

Strong, large, very *capable* hands anchor on his hips as he continues. "I respect that you don't have a recollection of our world, but let me remind you," he says in a low, measured tone, "I do not tolerate disobedience. Yes, from the people under my command, including my siblings. But most especially my wife. It's my job to protect you, and if you defy me, you make that job difficult or damn near impossible. I don't take kindly to defiance, Anissa."

So maybe I don't want to find out what he'll do.

"I don't think it's very good for you to control my life," I say defensively, but I feel like I'm standing at the edge of a tide that's sweeping sand from beneath my feet with every tug of the undertow.

He leans forward, his presence suffocating, and brushes a strand of hair from my face, almost—*almost*—tenderly. "This is me being patient, little Anissa." He shakes his head. "My little swan. I'm not threatening you. I'm giving you grace."

He leans forward, his breath warm against my skin. "Going forward, there will be no second chances. If you'd remembered your place, you'd already be over my knee."

My pulse races.

"You'll allow me to undress you, and that isn't a question. You're exhausted. Now come *here*."

My heart beats madly in my chest. I can't blame the medication, not this time. Being in the presence of a man like him is terrifying. Exhilarating. It's the top of a roller coaster before plummeting to near death. It's staring at a deathly predator eyeball to eyeball. It's the flicker of flame that could warm or cause utter destruction.

Of course I want someone to take care of me—I'm only human—but I want it to be someone I actually trust. This man is still a stranger.

"When you disagree with me, maybe you should pick your battles," he says, his voice low and firm. He told me he wouldn't warn me again, and even though he's a stranger, I've started to compile a small list of things I know about him.

Top of that list? He is a man of his word.

"I'm going to run you a bath. You have a waterproof cast. You can take a bath with the cast on, and I'll even allow you to wash yourself."

I swallow hard. "Very generous of you."

"I take very good care of what's mine."

Definitely true. I look at the ancient, polished wood. The immaculate state of his bedroom. His clothes folded in the drawers, and the laundry basket flush against the wall. I note his siblings, who have been under his care since he was barely past childhood himself. He does take very good care of what belongs to him, and that includes me. I may not like it, I may fight it, but there's no denying what's happening here.

Without a word, he leans toward me. His fingers brush bare skin. My nipples pebble as more questions bloom.

He says we've been together before. Was he telling the truth?

In the fog of not having any memory, this feels like the first time he's ever touched me.

I close my eyes against the rush of feelings. My heart pounds in my chest as I feel his hands on my skin. He takes his time, lifting the tee off, his palms on my bare skin leaving heat in their wake. He gathers my silky hair, pale as corn silk, against his rough, dark skin. And when my top is completely off, he grazes my bare shoulder with the hint of a kiss. I shiver, and pressure builds between my legs. Every biological need in my body screams for more.

Just surrender.

Just accommodate his dominance and command and let him bathe me as I know he wants to.

It's tricky, taking off the shorts with the cast, but he does so slowly, deliberately, and when the palm of his hand brushes the curve of my ass, heat and pressure build between my legs. I want him to touch me. I *want* him to take control.

When I sit in front of him wearing nothing but a sports bra and clean black cotton panties, he whistles.

"*Christ,* you're gorgeous."

Wait. Hasn't he seen me naked before?

I look down at my body and swallow hard. "Um. Thanks?"

I can't help the way I shrink when he sits beside me and

drags me onto his lap. "You fought me, but your body knows what it really wants, doesn't it, little swan?"

My body thrums with a rush of heat fused with desire.

My *god.* My breath catches, and my heart stutters when he dips his head, warm breath pebbling my skin. He nuzzles the damp square of fabric between my legs, breathing in the scent at the top of my thighs. My body throbs with need, my senses electrified.

I tremble against the raw heat of his body, flush against mine. The way he inhales me, the way he stares at me as if I am the most beautiful woman in the world. He says we hated each other, but the way he touches me tells me otherwise.

His hands, still grazing my skin, brand me with the heat of his touch. My breath catches on instinct, betraying me. I can't resist him—I know I can't—this dominant stranger who calls himself my husband is the one in charge here, the one with power. I'm not even sure why I *should* resist him, as primal need surpasses logic.

And as my body hums with need, craving what I fear and what I want, any protestation I may have begins to dwindle. His eyes darken as he watches me, slowly anchoring his hands on my hips, his thumbs pressing into my hip bones, firm enough to brand them. His fingers feel like hot pokers as they trace across my skin. He holds me in place, his gaze on me ravenous. When he brushes the bare skin of my thighs, I flinch, my mind screaming at me to run, to pull away, even as my body arches into him.

My limbs feel heavy, my consent blurred.

"Stop fighting me," he says in a rasp, his lips close to my skin. He bends and kisses the top of my thigh, and my body reacts. "You say you don't know who you are... But *I* do."

I swallow hard and lick my lips, trembling. The difference in power between the two of us is harrowing, terrifying, but somehow... exhilarating. I know I'm at the edge of that precipice, ready to tumble to my certain death, and yet... I don't care. His words linger in the air, somehow tightening the invisible shackle he has around my heart. My heart pounds, and I open my mouth to protest, but everything I was going to say dies on my lips. I don't remember who I am, and I have no choice but to accept this.

I could push him away.

Maybe?

But the way he looks at me, he's a wolf with ravenous eyes, and I'm nothing but his prey.

Who am I? Why does it feel like everything in me is tethered to a stranger?

He tilts my chin, his rough hand branding my skin as he forces my gaze to his. "You need to trust me. I know that's a hard thing to ask when you don't know me, but it's the only choice forward, Anissa." His grip tightens just a bit, enough to remind me of the power he holds over me.

Trust him? On the one hand, it feels almost logical to trust a man who has such power and control, but what if he's manipulating me? What if he's lying? Yet something stirs in the primal and wicked response to his command. It isn't trust or submission or anything logical but a raw, visceral attraction that needs no explanation, as if my body has already accepted what my mind refuses to.

"You want me to trust you, and I don't even know you," I say in protest.

Something that resembles a smile tugs at his lips. "You will, in time. We don't get a lot of firsts. We'll enjoy this one."

He pulls me to my feet, and it's the first time I'm standing in front of him. The last time, he picked me up and carried me, and we didn't stand together. This time, he braces me so I don't have to put weight on my cast, but there is no getting over the fact that he towers over me. The warmth of his touch burns through the thin fabric of my clothes, and his hands slide down my waist. I shiver when he grips my ass and cups it possessively.

"I'll give you a little time to adjust," he says as if he's granting me a favor, a boon, his voice deceptively soft, but the underlying edge of control remains. With two fingers on my chin, he lifts my face to his and presses his lips to mine. Every protest dies, and my body leans into him. My mind grows fuzzy, and my body heats with electric waves. He smells like clean mountain air and raw alpha male, and the way he touches me leaves no doubt about what he plans to do with me.

This is a man who has control, power, and knows his way around my body. Every nerve ending in my body is on fire, and I want to scream for more. I want him to lay me down and ravish me. I don't need to have even the slightest bit of memory to know what I want him to do because I crave primal, visceral need. There needs to be nothing between us. I'm starting to resent that I'm still wearing panties and practically grinding myself on him when he kisses me. He squeezes my ass, lifts me, and on instinct, I wrap my good leg around his torso. He's holding my weight so it doesn't hurt, bends, and kisses me as if he owns me.

Maybe he does. No, not maybe... He *definitely* owns me. My mouth opens. His tongue licks mine, and my pussy throbs. A rush of heat blooms between my legs. I'm aching for him. Is my response to him because I have some muscle memory of pleasure, or is it just that I know this is a man who knows what to do with me? I keen with pleasure as his lips continue, his tongue pressed to mine, and I moan when he pulls away.

"I'll give you time to adjust," he murmurs in my ear, his voice deceptively soft but the underlying edge of control undeniable. "My good, beautiful girl."

I swallow hard as he eases me to the corner of the room, where a large, overstuffed ottoman sits beside the couch.

"Sit," he commands, his voice hard. I am vulnerable, exposed, and incapable of defying him.

So I sit. His eyes sweep hungrily over me one last time before turning toward the bathroom.

The sound of running water soon fills the air, but I stay frozen, my mind a haze of desire, confusion, and fear. A part of me wants to run, to escape the suffocating presence, to find out who I am without being colored by his touch and his need for me. To find a place that's safe. Because he is anything, fucking *anything* but safe.

A sudden wave of nausea hits me, and I clutch my stomach.

I don't remember who I am, but I know this—when he touches me, I awaken. It's both scary and exciting.

I sit in silence, weighing my options. He's drawing a bath for me, that much is clear, but do I trust him enough to go to it? I glance at the doorway, then back at my reflection in the mirror across the room. I look down at my skin, pale, naked, save for the scrap of panties, bra, and my blonde hair that falls in waves down my face and shoulders. My icy-blue eyes are wide with uncertainty. And while my reflection is somewhat familiar, it's scary that I don't even recognize the person in the mirror.

Though I have no idea who I am, I do have the certainty of one definite detail—Rafail Kopolov is a man I cannot afford to disobey or cross.

"Your bath is ready. Come here."

CHAPTER 10

RAFAIL

I LOVE the way her body trembles when I touch her. The way she yields to me, soft and pliant. A surge of primal instinct slices through me. She's not really fighting me anymore. Her defiance crumbles.

She hasn't caved in, not fully, and my instincts rail against me. *You fucking know she isn't really your wife.*

I logic my way around it. By all intents and purposes, she is. She was given to me. She's my possession. And I will not make any excuses for what I do next because I fucking own this woman.

The difference between her and every other woman I've ever touched demands a different approach. I feel something deeper, something that claws at the edges of my control and makes me want to fucking ravish her. A primal part of me wants to please her, to see her lips part as she screams in pleasure. Somehow, that would be my greatest victory.

So I keep my hands steady as I touch her, relishing the way her skin brushes against mine. When my fingers graze her delicate skin, the warmth of her body sends my senses into overdrive. She's pale, soft, vulnerable. My little swan.

I admire the curve of her waist, the strong column of her neck, her pale porcelain skin. Wide blue eyes framed in thick blonde lashes. There's a little dimple in her chin when she smiles bashfully at me, but right now, she looks as if she's Little Red Riding Hood and I'm the Big Bad Wolf.

Everything about her calls to me, and I know it's not just my imagination the way she responds. Her mind is trapped in confusion, but her body knows exactly what the fuck to do. I can't help but feel twisted pride at that.

She doesn't remember, but her body knows.

Guilt makes me pause, but I quickly bury it because I have needs, too, and logic tells me she belongs to me. I don't want her afraid of me, necessarily, but I can't relinquish all my power. Not now. Not ever. Weakness gets you fucking killed. I've seen too much, lost too much to give in to weakness now. But something tells me she is my kryptonite.

Her eyes meet mine as I guide her to her bath, the raw fear in them whispering a plea. *Don't hurt me.*

I'll make no promises. I can't.

As I pull her closer to me, the scent of her arousal, sweet and seductive, fills the air. I take in deep, cleansing breaths, wholly unfamiliar to me. Steadying. When she looks up at me with those wide, blue eyes, her body slightly trembling, I know she isn't just afraid. There's more to it.

"Beautiful," I whisper, my voice thick with desire. I brush my knuckles against her cheek, and she shivers. I enjoy the way her skin flushes under my touch. My little swan is fragile, and yet... There's strength there, buried in the confusion in her eyes. This is a woman who ran from me, now dependent on a stranger.

She doesn't know her own strength, not yet. It's almost laughable that she, of all people—the one who's my victim, my possession—is the only one with the strength to fucking challenge me, and here she is... dependent.

She's mine now though. She was before, and she is now. No one will ever touch her. No one else will ever know her. No one else will even breathe the fucking air she does. She's clean, a blank slate, and I have a new chance. When she spares me a look, my hands tighten on her hips.

I've been almost gentle until now, but I've exercised virtually all my self-control. I want her to trust me, to look to me not just as a man but as her protector. The idea of her running again fills me with undeniable rage.

No one deserves her but me.

Steam rises in the air from the drawn bath behind us as I lean in closer, my lips brushing her ear. "You're mine," I whisper, a statement and a declaration. Her breath hitches, her eyes meeting mine. She opens her mouth as if to say something and hesitates, uncertain. I bend my mouth to hers and kiss whatever she was going to say away.

The less said, the better.

I need to erase every trace of doubt from her mind and make sure she knows exactly who she belongs to. My thumb grazes over her collarbone as I kiss her again and again, savoring the way she trembles.

"Trust me," I whisper to her, my voice softer this time, almost pleading. I hate that I'm showing any weakness because I am *not* vulnerable, but here I am, raw, exposed. I need her trust, her submission. Maybe more.

She doesn't pull away. I help her out of her bra and panties, then lift her in my arms, careful not to aggravate her injuries. She's light in my hold and fits perfectly against me. As I carry her to the bathroom, toward the waiting tub, my heart clenches. Grounding myself into my new reality.

I lower her into the water, steam curling around her. She won't slip away from me. Not physically, anyway. Pain is a tool, something to be used when necessary... But not now. Now she needs to be pampered; now she needs to know that she is precious to me. My prized possession. I kneel beside the tub, my fingers trailing through the water, brushing against her skin once. Twice.

My dick aches. Throbs. My jaw clenches. Control. I must maintain control. But it's slipping, little by little, with every look that she gives me, every soft intake of breath. Every time we touch.

"*Weakness gets you killed*," my uncle told me when I became guardian of my siblings and heir to the throne. "Never let anyone take your power." But I want to protect her. Control her.

She closes her eyes and sinks deeper into the water. It reaches her chin. For one brief moment, I imagine what would happen if she slipped under the edge, sinking into oblivion. I imagine yanking her out of the water, breathing life into her.

What the fuck is going on with me?

Her eyes open, and a look of challenge meets my gaze. "Well, are you joining me or not?"

The tension crackles in the air between us. For a moment, I don't move. I let the words settle between us, a challenge and an invitation. Her bright blue eyes are wide as if she's surprised even herself, but steady, waiting for me—curiosity tinged with a bit of defiance. My little swan is daring me to come closer, even though she should be running. She's inviting me into her space, laying down whatever fears she has.

"Is that a challenge?" My voice is a low, deep growl. I hold her gaze as I shed my boxers. The air is thick and hot with steam, and as I come closer, her eyes track the movement of my hands. I thought it was dumb as fuck to have this huge bathtub in here when I first took over this room.

My parents' room was on the first floor—not the primary bedroom because they wanted to be nearby when they were raising us. When I became guardian of my siblings and owner of this house, I took over the vacant main suite. I wanted space. This is a good vantage point, most importantly, overlooking the front lawn, with wide open spaces so I can see to the left and right of the estate. Now, having a tub like this doesn't seem like a waste. Even if we never use it again, it was worth it just to see her naked body submerged in its depths.

Her eyes track the movement of my hands as I brace myself on the edge of the large tub. The control I have over her with the slightest movement sends a surge of heat through me. "Are you impatient, little swan?"

"Why do you call me that?" she asks, licking her lips. She tilts her chin up defiantly as though she's brave, but I know that she's tumbling. I can tell by the way her fingers graze her neck and the way she gasps for air.

"Your nickname. You grew up in Siberia. It seemed fitting."

"Siberia," she says quietly. "I remember that." Fuck. I don't want to trigger her fucking memory. I need her aligned with me before I do. Her memory is going to come back, and I have no idea how or when, but I need her loyal to me before it does. "You're elegant like a swan," I say quietly, changing the subject. "Graceful."

I step into the tub, and her eyes continue to track every movement. I submerge myself into the water, and fuck, it feels good. Can't remember the last time I had a goddamn bath. I reach for her, my knuckles brushing her jaw. I watch as a droplet rolls down my finger and onto her chin. Quietly, I tilt her face upward so she has to meet my gaze.

The pulse in her throat flutters. Her chest rises and falls in the heated water, but she doesn't flinch. I don't see fear in her eyes like I did before, but now something more—a magnetic pull, as if she doesn't even know who she is, but her body does. And it's telling her she wants more. I watch as a flicker of something dark, dense, buried under layers of confusion, passes. She wants to understand, wants clarity, but maybe a part of her remembers I am not someone she can trust. I want to get her focused back on me.

"Up here," I say with a little growl. She flinches, and her eyes meet mine. The heat of the tub envelops us as I scoot closer to her. I reach for her and pull her over to me. She floats easily in the hot water and nestles against my chest, the warmth of her skin next to mine. My hand splays across her stomach, my thumb grazing the underside of her breast, my pinky right at the little V of her pussy. She has a small, tight, unshaven patch. I rub my thumb along the edge and feel the softness of her satin skin. Underneath the surface, she's strong. I feel her muscles tense beneath my palms, and she does not pull away.

"How is your pain?" I ask gently into her ear.

"It's there, throbbing in the background. But tolerable," she mutters.

"Let me take your mind off of it," I whisper in her ear.

Her eyes close, and she lets her head fall on my shoulder. "Deal."

My cock throbs beneath her ass.

I rub my thumb over her hard nipple in the water. I cup both breasts, weighing them in my palms and flicking water over them. I place one hand under her ass and lift her so that her breasts break through the surface. I bend and suckle a nipple between my teeth. I bite her lightly, and the way she moans—the sound in the small chamber—makes my dick hard as fuck. I lick and suck, tugging her nipple into the wet heat of my mouth until she's moaning, her mouth parted, her cheeks flushed, and I don't think it's from the heat of the water anymore.

"You have no idea how much I wanted this," I whisper in her ear. "You fought me. Wouldn't let me touch you anymore. Ran from me." I nibble her ear and tug the lobe with my teeth. She gasps, and my voice lowers again. "I should punish you for that."

She shivers, even though it's warm in here. "I should be afraid of your punishment."

I drag my mouth along her neck and lick the water off her skin. Her pulse quickens under my lips, her body shrinking against mine. I crave her submission, crave her taste. I crave the way she responds to me as though she wants what I can give her, even if her mind betrays her.

I cup her abdomen and slide my hand lower over the warm wetness of her pussy, drawing out a soft gasp from her. I tighten my hold, keeping her close to me, her back against my chest and my cock against her ass. Her breath stutters as I press a finger to her throbbing clit, just teasing, just skimming.

"Tell me you fucking want this," I growl in her ear, my voice a command. "Convince me not to punish you."

"Tell me what that punishment would entail first," she says.

Hot damn. My pulse races.

"You over my knee. My palm across your ass. You, tied to my bedside, naked, while I tease you and bring you to the edge of climax. You, wearing my cum down your neck, back, and breasts while I stroke myself off again and make you watch." She swallows with widened eyes as I continue. "You, sitting on my face, sucking my cock while I whip your ass, taste your cream, and don't let you come."

"Uhm. That sounds a lot more enticing than being locked in or grounded," she says with that humor.

"I can do that too."

She actually smiles at that, her laughter filling the small room.

"You want this. Admit it." My voice is a dark command.

When she doesn't respond with words, her body tells me everything I need to know. The way she shifts, opening her pussy to me, inviting me to touch her. I press one fingertip to her throbbing clit again and circle. Her head falls back on my shoulder, and she sighs contentedly. My other arm curls possessively around her waist, holding her tight as I press my lips to the hollow of her throat. She lets out a soft whimper, and a dark satisfaction and primal urge surge through me.

She's yielding to me, but it's more than that. So much more. She's *choosing* this. Her body knows what she wants, even if her mind protests, and she's allowing this.

It's a small win, but I'll take it.

My fingers close around her, my thumb brushing her nipples, one at a time. I bite back a groan of my own because the way she responds is addictive. Her fingertips curl against my thighs, and she tries to hold onto control, but she's slipping... slipping under my spell, and she's not going to get away. I trail my fingers down to the top of her, brushing water over her, fanning her. Her breathing grows heavier, and her hips shift against mine, pressing into me. My cock is at her entrance, hot, thick, and ready. My control hangs on by a thread. I want to take her and fuck her until she's boneless and screaming my name.

"Tell me you want this," I demand in her ear. "Fucking tell me, my little swan."

"No," she says, turning away from me with a teasing look in her eyes.

A spark of excitement fires in my chest. "So you *do* want that punishment I promised?"

She gives one noncommittal shrug of her shoulder. Of course she fucking does.

"Bad girls don't get pleasure, little swan. Only good girls do."

"Oh damn. I'll be a good girl for you," she says in a voice that melts every icy side of my heart. It's all I need. I turn her head and capture her mouth with mine, swallowing every sound, licking her tongue as I delve my fingers deep into her slick pussy.

I thrust, pressing her clit with my thumb, and thrust again.

She moans into my mouth, and I swallow it. Her hips rise, and I stroke again. I take her to the edge until she's tumbling, begging, and then I part her thighs and slide my cock into her slick, hot entrance. She's so fucking tight. A virgin.

Christ.

"Oh my god," she says in a whisper. I hold myself back so I don't hurt her as I thrust into her again, slowly, the hot water lapping against her bare chest and mine. "Oh my god."

"There's no turning away from me now, whether you remember who you are or not, Anissa," I say in her ear, my hand paused over her clit. My cock bobs inside her.

She nods. "I know," she whispers with a groan. "I won't."

I thrust again, and her head falls back in unadulterated bliss. She moans, writhing, water lapping in waves against her bare breasts and chin while my pleasure eclipses everything. I curse and thrust, claiming her. I spill into her, milking the tight walls of her pussy as she climaxes with abandon. My senses drown in pleasure as I hold her on top of me, thrusting into her hot channel with claiming strokes.

"Yes," she breathes, riding out her orgasm. "*Yes.*"

"Good girl," I breathe into her ear. "That's right, baby. Surrender. Confess you're mine. Let me hear who owns you."

Her response is breathless, choked, her voice thick with desire. "You," she gasps, drunk with pleasure and helpless to protest. "I belong to you. *Yours.*"

I hold her to me.

My plan is working.

Only I don't know what will happen when she remembers.

CHAPTER 11

"ANISSA"

I STIR IN MY SLEEP, somewhere caught between reality and a drugged state of consciousness.

There's... a woman in my dreams. A woman with silvery gray hair and kind eyes, and my heart aches because *I know her*.

"Mom?" I want to say, but that doesn't seem right; something's wrong with it.

"Where are you, Polina?" She wrings her hands, and she's crying. There's a man—no, there are *several* men, faceless but not quite strangers, there with her, comforting her. They're familiar, but I couldn't name them. I couldn't place them.

My heart aches. I reach for her, and I open my mouth to speak, but nothing comes out. I try, desperate to communicate with her as she gets farther and farther away from me. I can't see how she's drifting away, so I'm helpless to get to her or bring her back to me until her back is to me. The farther she goes, the harder I try to get her attention.

"I'm here," I want to say, which makes no sense to me, even in my dream, because... my name is not Polina. My name is Anissa. I have no mother. And who are the strangers?

Half waking, I feel strong arms around me, warm, comforting. Restrictive. I scream and thrash, but it does no good. I open my eyes and sit up, gasping for air.

I turn toward Rafail... my husband. He holds me. "You're all right," he says, and even though it looks like he's trying to soothe me, concern is written across his features. "I've got you. It was just a dream. Just a dream."

It's terrifying to wake from one dream only to realize that you're living in a nightmare. "It's all right," he says, his voice softer this time.

I remind myself over and over... My husband. This is my husband. I married him and wear his ring. I still don't remember.

There's some comfort in at least knowing who he is. *This is my husband.* I'm getting to know him, and I'm safe. I'm okay.

All right, I can do this. Just as a trial, I push one of his arms, which is wrapped around me, until he lets me go. He's only trying to comfort me, not restrain me.

This time.

Still, my heart is beating so fast that I feel a little sick.

I sit up in bed and look around the room. "It was just a dream," I repeat.

We had sex the first night, the two of us, and it's been a few days since then. He's touched me, talked to me, but mostly worked hard at making sure no one bothered me so I could "rest" and "recover."

I won't call it *making love* because I don't know him well enough to call this anything even close to that. There's something about the way he touched me, the way he kissed me, that spoke more to me than his harsh words and angry glares.

This man, who is still a practical stranger to me, is a lover. He knows his way around my body, and I definitely enjoyed the novelty of being with him. It was nice to lose myself in him for a little while.

"What's going on?" he asks in a low, husky murmur. "Do you want to talk about it? Was it a... bad dream or something?" he says. There's a little divot between his brows that tells how much effort it takes for him to be gentle. He's worried about me. Give Rafail Kopolov a sword and tell him to slay your dragons, and he'll do it without hesitation. Ask him to talk about emotions, and he's terribly out of his element.

I may not know who I am, but I'm starting to get to know who *he* is.

"It was," I say quietly, looking away because I'm still trying to sift through the memory of what happened. "There was a woman—an older woman, someone who could've been my mother. But you told me I don't have a mother."

"You don't," he says quietly. There's no sign of a lie.

"She called me Polina." I look at his face for some sign of recognition, but either he's a very good liar, or the name is unfamiliar to him too.

"I've never heard that name before," he says. "I mean, I don't know anyone who goes by that name."

I open my mouth to tell him, but something holds me back. I look away.

I am vulnerable, split wide open, and completely at his mercy.

Who is Polina?

Maybe I need to keep a few things to myself. Maybe—

His finger under my chin gets my attention. I swing my gaze to his as he cups my jaw. "You looked like you were going to speak and then stopped. What is it?"

"The name wasn't unfamiliar to me, Rafail. It felt... like it fit."

He stares at me and nods, perplexed. "That isn't your name. I know these types of medications can really wreck dreams. I'll ask the doctor to put you on something else tonight." He frowns. "How's your pain level?" He's eager to get answers, something tangible.

A dragon to slay.

"Manageable," I say softly because it is much better than it was. I sigh. I feel like one of those people in a movie, gifted with a vision and determined to get others to see what they can't. Any moment, he'll take my temperature to see if I'm delusional.

Quietly, thoughtfully, he pulls me over to him and holds me against his chest, then wraps one arm around me tentatively, as if he knows it's something he should do, but he doesn't quite know how.

I let him comfort me. It feels like a choice.

In the soft quiet of early morning, the memory of the dream fades until it's just that... a distant memory. A dream that I'll forget. I hope I do because it only makes me nervous, like a fear of forgetting something important on overdrive. I've forgotten *everything* important.

I try to go back to sleep, but after the shot of adrenaline and triggering memories, I am wide awake. I think with my eyes closed. Then I open them and stare at the ceiling. I enjoy the comforting heft of his arm strewn over me, but I can't tell if he's sleeping or not. I try to take a look—his eyes are closed, but he may be awake. I reach over, grab one of his small chest hairs, and give it a little tug. His eyes fly open.

"What the fuck?"

"Sorry," I say, trying to stifle a laugh. "I didn't know if you were sleeping or not."

"If I was, I'd be wide awake now," he says. His voice is still all sleepy-husky. It's sexy as hell.

"Sorry," I repeat. "Get some rest. I need to get up."

He grunts and closes his eyes.

An undeniable urge to run courses through me. I run early in the morning. I need that. I know that now. Impossible to do with this damn cast, but I'll get there again. I've been cooped up in this room, in this bed, and I'm ready to get out of here.

Polina—it's the one thing from my memory I can't forget. A name. It's mine. Somehow, the name Polina is more familiar to me than Anissa. It's like solving a riddle, and the answer to it is just beyond my reach. Rafail seems as clueless as me, at least when it comes to my name. Every once in a while, I get a hint he's hiding something from me, but right now, he seems genuinely confused.

As I still against him, watching light filter through sheer curtains, my thoughts are jumbled and confused.

Polina.

The name sits in my mind, clinging with the memory of something I can't shake. The older woman... her tears, stricken face... she *seemed* familiar, like someone I would know. But who? Not old enough to be a grandmother, yet the desperate way she called my name... she didn't feel like a stranger to me.

I push myself out of bed quietly, thankful I am not in as much pain as I was before. Maybe he was right about the medication. When I look over, one of his arms is across his brow, and he snores gently. I feel the urge to run again. I want to escape the confines of this room. The confusion. But I hesitate. I don't know who I am or even where I am, and it's dangerous out there.

Still, I need air and space to think. I tug on a loose pair of sweats with wide bottoms that fit over my cast and a T-shirt. I look around the room. Now that I'm dressed, I don't know what to do with myself. I need a damn pair of crutches.

"Where do you think you're going?"

I shouldn't be surprised at how easily he wakes.

I turn to see Rafail sitting up, his gaze locked on mine and that perpetual scowl on his face. Though his voice is calm as usual, there's an unstable edge to it.

"I'm just going outside," I say, trying to sound casual like it's not a big deal and I'm not trying to escape the suffocation of this room. "I want fresh air."

"How? You don't have any crutches."

"I can manage to hobble around outside."

"You're *not* hobbling around outside," he says firmly, swinging his legs out of the bed before he stands. "No way."

I cross my arms, defiance bubbling up inside me. "Why not? I need some fresh air. I need to clear my brain."

Fortunately for *him,* he has use of both legs, so he makes short work of closing the distance between us. As my heart beats faster, I hold onto a chest of drawers to steady myself. "It's not safe out there."

Now it's my turn to frown. "What am I, Rapunzel?"

He *glares* at me and doesn't answer.

I throw up my hands. "Where is it safe, then?"

I watch as he stabs a finger at his chest. "With *me.*"

Sadness settles over me as I look around the room. It's a prison in here.

"What's so dangerous out there?" I ask, and I try to be brave, but my voice trembles a little. Outside the window, the sun has begun to rise, bright light tickling the edges of the estate. And what an estate it is, at least based on what I can see from here.

There's hope in the air, promise, and I know then why I like the early morning. I stare out the open window like a bird in a cage, peering out into freedom and possibility. I swallow hard, my emotions wobbly and unpredictable. It's hard enough not knowing who I am. Harder still not knowing when or how I'll ever have freedom again.

"You'll do what I say, Anissa."

I sigh and don't respond as he continues. "I have enemies, and so do you. For now, we're keeping our distance. You've got a lot to do around here. You don't know anybody in this house, and before the accident, you had work you were going to do for me."

I feel his heat behind me as he approaches, but he doesn't touch me. Not yet. "What do you do for work?" I ask. "You said you're Bratva."

I see them then. Familiar faces swimming in my mind's eye. One with tattooed markings along his inner arm, another man so big he fills a doorway. I screw up my face, try to conjure up more vivid details, but it's gone as fast as it came. A flicker of memory, then.

I want to cry.

"Yeah," he says behind me. I hear the telltale squeaky sound of drawers opening. "My operations span a lot. Black market shit. Drugs. We own a few clubs and lots of real estate throughout all of Russia, not just Moscow."

"And Zalivka?"

"In our pockets."

I nod. "And America?"

"We have property in America, as well, yes, but I prefer staying here in Russia."

Right. I nod. He manages properties, clubs, and illegal activities that pad his family's pockets.

I take a deep breath. The scent of cinnamon and coffee lingers in the air, and my stomach rumbles. Someone's up.

I swallow, staring out the window from my gilded cage. Inside this well-appointed room, I have everything I could desire. It's a suite fit for a queen. I almost feel selfish asking for more, but it's normal and natural to want freedom, friends... family.

I let my gaze wander outside. A wall of tall, sturdy pines, as dependable and impenetrable as he is, line the estate.

I hold my head up high and stand to my full height, bracing myself on the windowsill. "You said I'm your wife. Then maybe it's time you treat me like that." I turn to face him. "I want out of this room. Crutches. An appointment with the doctor so I can ask my questions." I swallow hard. "I want to meet your family."

A shadow crosses his features before he answers.

"There's always a threat, Anissa," he says. "I'm not letting you walk right into danger. You don't have to work, but I've already accepted that you'd want to."

He's bare-chested and sexy as fuck, as he prowls over to me.

I turn away from him, purse my mouth, and gaze out at the evergreens. "Very generous of you," I mutter. "For fuck's sake. I'm so over—" I gasp when his palm slams against my ass. I turn around, my cheeks flaming.

"Hey! You can't do that!"

"I just did. Don't sass me, and I won't."

"Oh, is that all?" I ask as his eyes flash at me.

"No. Definitely not."

I scowl at him and open my mouth to argue—to tell him he has no right to tell me what to do, but something in his expression stops me.

This... bossiness... I've encountered it before. This feeling of imprisonment... it isn't foreign either.

Who else made me feel this way? Was it him? Or someone else? I don't know.

I cross my arms on my chest, even as heat rises in my belly, and I feel a strange, albeit maddening, attraction to his dominance. "Just so you know, when I get stronger? I am *not* helpless."

"I know," he says, his tone softer but still rigid. "But until we know more, you're staying here where I can keep you safe."

This feels familiar... the same story, just a different day. Every response, every feeling... I've felt it all before.

The delectable smells wafting from the kitchen make my mouth water. My belly flips. I'm hungry. "Do I get to eat breakfast, or should I wait until you spoon-feed me?"

Why does that narrow-eyed look make me shiver?

"Watch it, beautiful," he says, shaking his head. "You know what I said about disrespect." I toss my head to cover up the feeling of the blood rushing in my ears.

"Yeah, we'll go downstairs and eat breakfast. I'll help you with the stairs and get you a pair of crutches. It's something."

I jump at the sound of a knock at the door. My frustration flares as he turns toward it.

"Come in," Rafail barks in a tone that would make anyone cower. The door opens, and one of his brothers—Semyon?—stands awkwardly in the hallway. He's tall and lean, looks a lot like Rafail, but slightly younger, his beard a bit more scant. I don't think he's much older than I am.

"I need to talk to you," he begins, but Rafail cuts him off.

"Not now." He runs a hand through his hair, his patience frayed. "I'm busy."

His brother frowns, his eyes flickering to me, then back to his brother. "It's about the shipments. You told me to keep track of them—"

"I said not now," Rafail snaps, his voice sharp like a whip. His brother visibly flinches. "Stop asking questions and leave us. I'll talk to you over breakfast." He gestures angrily at the door.

The harshness in his tone catches me off guard, but his brother doesn't seem surprised. His mouth opens and closes like he's trying to find the right words but knows better than to cross the beast.

"Rafail," I venture. "We're just going down to breakfast. You probably have to put a T-shirt on or something," I add, glancing at his bare chest. "Maybe you should let him speak."

Rafail narrows his eyes at me, jaw clenched, but after a moment, he steps back and looks to his brother. Turning his back to him, he opens a drawer and grabs a white tee. "Fine. Make it quick."

His brother stares at me, his jaw unhinged. I smile at him. "What do you need help with?"

He speaks in a rush of words, making sure he can get it all out before Rafail cuts him off impatiently. "We were supposed to receive thirty crates. Usual supplier. But only twenty showed up, and there's something off about what came. The stamps on the crates don't match the manifesto, and half of the supplies are from another manufacturer."

"Motherfucker," Rafail mutters, tugging his shirt on. His gaze darkens as he thinks this over.

"What do you think I—" his brother begins, but I cut him off with a sharp shake of my head.

"I got you a chance to talk to him. Don't push your luck. Sounds like a good catch, but I'm sure your brother can handle it from here."

Semyon blinks in surprise. I gesture toward the door, a silent command for him to leave the way he came. What does he think this is, a democracy? I'm still getting to know Rafail, but even I can see the fire building in his eyes, coiling like a dragon ready to snap its jaws and burn him to bits with his fiery breath.

"My wife is right," he says in a very dragon-like voice. "Now get the fuck out of here."

"But—" his brother continues. I actually flinch. There's only so much I can protect him from.

"I said I'll handle it," Rafail barks, and finally, thank god, Semyon bolts when Rafail takes a step toward him, his body tense with barely controlled energy.

"Keep up the good work!" I yell after Semyon because I feel as if I need to protect him or something.

I turn back to Rafail, who is staring at me with a mixture of frustration and something else on his face. "What? Do you always talk to them like that?"

Somewhere in the back of my mind, I feel like it's familiar... having siblings. *Siblings*... sometimes harsh to each other but loyal to the core. It's all familiar too—a dance that I've danced once before and maybe still know the steps—as if from another life.

His low growl of a voice doesn't surprise me but catches my attention. "Don't do that again."

"Now, listen," I say, meeting his gaze head-on. "I'm not going to stand by and just let you bully everybody into submission. That's not how this works, not if you want me to actually like you."

"Bully everybody?" he says, as if shocked I accused him of such a thing.

I catch a flicker in his eyes, but there's something beneath the surface that tells me I hit a nerve, that I'm standing on quicksand, and one step further, I may not be able to yank myself out.

Oh well.

"Yeah," I continue. I can *feel* my eyes dancing at him. "Bullying. You've tried it with me, but luckily, I... kinda like when you get all bossy. *Sometimes.*"

What? Why did I turn this into flirtation?

He gets in my face, his breath hot on my chin. I can almost see fire dancing in his eyes. I reach my hand to his face, loving the way the rough stubble's grown a little thicker. I shiver. *Yum.*

"I detailed what punishment looks like, Anissa. Maybe I've changed my mind about going down to breakfast." He takes me by the hand and then, in one swift motion, lifts me into his arms, marches to the bed, and tosses me down.

"Rafail—" I go to protest, but in the next minute, my wrists are bound in front of me with white satin. *Jesus.* "What are you doing?"

"Teaching you your place," he snaps, rolling me over to give me a sharp slap to my ass before he's gone in a flurry of temper and heat. The door slams shut behind him.

"Very charming!" I yell after him before I let out a scream of frustration. God, just when I think I'm starting to see a little side of his humanity, that there's maybe hope for the two of us? He pulls this shit.

Voices rise and fall in the hallway. Well, fine. He can tie me to the bed, therefore I can eavesdrop, dammit.

I recognize his voice, engaging with a female one, but I can't tell if it's Zoya—the one who's quickly become my favorite. He's protesting something, and from the sharpness in his tone, I can tell he's telling someone off again. I haven't even met his second sister yet. Yana?

The other night, in the bath, for a moment, I thought that there was hope. I thought that maybe there was a chance that my brutal husband... maybe wasn't so brutal.

Perhaps I was wrong.

Or maybe we need sex to bring out the humanity in him.

I stare up at the ceiling and assess my pain level. My leg does hurt, and so do the lacerations on my arm, but the medication he gave me is starting to kick in. The lingering memory of the dream I had last night is only that now—a memory. I can't remember the details, and I'm not sure I want to. There's something about it that was unsettling, something about it I can't quite shake, though I'd be hard-pressed to even tell the details now. My stomach churns with hunger, and I definitely need some food. I need to settle my stomach, though, so I'm not sure food is what's going to do it for me.

I close my eyes. I'm still tired. Always tired. Maybe I can get some rest.

I need a purpose here, eventually. Obeying my bear of a husband or whatever it is he demands is hardly enough. I roll my eyes to no one.

When the door opens, Rafail stands in the doorway, glaring at me. "Fine," he growls. "You can come to breakfast, but you'd better behave yourself."

If by behaving myself, he thinks I need to keep my mouth shut, then I believe there are a few things my new husband needs to learn about me.

"Did somebody out there remind you to be human again? The full moon's gone, and you can put away your werewolf?" I jerk my chin into the air.

His response is a low growl I feel in my bones. "Watch it. I came to bring you a present, and I'll take it back if you sass me."

Even when I'm mad at him, I love the sound of his voice. That's when I realize he has a pair of *crutches* with him. Whoever he saw in the hallway had these for me. My heart soars.

"You're sure you're alright with giving me some mobility? Thought you'd have me depending on you for life. Thought *you'd* be my crutch."

He smirks at me, and my belly swoops. I swallow hard, pretending he doesn't have this hold on me. "No, baby," he says, leaning close to put his mouth to my ear. "I'm your husband. And when you realize what that means, you'll see it's all I need to be."

I forget his domineering tone as he unties me and helps me to my feet, then hands me the pair of crutches. I'm clumsy at first, and it's awkward with them under my arms, but I quickly make my way to the door. *Yes.* I can move, and faster than wobbling and feeling like I'm going to tumble over.

"Also, don't forget you said I can talk to the doctor."

"Yes," he says distractedly but doesn't offer any details. "How are you going to manage the stairs?" he asks with another frown, holding back.

He holds the door wide open, and my heart *soars.* I was so tired when I first came to this room that I barely paid attention to the details of his home. Now I'm struck with its beauty—high, vaulted ceilings, marble floors, and large windows that flood the space with light.

"This home is *gorgeous,*" I breathe, looking around like a kid in a candy shop.

He gets a sheepish smile and puts his hands in his pockets. "Thank you. They call it The Cottage."

I snort. "The Cottage? I love how Russians have a dry sense of humor. This place isn't quaint or small but *enormous.* At least it looks that way."

I make my way toward the top of the stairs. He reaches for me and then holds himself back as if reminding himself to let me go.

"I've made sure it was safe and secure. My sisters are the ones who keep it… homey."

I breathe and soak in every detail. Beyond the large windows are stone walls and intricately carved iron gates, lush gardens outside with greens and blooming flowers. The sprawling mansion seems to balance old-world elegance with modern charm.

"You alright?"

"I've got it." I put both crutches in one hand and hop one step at a time. My husband stands just in front of me, clearly using all his self-control not to help. Resisting the urge doesn't come naturally to him. I can tell by the tension in his jaw and shoulders he's not too crazy about this plan, but it's working. He grits his teeth, standing just in front of me and takes a step forward just before I do.

"Are you standing there so that if I fall, you'll catch me?" I ask, huffing and puffing and sweating from the exertion.

He shrugs, his eyes meeting mine only briefly before he takes another step back. "Yeah, baby. That's a husband's job."

Something like pleasure weaves its way across my chest, and I swallow a lump in my throat. So damn emotional on these meds. I want to get off them soon.

"What did you give me for pain meds?"

He lists off a bunch of names, things I've never heard of before.

"I want something over the counter. Please," I tack on as an afterthought. "Something tamer."

Step. Hop. Brace.

"They won't work as well," he mutters, still frowning.

"I know, but that's a risk I'm willing to take."

I don't want another dream like the one I had last night. Something tells me it may have been the pain meds.

Finally, we reach the bottom of the stairs. "I can't believe I was a runner, and I can hardly handle a flight of stairs without being winded." It's frustrating as hell. I place the crutches back under my arms and glide my way next to him.

"You'll get back there. Patience."

"Ah, something else you'll teach me?" I ask with a playful smile.

Rafail grunts in response as he walks, and I hobble across a formal dining room. The polished table is covered in textbooks at one end, with coloring pencils and doodled-on papers scattered around them. It's clear this room sees more homework and art projects than actual dinners. To the right of the table stands a sideboard with a few cases of sports drinks and soda.

"Careful," Rafail says with a frown. "I told Rodion to put those away." Shaking his head, he lifts a notebook. "And Zoya was supposed to get this project in yesterday. She's been distracted."

"How old is Zoya?"

"Seventeen."

He's been her guardian since she was only a small child. No wonder he has a soft spot for her.

No wonder she's as timid as a little mouse, poor girl.

"Are those her schoolbooks?"

"Yes. She's got a big exam coming up."

Just then, voices ring out from the kitchen, followed by the unmistakable sound of a scuffle—thumps, grunts, and a clatter that makes my heart skip.

"Jesus," Rafail mutters, striding toward the commotion.

As soon as we round the corner, we find two of his brothers locked in a wrestling match, grappling and shoving each other dangerously close to the counter where a bowl of dough sits, perfectly risen and ready to bake. Zoya's precious bread.

Without a word, Rafail steps in and grabs them each by the collar, yanking them apart as if they weigh nothing. He gives them both a quick, firm shake, his glare cutting through their adrenaline-fueled grins.

"Alright," he growls. "Which one of you needs to get your ass kicked first?"

The brothers exchange glances, their faces suddenly sheepish. From behind him, someone I haven't yet met peeks out, barely containing a snicker.

"Well, Yana?" Rafail prompts, raising an eyebrow at her. "Who's getting it first?"

Yana crosses her arms, smirking. "I'd start with the one who nearly knocked over the bread."

Both brothers freeze, eyes darting to the delicate bowl of dough. They gulp in unison, and Rafail gives them one last shake before finally letting go.

"I brought my wife down to breakfast," he warns, "behave yourselves."

They're hardly children, but the brothers quickly back away from each other, Semyon's cold gaze still fixed on Rodion, Rodion's jaw clenched. Rafail just shakes his head, muttering something under his breath as he straightens his shirt.

Yikes. He had his work cut out for him with this crew.

"Sit down," he barks before he turns to Zoya. "Did you forget to hand in your assignment?"

Zoya flits around the kitchen, straightening things out, and doesn't meet his eyes. "About that," she says as she places a crock of butter on the table and a loaf of bread. "I've been meaning to ask you to help me with it. There's all these questions about... well, family history and stuff."

Rafail stands taller and crosses his arms on his chest. "What do they want to know?"

As they talk over past history, someone clears their throat. Yana stands in front of me. A young woman a few years older than Zoya but younger than Rafail, she smiles softly. Her presence has a calm, almost regal quality, with a confidence that's both subtle and undeniable. Her hair falls in loose waves around her shoulders, framing her face. I notice the faintest trace of makeup—a flick of mascara, magnifying her electric-blue eyes, and a hint of pink lip gloss—matching her understated elegance.

Her eyes meet mine with an openness that catches me off guard. There's a quiet strength in her gaze like she's weathered storms that only she fully understands. When she tucks a strand of hair behind her ear, a glint of gold on her finger catches my attention.

Is that a wedding ring?

"It's nice to finally meet you," she says, her voice gentle yet unwavering. I'm struck by the warmth and steadiness in her tone, and there's something about her that feels both grounded and fiercely resilient. "My brothers have told me all about you, but Rafail's been possessive, hasn't he?"

My brothers. For some reason, it makes my heart ache. He says I don't have siblings, but I know that to be... a lie.

I did. I do. And I'll find them.

"I don't remember who you've met or who you remember," Rafail says.

I shake my head. I had too many meds and was confused and disoriented.

"A proper introduction would probably be a good idea," I tell him with a shrug.

"Right. This is Semyon," Rafail says, gesturing toward the man I encountered upstairs. He stands just a step back, arms crossed, his gaze dissecting me with unnerving precision.

Semyon has the sharp, chiseled features of Rafail but wears them with a colder detachment. He pushes his glasses up the bridge of his nose, his expression clinical as if he's calculating exactly who I am and what I might mean to his brother. His eyes are ice-blue, unblinking and methodical, and he gives off an aura that's almost surgical—analyzing, cataloging, already figuring out the quickest way to manipulate or dismantle me if it ever came to that.

"Hello again," he says, his voice low, each word deliberate. There's no warmth there, only a distant courtesy. "Welcome."

I manage a nod. "Hello."

For a moment, his gaze flickers past me, locking briefly with Rafail's in what seems to be a silent exchange. I can't quite read it, but the corner of Semyon's mouth quirks, almost as if in approval, before he turns his attention back to me with that same unnervingly calculated stare.

He's less angry than Rafail. Hell, they all are. Maybe they haven't had to face what he has. Anger radiates off Rafail in waves—it's in the tone of his voice, the cut of his eyes, the familiar downturn of his lips. Even without my memories, I'm sure I've never known anyone as angry as him. And, yeah, there's a part of me that can't help but want to fix him. Not my job, I know, but... it's only instinct, really.

Rafail pulls out a chair for me, his grip steady and commanding as he helps me sit. His voice is calm but carries an edge as he continues the introductions. "This is Rodion," he says, gesturing to the man standing just behind him.

Rodion's stance is deceptively relaxed, but there's a tautness in his movements like he's ready to strike at the slightest provocation. His scant beard shadows a face that holds a mix of mischief and menace, his sharp eyes flashing with a dangerous gleam. For an instant, a smirk pulls at the corner of his mouth, but it vanishes as quickly as it appeared, replaced by a look that seems both appraising and faintly amused as if he's already one step ahead of everyone in the room.

He gives me a single nod. "Hey," he says, his voice low and casual, but there's a note beneath it that's almost predatory, and I don't trust the way his gaze shifts away from me as though he's afraid I'll see who he really is or Rafail will.

"Hey," I reply, my voice softer than I intended, the intensity in his gaze unsettling.

I glance back at Rafail, catching a flicker of something sharp in Rodion's eyes when he looks at his brother. Respect, perhaps, but tinged with something darker—a wary kind of fear or maybe an unspoken rivalry.

"You met Yana?" She nods and gives me a small smile. There's a reserved pain behind her eyes, the kind that only comes from experience. I get the distinct feeling she keeps her life close to the vest and only trusts a select few. I want to be one who she trusts.

"And you know Zoya," Rafail adds. The sweet girl, wearing jeans and a modest tee, her hair in a ponytail, smiles softly at me. You wouldn't know who she was—or, more accurately, who her brothers were.

"How's your pain level, Anissa?" Zoya's voice is soft, full of concern—always the caretaker, always the one trying to mend what's broken. Her wide, watchful eyes track my movements as if she's afraid I'm going to fall apart.

I smile, trying to ignore the throbbing in my temples. "Better with the meds." I glance down at the table, at the plate of slightly overdone eggs and dark-brown toast that's barely edible spread with butter that's still lumpy. "Did you... cook breakfast?" I'm trying not to be insulting, but it's hard to imagine the feast of the other night was prepared by the same hands.

"Oh, um, no," Zoya stammers, shifting nervously, her hands clasped together as if she's trying to hide something. "It was Rodi's turn today. I like when it's my job, but we take turns. Rafail's rules."

"She's being modest," Rodion mutters from across the table,

leaning in with a crooked smile. "We *all* prefer when it's her turn."

Rafail smacks Rodion's arm. Rodion snorts and buries his face into a cup of coffee, but the smirk remains. He fears his older brother, but not so much that he doesn't speak his mind or forget his sense of humor.

Semyon, the family observer, it seems, chuckles. "You can thank *him* for this." He nods toward Rafail. "He decided learning how to cook was a life skill we all needed. Said something about not being reliant on others. And some of us are... well, better than others."

"I can grill steak," Rodion offers with a shrug. "That's all I can cook, but it's a good one."

"I'd... eat steak for breakfast," I say helpfully.

The others snicker, except Rafail, who blows out an impatient breath. It feels like a normal family for a brief moment —if not for the dark undercurrent that flows through the room. They hold secrets and fears they haven't yet revealed to me. Rafail's face is unreadable as he fills a plate and pushes it in front of me. He pours himself a cup of coffee, then turns to me. "Do you like coffee?" His voice is low and controlled as usual, his dark gaze flickering to me before he amends his question with an almost uncharacteristic stammer. "I mean... today. Sometimes you drink it, and sometimes you don't."

Awkward silence hangs in the air between us before I nod. I'm not used to him being unsure, much less deferring to me. Silence stretches before I shrug. "I think so. It depends."

His brow furrows. "On what?"

"Um, who made it?"

Laughter erupts around us, and something loosens in my chest. Zoya's eyes dance at me. "I made the coffee."

I nod seriously. "Then yes, please."

I take a sip of the coffee. It's black and bitter, and I wince at the taste. Rafail slides a carton of cream toward me without meeting my eyes. "You like it with cream," he says, his voice low. I pour it in and give the cup a stir, finding the taste much more bearable now. "Yes, I like it."

"You don't remember what you like or who you are?" Zoya asks gently.

"Yes, and it's unsettling," I admit. "I had a dream last night that felt so real before I woke up and realized that waking up feels like a dream too."

Zoya gives me a sympathetic look, but Rafail cuts in, shifting the conversation. "Let's go over the plans for the day." He turns to me. "Today, you'll have that appointment with the doctor. Yana, make the appointment." He goes off on a litany of tasks for all of them. Some make sense to me, and some don't.

"Zoya, reach out to the Popovs today. I want them to know we still honor our agreements despite everything going on."

She nods and says something quietly with her back to us. "On it."

"Semyon, circle back and make sure that shipment arrives tonight without a hitch." His voice lowers. "*No* mistakes this time."

Semyon nods but sits straighter, clearing his throat. I can tell he's the type who rarely makes mistakes, and definitely not the same one twice. He takes pride in perfection and doing his job. "Of course."

"Rodion, I want you to meet with Vory and let them know we're watching." He holds his youngest brother's gaze. "Make it clear I don't trust them, but remember you're the messenger."

Rodion blows out a breath, his shoulders slumping as he opens his mouth to protest, but Rafail cuts him off, sharp and direct. "Don't fuck this up, Rodion. I'm not saying it again." He leans in closer, his eyes narrowing, his voice low and dangerous. "You remember what happened last time, right? If I have to leave Anissa to drag your ass out of another mess, you're gonna wish you'd never left the house."

His glare is so intense that even I shrink back in my chair, a little voice in my head already whispering, *Whatever you do, just don't get on his bad side.*

Rodion lets out a long, dramatic sigh, rolling his eyes but eventually nodding. "Alright, alright. Got it." He glances at me, giving a half smirk. "See what I have to put up with?"

Rafail ignores him and goes back to issuing orders. "Yana." She's on her phone, presumably pulling out the number he asked her for. "Check on the financials for the front companies. Make sure everything looks clean as hell. I heard rumors of auditors breathing heavily down the neck of a few friends. We're squeaky clean."

She nods and crosses her legs gracefully. "Obviously."

“And I need to talk with Danila. He reached Bangkok this morning, yes?”

Her eyes meet his warily. “About what? You promised me he wouldn’t get involved in family business.” Her wedding band glints in the overhead lighting. I’m gonna guess Danila is her husband.

“And I’ll keep my promise. That doesn’t mean I don’t get to talk to him about *you.*” He holds her gaze. “You’re my sister. I don’t care if you’re married. You’re part of this family, and I want to make sure you’re safe, especially when your husband is traveling.”

My heart melts a little.

The rest of them begin clearing the table, but Zoya stays near me, always eager to help. "I'll help in the kitchen," she says, but Rafail snaps again. “No. Sit.”

She quickly takes her place and sits.

I turn to him with a raised brow. "Do you always tell them what to do like this?” I bite back a sarcastic reply that I don’t think he’d appreciate and remember his admonition. “Rafail… relax.”

“Listen,” he says, leaning forward, his eyes dark and unflinching. The blunt tips of his rough fingertips press together. “This isn’t a request, Anissa. It’s a partnership, one my siblings will be as familiar with as you. You’ll learn how things work around here and fast.” His voice drops, cold and sharp. Poor Zoya flinches. “I *always* take care of what’s my responsibility—but you give me *everything* in return. No questions.”

“Zoya, help me with the dishes?” Rodion asks. She scurries out of the room before Rafail can stop her.

I find myself asking, “You don’t have staff that work for you? With a house this size, I would've thought you’d have people to cook and clean.”

“We do,” Rafail admits. “But my parents taught us the value of hard work. Independence is important.”

I nod, digesting this. "Interesting, Mr. Self-Sufficient. And yet, we seem to be getting along quite well."

Rafail smirks but offers no more details. I feel more awake now, the effects of the medication wearing off, and I’m starting to orient myself. The memory of who I was still escapes me, but I can feel bits and pieces slowly resurfacing.

I sit quietly. My job for today is observation, and one thing I note with certainty is that while everybody jokes and laughs with a camaraderie that is fitting for siblings, there's an underlying tone of respect they all have for Rafail. He's definitely more father figure than brother.

Even though we haven't been at this very long, the exhaustion from having to keep up with everything is starting to wear on me. I know he notices this when he places his hand on the small of my back. I don't even know if he realizes what he's doing as he draws small circles with his thumb, soothing, and I wonder which one of us he is trying to calm.

"Get the doctor on the line," he snaps to Semyon.

"About that... Yana said he’s, um, traveling," Semyon says with a cringe that tells me he is very well aware of the fact that his brother is definitely the one who will murder the messenger, regardless of the message.

"Have you asked how long? How far?"

"Not sure."

Rafail blows out a breath. "Find out."

I bite my tongue, just about to tell him that maybe he should say "please" once in a while, but I remember that he tied me to his bed stand for giving him shit earlier, and I'm not quite sure I want to test him already.

"It doesn't have to be your doctor," I tell him with a shrug. "I just want to talk to a doctor about what I can expect and what's happened."

"I want someone to understand the history and who they're dealing with," my new husband says, his eyes locking onto mine.

Semyon talks on his phone while Zoya and Rodion do the dishes. Glad to know that Rafail is an equal-opportunity employer, and that the men do shit right along with the women. But I guess that makes sense when you had to be both mother and father for many years.

A sharp knock at the door catches our attention. I stiffen when I realize that everyone—and I do mean everyone, even little Zoya—snaps to attention. Rodion's hand is at his waist as if ready to pull a gun, and Semyon's knees are slightly bent. Rafail has gone as still as a statue and already holds a gun in his hand.

Where did that even *come* from? *Jesus.*

Once again, that flicker of familiarity ignites in me. Déjà vu, you could even call it. They've been here before, and so have I. Then why are none of them familiar?

I glance down at my hands, the sensation of cold, hard steel lingering as I remember… I know how to hold a gun. My fingers twitch involuntarily, and the question rises in my mind: *Do I know how to use it?*

Before I even realize what I'm doing, my mind is already running through a series of instinctive motions as if coldly calculating how to survive.

I belong here. I'm not a fish out of water like I thought. I'm missing parts of the puzzle, but this life—this life is not unfamiliar to me.

My gaze flicks to the wooden rolling pin hanging on the metal rack by the wall. It'll do. I could grip it tightly, let its weight settle in my hand, then swing it hard—I'd aim for the head or temple, and if they got too close, I could drive the handle into a pair of ribs and feel the crack of bone. If that didn't drop them, I'd use my good knee—hard and fast—to the groin. That would give me an opening. Then, a swift elbow to the jaw, a strike at the part of the throat, and find a way out.

Flashes of muscle memory flood my mind. My pulse races. Twisting, countering, neutralizing. The shadow of a figure in my mind was my trainer, but I can't see her face. A woman's voice, sharp and commanding. Her name is out of reach, but her lessons remain. She taught me how to fight. How to survive. Her voice, strong and distinctive but feminine, guides my instincts even now.

Was she a sister?

Always go for the joints. Knees can buckle. Elbows can be broken. Eyes can be blinded.

This all flashes in seconds before someone shouts, "Don't shoot," an older male voice says. "It's just me."

Rafail growls and puts his gun away but still looks wary. The rest of them don't look so eager to do so. Two steps, and Rafail's at the doorknob, turning it.

"How many times have I told you to use the front door like civilized people?" Rafail growls. He blocks the door so I don't see who it is until he steps aside.

An older man, with the slightest resemblance to Rafail, stands in the doorway. He has salt and pepper in his hair, slicked back from his forehead, revealing tanned, well-worn skin that's cracked like leather, calculating eyes, and a cruel mouth that tells me he is very familiar with what these men do. Next to him stands a blonde woman with bright-red lipstick and false eyelashes that border on wings, wearing a red cardigan cinched at the waist with a gold belt, paired with dark-blue jeans and a pair of heels.

She stares at me, her eyes sweeping over me in a slow, deliberate, uncomfortable once-over, scrutiny the other two women spared me from. The frown that follows is unmistakable when she takes in my rumpled clothing and bare face—disapproval, maybe even something stronger. Like I don't measure up. I feel smaller under her perusal. Exposed.

I stand taller and meet her gaze. I may not remember who I was, but I know who I am now, and I will not wilt under the scrutiny of anyone.

"Is this the new bride?" she asks, snapping her gum.

Rafail's jaw clenches. "Yes. This is Anissa. Anissa, meet my

Uncle Eduard and his wife, Irma." He turns to Eduard before I can respond. "Listen, I need a lead on a doctor."

Eduard nods, helping himself to a cup of coffee. "I've got you one, but you'll have to go there in person. He doesn't do house calls."

"Did you make these?" Their aunt pokes at a container of last night's cookies.

"Zoya did, but easy, they're *loaded* with sugar and fat," Yana says, her eyes thin slits, hands on her narrow hips.

They don't like this blonde. I'm not surprised.

"That's fine," I say to the uncle just as Rafail shakes his head and says, "No way."

We glare at each other. In the presence of witnesses, maybe I can push my luck.

"I'd like to go, please," I say, more friendly this time.

"No. Not if it involves leaving the house." He looks at his uncle. "Give me his number. I'll convince him to come."

Something tells me he definitely *could.*

"This particular doctor takes a neutral position on all things related to..." he glances at me, "our world. It's likely in our best interest to keep it that way."

Rafail scowls before he turns to Semyon. "Find the doctor on vacation."

"Tried, brother. He has no reception. Can't reach him." Rafail's eyes darken, and his lips thin. Oh, for the love of—

I throw my hands up in the air. "Rafail, you told me I would get some answers. You *promised*."

Narrowing his eyes at me, he gives me a silent warning. I know what he said, and I heard him, but dammit, I want answers.

And how bad can disobeying him really be?

"I promised to get answers, but I never said that doing so would actually be an opportunity for you to get injured again."

"You know," Semyon says. "Might be a good idea for you to go there." He thoughtfully strokes his chin. "You'd be right in the vicinity of the docks, where the shipment's set to arrive tonight. Not to mention, where Popov's men were last seen snooping around. You could kill two birds with one stone."

Rafail draws a breath through his nose and clenches his teeth as he exhales. He absolutely doesn't like the position he's in.

"You're not well enough to travel," he snaps, but I know this is just a sham. He doesn't want me to leave the gilded cage.

"I'm fine," I say, pushing myself to stand. "Stronger now that I've had an excellent breakfast."

Rodion snorts but quickly shuts up at Rafail's murderous gaze.

"Fine," Rafail finally says through gritted teeth, obviously outnumbered. "I want to go now. You're going to need to rest later. Give me the number."

He hasn't even called to see if the doctor would have time for him, but apparently, he doesn't need to, not with that much power.

I watch as his aunt traipses across the kitchen, high heels clicking. She sniffs at the carton of cream. "Don't you have any low-fat creamer? Skim milk?"

"Eh, drink it black like a real man," Rodion says, his eyes challenging her, and his uncle snorts.

"Let's go," Rafail says as he wraps an arm around my shoulders and helps me to my feet. "Now."

I reach for my crutches, and he lets me, even though I feel the tension in his hands as he loosens his grip, reluctant to let go. I hobble toward the door, but just as we're almost there, my ankle wobbles. *Shit.* His arm wraps around my waist in an instant, steadying me as a low curse slips from his lips, warm against my ear.

"You okay?" he murmurs, his voice rough but laced with concern. A shiver runs down my spine, instant heat coloring my cheeks.

I swallow, feeling the heat of him close. "Yeah," I say softly, trying to smile. "I just need a little practice."

Rafail opens the door, scowling at the darkness in front of us. A car already waits right at the edge, only a few feet from our home.

Am I already thinking of it as "our" home?

So now I know what the phone call was. I'm starting to get the hang of these crutches—they aren't as bad as they seem.

I place them under my armpits and swing my legs out, one after the other. After he opens the door for me, I slide into the passenger seat.

But as soon as the door shuts and we're alone, he yanks me onto his lap, careful not to jostle my leg, and turns me to face him. His grip on my jaw is painful as he locks eyes with me.

"Do not ever, ever do that again. The only reason why you're not over my lap with your pants around your ankles learning your place is because I'm giving you this one warning."

My heart thuds in my chest as I stare at him. "What?" I swallow hard, trying to muster my courage.

His voice drops to a low, dangerous register, cutting through the air like a blade. "I've given you fair warning, and I do not repeat myself." He drags me closer, his fingers tightening, just harsh enough to remind me who's in charge. "I expect your obedience, just like I expect theirs. I'll risk fucking *everything* to keep you safe. But if you think talking back to me in front of my family is how you'll help me do that, you're dead wrong."

Leaning in, his breath is hot against my ear, the menace in his voice sending an undeniable shiver down my spine. There's a fine, fine line between fear and excitement, and every second I'm with him reinforces that. "You don't contradict me. You don't talk back to me. You do what I say, the way *they've* learned to, and I promise, you'll never have to worry about a damn thing again."

His grip tightens, his fingers digging in deeper, the pressure almost painful. "Is that clear?" His eyes bore into mine.

"You've pushed, Anissa. You've tested how far you can go, and right here is the edge of where your boundaries end."

I swallow hard.

"Tell me you understand."

I nod, my heart pounding, the thought of softening this beast of a man a distant memory.

"Yes," I whisper, my voice shaking as I ask myself what the hell I've gotten into.

He leans in, his devastatingly handsome face mere inches from mine. He lowers his hand to the small of my back, drawing me close. Almost caressing me. A reward for obeying.

"Yes, what?" he demands.

I swallow and give him the only possible response. He doesn't need to ask me twice, as the vision of what he threatened plays itself out in my mind. "Yes, sir."

The approval in his eyes warms me as his hand dips low to the small of my back and flexes. "That's my good girl," he whispers, his voice low and rough. And then his lips are on mine, and I'm melting, lost in the raw, intoxicating scent of him, the rugged yet somehow tender strength of his hold. Heat pulses through me, responding to the possessive way he claims me with a promise of protection and so much more. My mind wavers, torn by the intensity of his demands, but my body yields, melting into him like wax to an open flame.

I'm a stranger in a foreign land who's starting to feel as if she might belong, even as the questions of my past remain unanswered. Something in me warns me to resist, but I'm realizing with every passing day... I'm not sure I want to.

He touches his forehead to mine and pushes a button beside us. "Pull this fucking car over and put up the privacy screen."

CHAPTER 12

RAFAIL

I WANT to lay her down and fuck her until she screams my name. I want to wrap my hand around her throat as she comes, giving her a taste of how yielding to my control can bring her pleasure.

I hold her to me and watch as her eyes widen. The flutter of her heartbeat at her throat excites me. She'll learn what I expect, and fuck if it doesn't make my cock hard as fuck knowing I get to teach her.

I grab the back of her neck and drag her mouth to mine. I bite her lip and lick where I bit, eliciting a moan from her that makes my cock press to her ass. Her skin is warm to my touch. I love the way her body melts against mine, how the slightest brush of my fingers makes her flush and press closer to me.

"Touch yourself," I whisper in her ear, cradling her against me so she can slide her hands to her waist.

"Rafail," she says, her voice shaking. "I can't do this. Here? *Now?* I don't—"

My palm slams against her ass before I grip her hair in my fist. "You'll do what you're fucking told. Go ahead. Give me a reason to take my belt across your ass before we go to the doctor. I'd fucking love to see my stripes on your naked skin when you sit on my face tonight."

Her jaw drops, and her eyes go wide. She has one more second before I make good on my promise. I fucking hope she does.

I savor the way her breath hitches. The way her hand trembles over her sweet pussy. The way she obediently slides her fingers down to her bare skin. She moans when she finds her own wetness. My mouth goes dry. I can only imagine how fucking good she tastes.

I'll taste her tonight.

Her pupils dilate as she strokes her wet pussy. I wrap my fingers around her hair, yank her head back, and bring my mouth to the bare, throbbing skin at her neck. My eyes close, and I moan at the salty taste of her skin while she trembles and strokes. My breath hot on her ear, I talk her through it.

"Faster. If you stop before I tell you, I'll whip your pussy and lick you until you're ready to come, then make you sit there, right in the office, wet and aching for me."

I'm a fucking bastard, and I make no apologies for it. I won't. She's my wife, and she fucking earned this when she ran. When she put my family's legacy at risk. When she made a mockery of our vows. She'll learn her place by my side, and she'll *feel* it. Pleasure will be her reward, but not before she takes the pain along with the punishment she deserves for defying me. And she'll understand *exactly* who's in control.

I'm half-drunk on the smell of her arousal in the small confines of the back of the vehicle. The car hums beneath us. It's hot as hell in here. Her skin's slicked with sweat as she strokes herself. I bite her tender flesh, and her head tips back.

I lick and suckle her earlobe, her lips, and she arches her back as if on the cusp of coming. "Faster," I order. "Do it."

I yank down her top and reveal her perfect naked breasts. I pinch one nipple between my fingers and clamp down on the second with my teeth. I lick and bite, my dick painfully hard as she releases a soft moan. "Come, Anissa. Come now. And I want to hear it again. Say *yes, sir,* as you come, my little swan."

"Oh my god," she whispers, stroking herself. "*Yes, sir,*" she says before she screams, her body shaking. I hold her as she comes and murmurs her promise of obedience. Her face flushes, her mouth parted in a gasp. I hold her to me.

"Good girl," I whisper as her breathing slows and her head falls to my shoulders. I right her clothes, and her hands come to rest in her lap. Her breathing's ragged as she comes down from her climax. "Good girl," I repeat. "That's what I want to see, my little swan."

I tap on the privacy screen and hit the speaker button. Her face is tucked into my arm as if hiding from the world.

My chest swells with pride.

"Let's go."

CHAPTER 13

"ANISSA"

I STARE up at my husband, that wicked glint in his eyes and the smile that curves his lips. My god, I don't know if he's a demon or an angel.

Maybe neither.

Maybe *both.*

He's wicked and sexy, and he makes every nerve in my body sing, even as my heart beats frantically at his issued commands and utter demand for compliance.

I won't let him know how much this exhausts me, how tired I am just going from one place to the next. I won't tell him how much the pain is either. I wanted to see the doctor, and I'm getting my way, so there's no need for him to get all smug about it. Still, I can't help but lean my head against the seat and close my eyes, still sweaty and panting from my climax.

But as the wheels crunch over gravel and we continue toward wherever the doctor's office is, I can't help but wonder what else he has planned for me. What he's threatened. What he's promised.

Gah.

"This was a bad idea."

"It wasn't. It was an excellent idea," he says with no small measure of smugness.

I open my mouth to protest when I decide it's probably smart for me to reserve my energy. Bide my time.

See what else he has up his sleeve.

We're silent for long moments, and I'm half-asleep when he finally speaks. "Don't fall asleep. We're here."

"I'm not asleep," I lie, even though I think I was almost dreaming. I pry my eyelids open and find us at a small residence.

This is nothing like what I expected. I thought he'd bring me to some type of office, but instead, this is a little house with wooden clapboard siding and a faded sign.

"Wow. Um, this is it?"

He frowns at the age-worn building, eyes narrowed. "I suppose so."

"Do you trust your uncle?"

He shakes his head. "That's a complicated question." I don't push. "Hold my hand when we go in. Don't talk to anyone. Keep your eyes in front of you."

What?

I want to ask him why he's so afraid. Even though I think I already know, I want to hear it from him. For someone like him, just taking me to the doctor means he's already given me what I want—and let the doctor take the upper hand.

What's it like to need to control things so tightly? What will it take to make him crack? I feel as if I've already gotten a taste of it. He looks from left to right as though waiting for someone to leap at us from the shadows. What is he hiding? Or is he really just fearful in general?

Not surprisingly, we manage the short distance from the car to the entryway without being bombed by a terrorist, attacked by a madman, or swept away in a hurricane. I am clumsy on my crutches, but he is sturdy by my side.

Inside, it's clean and vacant, a sterile waiting room with a few chairs and end tables strewn with glossy magazines. It's so normal, so natural, it feels a little odd to see after the total isolation of the past few days. "Huh. No other patients?"

"Obviously," he says, scowl in place. "I won't take unnecessary risks."

Oooh. Right. "So you made sure nobody else came here?" I ask him, but the wide-eyed look of the receptionist sitting at the desk is answer enough for me. She stares at him as if he's a ticking time bomb. "We have an appointment with the doctor," he grunts.

"I-I know. Yes, sir."

My cheeks flame at the wicked hint of a smile he gives me. Those words will never have the same effect again. I turn away, cheeks flushed.

The assistant grabs a clipboard, fumbles awkwardly with it, and then drops it on her desk with a loud clatter. She jumps, her face flushing as she scrambles to pick it up again. Her hand shakes so much she can barely hold on. Rafail blows out a breath, grabs the clipboard from her, and thrusts it into my hands along with a pen.

I look at the sheet in front of me and scan the questions. A lump rises in my throat when I realize I can't answer half of these questions. Date of birth? No idea. Medical history? I haven't a clue. Blood type?

Beats me.

I turn away. The page in front of me blurs, my eyes filling with tears of frustration, when Rafail pulls it away from me and tosses the clipboard back on her desk.

"This is unnecessary. Open the fucking door, and let me see the doctor. He can shove this paperwork up his ass."

One thing's abundantly clear to me: Rafail didn't get where he was by being *charming*.

"Of course, Mr. Kopolov," the assistant says. She's stunning, dressed in a tight pencil skirt and V-neck blouse that shows every curve. Her calves look amazing in those heels, but he doesn't even look at her. He turns his head and peers in the other direction, a muscle ticking in his jaw.

"Mr. and Mrs. Kopolov."

It's the first time I've heard both of us addressed like that. Did they announce us that way when we were married?

A young doctor in his mid-thirties stands in the doorway. Tanned skin and short hair—he looks as if he just got home from a trip to the Caribbean. "I'm so sorry for the confusion," he says, gesturing for us to come into the office. "Please, come in. If I'd known it was you making an appointment, sir, I'd have come to your house."

Oh Jesus. All this *compromise* from my unyielding husband for nothing.

"Next time, you will," Rafail growls.

I place a hand on his arm to calm him. Maybe more sex will help.

Jesus, did I really just consider that?

"Mr. Kopolov, I have your family files here."

Rafail goes rigid. "Who sent those?"

The doctor frowns, looking over them. "No one. These are public record." He's quickly reading through things. "Ah, I remember this story. You became legal guardian to your siblings when you were barely an adult yourself." Nodding, he flips through. "There were three brothers and a sister. You—"

"Strike that." Rafail cuts his eyes to the doctor, who pauses mid-sentence and stares at him. I stare too. Three brothers and a sister?

"I have two sisters and two brothers. My sister Yana is now legally married to Danila Sanchez, though she kept her legal name."

I stare, but I don't say anything. I've seen Yana's ring but haven't met her husband. She doesn't live with us.

My mind whirs over this news as I piece it all together.

Rafail *has* had his work cut out for him as guardian. The laws in Russia are draconian, with few rights for people who don't meet the status quo.

Again, more questions surface, but I watch as the doctor makes the necessary changes to the paperwork before we move on.

"What can I help you with?" the doctor says.

"My wife has amnesia," Rafail says at the same time I say, "I have amnesia." The doctor nods. "Yes. I read the report."

"Where was that report located?" Rafail asks, his eyes narrowing on the doctor. The doctor doesn't fluster, but I watch him nervously eyeing the doorway as if estimating the distance between him and Rafail in case he needs to run. Good luck with that, buddy.

"A secure, encrypted file," the doctor says. "I promise, no one else has access to it. Your brother sent it to me." He turns to me. "I know you suffered retrograde amnesia due to head trauma. Are you here because you have questions about this?"

"I do."

Leaning back in his chair, he taps his fingertips together. "What can I answer for you?"

My mind goes blank. I begged—damn near demanded—for him to take me to a doctor so that I could get answers to my questions, and now that I'm here, I don't know what to ask. I open my mouth, but the problem is I have so *many* questions that I can hardly form a coherent thought.

"How long can she expect to have memory loss?" Rafail asks. His voice is calm as always, but there's an underlying tension when his hand grips mine. Maybe he doesn't like that I don't know who I am.

The doctor adjusts himself in his seat, glancing between the two of us as if weighing his response versus his need to relay accurate information. "Retrograde amnesia varies greatly from case to case. There's no promise of a full recovery, and in some isolated cases, certain memories will never return. The brain can be unpredictable."

Rafail's jaw tightens, his fingers flexing against my skin. "So there's nothing concrete? We came out to see you, and you don't really have any answers?" His questions become more detailed and pointed as he drills the doctor on every angle—treatments, triggers, even the possibility of sudden recovery. I watch as his need for control clashes with the ambiguous answers. I almost feel bad for the doctor. God help any doctor who will deliver my baby if I ever get pregnant.

Pregnant. Babies. Something flashes in my memory again, a triggered memory of wearing scrubs in a hospital as someone prepared to birth a child. Huh.

I watch as the doctor flips through a manila envelope, reading the chart, his brow furrowed. "This type of amnesia impacts your ability to recall memories from before your accident."

I know. That seems obvious.

"I remember... some things. Little bits. Pieces." My voice breaks. "Not enough."

"That's typical," the doctor says, almost methodically, tapping the file. "Your memories are fractured, and we've found that memory loss is sometimes tied to the emotional intensity of an event. It's the brain's way of protecting itself from trauma, and we don't even need to have physical impact for such a thing to happen."

"So someone can be so traumatized that they have amnesia?" I ask, staring at him. "Without any impact?"

The doctor nods. "In your case, it seems as if the trauma was significant."

"She was hit by a car," Rafail snarls. The doctor jumps in his chair, but I just give Rafail a withering look and squeeze his knee. *Relax.*

"The brain has its way of protecting itself from trauma, is all I'm trying to say," the doctor says, glancing briefly at Rafail before continuing.

"Will I... remember? When will I know?"

"Know what?"

I try to swallow the lump in my throat, but it doesn't work. My voice wobbles. "Everything."

The doctor hesitates. "Remembering is possible, but with retrograde amnesia, memories often return in fragments. But to reiterate, there's no guarantee."

My jaw unhinges. My heart pounds so hard I feel nauseous. Hope sinks as I shift in my seat. "Do you mean to tell me I might never remember who I am?"

He sighs. "It's hard to predict. You may get some memories

back, but if we push too hard, it could cause things to be much worse."

"What could make it worse?" I ask as the room begins to spin, and it feels too hot in here.

The doctor pushes his glasses further up his nose with a furrowed brow as though trying to determine his next move in a game of chess. "Stress, trauma, trying too hard to remember things. All can complicate your recovery. If you want to make sure that you remember, don't push yourself. You don't want to shut down the process. Let things happen naturally."

I can tell you this—I'm not somebody who lets go easily. My hands clench into fists. "You're telling me I could break my brain?"

The doctor looks at Rafail again before he responds. "To be perfectly honest, I can't make any guarantees. There's no way to truly break a brain," he says, quoting me. "But we want to make sure that you have proper healing."

He's raised more questions than he's given answers. "But I need to know. I need to remember. It's like I've been dropped in a foreign land, and I don't speak the language."

Something like fire ignites in Rafail's eyes, but he doesn't answer or say anything.

The doctor leans back, his expression vaguely sympathetic. "I understand that, but you must be cautious. You don't want to force a memory to come back and trigger more confusion or even introduce false memories."

My stomach plummets. Before this conversation, I had no idea that was a possibility.

The truth is... the man beside me is the biggest question of all.

He tells me I'm his wife, but I don't *feel* that way.

Why was I running? I need to know.

His answers have been fruitless so far. I turn to Rafail. The brief silence that follows is heavy, nauseating, as Rafail's eyes darken, and when he speaks, his tone is typically cold and chilling. "You were running," he says softly. "I told you that."

"I know, but *why*?" Surely, there was a better way to handle things.

He doesn't answer right away, his jaw clenched. Finally, he says in a low but clear tone, "You didn't want the life we had, Anissa. You were trying to escape it."

I can almost hear the words he doesn't say aloud: *but there is no escape.*

The doctor interjects, "I understand this is a lot, but I recommend you just focus on resting your brain right now. Give yourself time to heal."

Give myself time to *heal*? Take this easy? I balk at him. "What if I *never* remember?"

Rafail shakes his head. "I promised you we'd ask questions, but we need to leave now."

Suddenly, my husband's phone buzzes. His brow furrows as he pulls it from his pocket and shakes his head. "We need to go. Thank you for your time, doctor. I wired the funds to your account."

The doctor's brows shoot up. Wired funds sound like some underground negotiation, not a medical consultation. I wonder how much he paid him.

When we're outside, I stare at Rafail, eyes wide. "What happened?"

He smiles at me, bends, and kisses my cheek. "Nothing out of the ordinary. Not yet, anyway." We walk toward the car. "Semyon saw a threat retreat, one I feared." He turns toward me with a soft smile on his lips. "You said you wanted to go see the city? Let's go, Mrs. Kopolov. You *own* this city."

CHAPTER 14

"ANISSA"

Snow falls like starlight, dusting the narrow, cobblestone streets of Zalivka. The buildings rise close around us. It feels familiar yet different, like visiting a city in a foreign country that resembles home, but the locals speak another language.

This is a place that has seen centuries pass and keeps its secrets hidden within stone walls and narrow alleys. I feel both curious and cautious as I walk beside Rafail, his presence a shield. I wonder how much the Kopolovs have played the part of gatekeeper.

I note as people stare in his direction with wary respect, and a few nod to him, casting glances toward me as if to assess my role beside him. I can see it in their eyes—they know him as something of a myth here, feared yet respected, the kind of man who could command a whole town's obedience with a mere look. Naturally. His reputation precedes him, and with each step, I feel it pressing down on me like a weight. In this world... in these streets, filled with old-world charm and traditional values he both embraces and challenges... where does he fit in?

Where do I?

Rafail keeps his hand on the small of my back, guiding me forward with a firm, possessive touch. I wish I could skip these crutches and be less conspicuous, but I'll have to deal for now.

I try to push my doubts aside and lose myself in the sights around us, but they resurface when a frail, elderly woman catches my eye. She stares at me and then looks at Rafail, her brow furrowed in concentration. Someone talks to her, but she ignores them while she hobbles toward me. Bundled in layers, her small, frail hands tuck the scarf around her neck.

I open my mouth to speak to her, but I don't even know what I'll say.

Do I know you?

Do you know me?

But a large crowd of university students push past us, nearly jostling me.

"Watch it," Rafail growls, parting them so I can walk safely. And when they're past us, the old lady is gone.

Once again, I feel like I'm trying to reach for something I can't quite grasp. Rafail notices my distraction and steps in close, his voice a low murmur as he nudges my chin up with a gloved hand. "Distracted, little swan?"

I smile, managing a nod, but he watches me with a hint of calculation in his gaze as if he's measuring my reaction to everything we pass. He presses a soft kiss to my forehead and takes my hand, leading me into a nearby café, the words *Zimnyaya Roza* emblazoned out front.

"Anything you need?"

"Hot coffee and something buttery and sweet," I say in a rush of words. I feel anxious and weighted down. I want some reassurance.

"This city is charming," I tell him as he opens the door, the warm, powerful scent of strong coffee enveloping us. Orthodox churches stand beside sleek, minimalist buildings. The cityscape is dotted with old-fashioned iron street lamps and faded stone archways leading into courtyards, a slower-paced life compared to Moscow, not far from here.

"I love Zalivka," Rafail says with feeling, eliciting a fist bump from another patron who overhears. "Here, we've managed to keep small businesses operating that have been owned for generations."

"Mr. Kopolov." A burly man with a ruddy face and red nose, wearing a flour-covered apron, wipes his hands on it and comes to see us. "Welcome. You pay nothing when you're here, sir, you know that." He turns his attention to me. "And is this your wife?"

Rafail's arm comes around me with pride. "Meet my wife, Anissa. Anissa, Cecil is an old friend."

I smile shyly as others glance our way, and I pretend to look over the menu. I can't help but wonder how much the

Kopolov family had to do with any of that. Keeping large businesses out of town is in their best interest.

They talk to each other like buddies, and it's good to see Rafail's stern gaze soften a little. "We have a stall in *Old Square* at the festival," Cecil says. "We hope to see you there."

Rafail nods. "I'll do my best."

Cecil claps him on the back. "It would do well for our biggest benefactor to come so we can thank you."

"Precisely why I'm not sure I'll show," Rafail says wryly.

Cecil goes to the back, and I turn to Rafail. I'm seeing him in a whole new light.

Benefactor.

First, Yana's biggest support, and now this.

"Tell me about the festival?" I ask him as he steps up to the counter to order. "I'll have a hot mocha latte and one of the chocolate-covered biscuits, please."

Cecil has a sharp word to the cashier, who promptly declines any payment.

We walk back to a table and sit. "The festival has handcrafted goods and artisanal gifts in outdoor stalls, everyone haggling over prices.

"Oooh. I'd love it. It's gorgeous here." Familiar yet... not.

Wordlessly, he takes my hot latte and blows on it to cool it down before he hands it to me. My heart melts a little.

"When your leg is better, I'll take you to the river. There's a bridge that connects the city center and all the bustle and stands to the quieter residences. When the river freezes, we ice-skate across, and in the summer, it's in full bloom." He takes a sip of his coffee. "My family loves it. Zoya is all about the shops, and Yana is all about the flowers."

I swallow a bite of my food. "And Rodion likes it because there are local ladies?"

Rafail snorts. "Exactly."

When we leave the shop, thick snowflakes still come down. They melt on my warm cheek as Rafail brushes stray snowflakes from my coat with a gentleness that surprises me. His hand lingers on my shoulder, his touch unexpectedly tender, and for a moment, I feel like we're not two people wrapped in secrets but simply... together.

"You like it here," he remarks, watching me with an almost bemused expression.

"Yes, I do," I say softly, and I feel my guard slipping under his gaze. "It's beautiful, even if a little... heavy."

He laughs, a sound low and warm. "That's Zalivka. Heavy with history, yes. But it's a good place, full of loyal people. People who know how to survive."

But as we walk, a prickle of unease crawls over me, like we're being watched. Rafail feels it, too, his grip on my hand tightening as his gaze sweeps the street with a hardened look. He pulls me closer, his arm wrapping protectively around me.

"Stay close," he murmurs, his tone unreadable.

I reach for Rafail's hand. The cold air sharpens my thoughts, and without fully realizing it, I find myself saying, "You had so much to shoulder as a guardian. You still do. Not just running an empire but... your family. And Yana. It couldn't have been easy."

Rafail's gaze sharpens, his jaw clenching for a moment before he nods, an almost imperceptible gesture. The doctor's questioning made it easier for us to broach this subject. "Yana has always been my sister," he says, his voice quieter than usual as if sharing something fragile. "But... if my father had known she was different—if he had known she was truly herself—he would've killed her."

The way he says it, without dramatics, as a cold, unyielding fact, sends a shiver through me. I tighten my hold on his hand, sensing the fierce protectiveness beneath his composed exterior.

"And when she fell in love..." My voice trails off.

"In love with someone outside our circle? It was the best possible scenario for her. In the underground world, marriage is a strategic move. Those who don't fit the status quo are summarily ostracized, punished, or killed. Yeah. Yana needed to stay out of that fray."

I nod. She really did.

"I only wish I could do the same for Zoya," he says with a sigh.

"That's why you're so strict, isn't it?" I say, realizing it even as I speak. "You demand loyalty and hold everyone to these intense standards, but it's because you're trying to keep them safe. To give them what you think is... best."

He glances down, his expression a strange mix of pride and weariness. "I won't let anyone destroy what I've built, Anissa," he murmurs. "And I'll do whatever it takes to keep my family strong—even if that means holding them to standards no one else would dare impose. Yana, Rodion, Semyon, even Zoya... they don't understand it, not always. But I'd die for them."

A softness emerges behind his hardened gaze, something almost vulnerable, like he's peeling back a layer of armor just for me.

I hesitate before I ask, "Did Yana understand? Does she know how much you risked to protect her?"

A ghost of a smile tugs at the corner of his mouth. "Yana always knew. She's more perceptive than all of them put together." He pauses, watching me carefully. "I do push her harder than the others, yes. I demand her loyalty, her strength—but I want her to know that I see her. That I love her, not in spite of who she is, but because of it."

"Does she know that?"

His gaze shifts to the snowy street, contemplative. "Maybe. She's quiet, like she's always taking everything in. But she understands. More than anyone, Yana knows how much I care for this family, for every one of them."

I nod, feeling my heart tighten, admiring the fierce loyalty in him, seeing now that every hard edge in Rafail isn't just about power or control—it's about survival, about a love so intense he doesn't know how else to express it.

We walk in silence for a few steps before I whisper, "You're a good brother, Rafail. A good man, even if you don't see it."

A flicker of something raw crosses his face, but he only nods, his hand firm and steady in mine. And for the first time, I see a hint of the peace he's rarely allowed himself to feel.

As we approach the car, a rush of relief settles over me, but so do the questions that keep surfacing in my mind. I cast him a sidelong glance, my voice tentative. "Rafail... what if... what if I had another name before I met you? Another life?"

He pauses, looking at me with something between surprise and suspicion. But before he can answer, his phone rings, shattering the moment. His face goes dark as he listens, and I catch only fragments of the conversation before he hangs up.

"Romanovs... cartel... missing sister..."

The words chill me. They strike something deep, something that pulses with familiarity, even as it leaves me more lost than ever.

"Romanovs?" I whisper, my voice barely audible, but Rafail's grip on me tightens as he meets my gaze, his eyes cold, guarded. "We need to move *now*," Rafail says, taking my hand.

"What happened?" I ask, hobbling toward the car on my crutches, but he has no patience for my slowness. He sweeps me up off my feet and holds me with one arm against his chest while he takes my crutches in his meaty hand.

"A rival group is moving against us. I feared this—that once word got out I was married and we left the house, we'd have some pushback. We have no fucking time to waste. I need to move. We need to secure you and everybody else at the house."

My heart pounds. Is this the new life that I lead? Leaping from question to question without ever having answers? Moving from one dangerous scenario to the next?

My leg throbs under the weight of the cast as he speeds back home in silence.

"We had a driver on the way here."

"We did. I dismissed him. We need to drive fast, and that's on me."

I nod silently, gripping the door until my knuckles turn white. He drives at a breakneck pace, breathtakingly precise, pressing the gas without a hint of hesitation. Each curve is taken with terrifying speed, his control effortless, as if he knows exactly how far he can push us. The sharp turns press me into my seat with the force of a roller coaster. It's not just the speed that astounds me—it's the sheer certainty in his every move as though the rules don't apply to him.

It's exhilarating yet terrifying. My mind races as the car's wheels spin, and we hurtle toward home.

Why is he still wholly unfamiliar to me? Even if he was someone who I was running from, I should have some recollection of him... Shouldn't I?

The doctor's words linger in my mind.

There's no promise of a full recovery.

Your memories are fractured.

Stress, trauma, trying too hard... all can complicate your recovery.

The sound of booming gunfire shatters my thoughts. Instinctively, Rafail grabs for me and shoves me to the floor while keeping effortless control of the car. I scream, and my leg slams against my cast.

An explosion rips through the air just behind us, and Rafail turns the wheel so hard I'm pressed to the ground with the weight of gravity. My heart thunders in my chest, adrenaline flooding me as the sound of bullets ping off the car.

"Stay down!" Rafail barks at me, his voice sharp and controlled. Panic rises in my chest. I'm shaking. I watch as he continues to effortlessly guide us to a stop. My mind reels.

We're being shot at, and instead of outrunning them, he's *stopping*? I watch in breathless silence as he pushes my head down with one hand and opens the glove compartment. It clicks shut. I stare up at him holding a huge black handgun, its cannon-like barrel glinting in the overhead light. My mind snaps to attention because I know exactly what it is—a *Desert Eagle*. I've held one before, its recoil so strong as to make it almost unusable except to the strongest and most capable of shooters. The way he casually wields it makes it look like a child's plaything in his hand, his finger already on the trigger as his dark eyes narrow with cold decision, the promise of violence spiraling out of him like an uncontrollable wave of hatred and death.

I cling to his arm and watch him scan our surroundings.

Why is this... vaguely familiar to me? Why do I feel this has happened before? A memory flashes through my mind, familiar faces I can't place, and a name...

Polina...

My name.

It was my name from a different place in time. I feel as if I've been rebirthed into a second life, as if I've been reincarnated into who I am now.

Voices sound all around us, but my head is spinning as I try to focus.

"*Stay down,*" he growls. His body presses against mine, keeping me behind him. One hand is flat on my chest, holding me in place before he goes back to gripping his gun with deadly precision.

Tires screech toward us. My heart stutters, and he throws me his phone. It's on speakerphone, Semyon's name at the top. "They're coming in at three o'clock," he yells. "*Stop them.*"

A deafening boom like a cannon sounds ahead of us. Someone screams with maniacal glee, and Rafail shakes his head, cursing. *Rodion.*

A car races toward us at breakneck speed, tires squealing on pavement . Rafail leaps to his feet, heavy boots planted as he stands facing the oncoming car head-on, gun blazing. Fire spits from his weapon. Windows shatter. A tire explodes. I'm frozen in place, my heart racing, when it dawns on me with crystal clarity: *they're going to hit us.* In that moment—with the vehicle hurtling toward us and the knowledge that I'm going to be hit—a memory flashes in front of me.

I'm running. Running away from a nameless captor who's going to hurt me, running away from... Rafail? I can see the dark intensity of his gaze, even feel the heat of his fingers on me, but... he's a stranger to me. He isn't my *husband.*

The memory of the accident comes back with brutal clarity. All of it. The screech of tires. The impact that shook my bones and rattled me into unconsciousness. His bellow of rage from behind me. Vague voices over me.

Another deafening boom rattles the ground beneath me. Then another. The car in front of us explodes as Rafail hits the ground and covers me.

"That's it, Rodion," Rafail says with dark approval. "Atta boy."

Metal and glass fly over us. In an instant, Rafail presses me beneath him, shielding me with his body.

Bloodcurdling screams.

Boom.

Then... nothing.

Nothing but eerie silence.

I close my eyes, assaulted by memory after memory.

My mother.

My home.

I am Russian, and I...

It's on the cusp of my consciousness, so close I cry out loud and reach for the air in front of me just before I collapse against Rafail, and my world fades to emptiness.

CHAPTER 15

RAFAIL

The heavy silence after the gunfire weighs on me like bricks on my chest.

"They're gone," Semyon says from my phone. "We got them."

I need answers.

I need her safe.

I need names.

My ears ring with the silence as I glance down at my wife. Panic sweeps over me when I realize her eyes are closed.

"Anissa!" I lift her slender shoulders and shake her. At first, she doesn't answer, but after another shake, she blinks up at me, her eyes clouded with confusion and fear. Her chest rises and falls too quickly. It's too much.

Can I break my brain? She had asked.

Am I losing my mind?

Did she?

She's shaking, but she's okay, I reassure myself as I run my hands around her body. "Are you all right?" I ask, my heart pounding.

I feel helpless, afraid. It drags me back to years ago, back when I was barely old enough to understand what it meant to be in charge. I'd lost track of my brothers and sisters, and a cold dread settled in as the hours ticked by with no sign of them. They were supposed to be home, and with every minute they were missing, the fear clawed deeper. When I finally found them, swinging like idiots on a rope over the ravine, I was raw with fury. Zoya was soaked and shivering, the others laughing, oblivious to the hours that had passed.

I'd promised myself that when I found them, there'd be hell to pay. They'd know the consequences of making me think I'd lost them. But when I finally reached them, rage left me in a rush. All I could do was fall to my knees and pull the smallest ones close—Zoya in one arm, Rodion in the other—and make them swear to me, my voice hoarse with worry, they'd never do anything like that again.

I felt helpless then, and I feel helpless now. Hell, it's half the reason I'm so fucking hard on all of them. She's not wrong—the thought of losing everyone I love petrifies me.

Damn it. I've done this to myself. Every instinct in me screams to stay distant, to harden myself against anything even close to feelings. She's not my lawful wife but someone I forced into a fake union to suit me and to punish *her*.

But then the other part of reason kicks in. *She's my wife now.* My wife. The word feels heavier, more significant than any other in my life. It's not like my siblings or my family. I love them with all of my heart, but *wife*...

Flesh of my flesh.

I'm not a religious man, but there's something sacred to the ritual of marriage, to our bond.

I tell myself to keep my distance, but when she looks at me the way she's looking now, like I'm her savior, and no one else in the world can protect her like I can. That look...

She lifts her small, blood-streaked, trembling hand to my face and brushes her thumb along my jaw. "You're cut, Rafail," she whispers, her voice soft with concern. "Are you alright? Let me doctor you up. Please."

"I'm fine." I stand, holding her behind me. "It's just a scratch."

The car that barreled toward us is now a twisted wreck, its occupants either dead or captured. My team saw to that. Who were they? Does it matter at this point? Stupid fucking rivals.

My phone vibrates in my pocket, and I pull it out. My eyes scan the phone three times before I actually read the message because I know. It's only a matter of time before enemies regroup. They strike again. They always do. But now, so much more is at stake.

So much more.

I can still hear the screech of tires and her scream when she was hit. I don't ever want to experience that again.

This was not supposed to happen. I'm supposed to keep her away from everyone. Keep her away from the world. Safe.

Safe from everyone... even *me*.

But now that she's here, she's in greater danger than ever.

"I should have kept you in the house," I say, my hands gripping her as tightly as I can without hurting her.

"I'm fine," she insists. "You can't exactly keep me in a bubble, no matter how much you wish that you could."

"I can fucking try," I insist, which makes her clam up.

I remember what the doctor said.

Her hands tremble slightly, and it annoys me. She needs to be safe. She needs to be protected. She's *mine.*

And for a moment, I allow myself this weakness and pull her close to me. I cup the back of her head with one hand and her slender body with the other.

"Are you sure that you're not hurt?" I ask, my voice harder than I intended as my gaze roves over her, probing, seeking any sign of distress or injury. She shakes her head, her eyes still wide and stunned.

"Rafail, I'm fine. Let's get you to safety too."

I almost laugh. *Fine.*

Nothing about this situation is fine, and I damn well know she's not fine. She's trying to piece together a life she doesn't remember, and as her memory returns, the threat of her realizing that she ran from me—not her husband, but from the man who was supposed to marry her—looms. What is she going to do when she remembers that? How long can I keep her with me? No. I need to find a better way.

"Let's get you inside."

She stares at me as if searching my face for answers I don't have. Her voice is small and shaky.

"Who was it? And why were they shooting at us?"

"I have enemies." I blow out a breath. "So do you. They don't want us to be married. We'll look into it and have swift retribution."

Pushing herself to standing on wobbly feet, she looks at the simmering remains of the car. "If there's anyone left after that." I don't offer more, and she doesn't press. Not this time, anyway.

She will. She fucking will.

As we walk toward the house—my guards surrounding us, wielding weapons as they come too late to protect us from any blowback—her silence is unnerving.

Wordlessly, I snake an arm around her shoulder when she trembles and draws closer to me. Leaning heavily on me, she lets me half carry her. How do I keep her from leaving me? Threats only go so far. How do I make sure that she stays?

She doesn't remember.

I can never let her remember.

Back at the house, I lead her to the living room, the closest to the entrance. Yana flits around, wringing her hands, and Zoya watches us silently, her face drawn and pale.

"Are you going to lock me up again?" With a pout, she turns away. "Somebody tried to hurt me, and I have to be locked up again?"

I frown. "Is it that obvious?" She sits down, cradling her injured leg, her face pale.

"Our enemies..." I begin. "Now they've seen me with you..."

Rodion stands at the desk near the bookshelf, his narrowed gaze a promise of retribution as he lovingly caresses his switchblade. "One more call, and I'll have names. I've got this." He nods to Anissa. "Go, take care of your wife."

And for the first time in a long time, I don't see him as my kid brother who needs to be taught how to behave. He's my ally. My right-hand man.

I settle beside her, resisting the urge to prowl the room like a caged lion. I pull out my phone, forcing my focus into sharp resolve as I arrange for more security. Every call is a demand, every message a promise backed by power and wealth. I leverage every favor owed, tossing money and influence around like weapons. I have to fortify the walls between us and the dangers closing in.

I push to my feet and pace.

My gaze roves over her—she's troubled.

"Rafail," she says softly, her tone steady but insistent. "Come back here." She pats the chair beside her, eyes fixed on me. She's seated in the large living room, usually so watchful, taking in every detail—but right now, her attention is all on me.

I don't want to sit right now.

"Rafail," she says, more insistently.

"What?" The steel in my voice somewhat hides the edge of panic I'm barely holding onto. I can't let her slip through my fingers. Not again.

"I want to talk to you," she pleads. "Please. Just sit down."

When I sit down beside her, our knees brush. Her hand comes to mine as she holds my gaze.

We sit in the silence, alone. Me and my beautiful, stolen wife. The reasons why I took her elude me when I look at her winsome face, her trusting eyes.

She's not here of her own accord, and when she remembers, she'll want to leave.

I need her to want to stay.

"You look so desperate," she says softly. "Why?"

Her eyes are blurry, and when she blinks, the unthinkable happens. A fat tear rolls down her cheek.

I take a deep breath and decide to tell her the truth. "You ran from me once. And there's a part of me that's scared that when your memory comes back, you'll want to do it again."

The wide look in her eyes tells me it wasn't the answer she was expecting. She doesn't say anything at first but looks away thoughtfully as if choosing her words. When she turns back to me, she squeezes my hand, her fingers curling around my larger one. "I understand," she says, her voice calm and steady. "That's a reasonable fear."

It's not what I expected her to say. Hell, I had no idea what she'd say.

For the first time in a long while, I feel a small smile tug at my lips.

“I wish I could tell you more about why I ran,” she adds, her eyes searching mine for answers I can’t give.

I shake my head. “I don’t have all the answers,” I say, aiming at honesty again. And damn, it feels good to finally tell her the truth. "I really don’t know," I tell her honestly. "I had no intention of hurting you. Well, not at *first.*” I run a hand through my hair and still, she continues to stare. “I’m not a good man and never pretended to be, but I had every intention of taking good care of you." It’s the truth. I did.

"I can see that. I see how you take care of your brothers and sisters. I know that now.” She blows out a breath. “So why don’t we let this lie? Forget about the past. Let’s move forward.”

Fuck, but I wish we could.

"Maybe I was afraid of change," she says softly. A small, hardened crevice of my heart melts a little.

Maybe she was.

I reach for her and drag her onto my lap. Her fingers graze the stubble on my chin. I lean in, and she kisses me as if she really wants to forget the past and move forward. I kiss her back like it’s a promise, as if it will hold her here, right here, in this moment. Her tongue slides into my mouth when someone clears his throat behind me.

“I’m gonna fucking kill you for interrupting me and my wife,” I growl, not bothering to confirm it’s Semyon. I’d know his throat clearing anywhere. “What is it?” I touch my forehead to hers, relishing the weight of her hand on my arm.

"Rafail," she whispers, a plea. "No more violence today."

Somehow, her touch has the strange ability to silence murderous thoughts.

Semyon shifts nervously. "Sorry. I have to tell you..."

"What?"

"We let the news spread. They all know you have a wife, and some aren't taking too kindly to it. The Popovs are willing to meet."

Tension coils thickly between me and Anissa, a silent pull that neither of us dares to sever. She doesn't say anything, but the fear in her eyes speaks volumes, flashing in those brief, stolen glances. Her back is rigid, her body betraying the doubts she doesn't voice. I refuse to look at her too long —if I do, I'll see that flicker of uncertainty in her eyes, the same doubt that gnaws at me like a curse. I can't let her leave. I *won't.* But the harder I cling, the more I can feel her slipping through my fingers, like smoke dissipating in the night air.

"Maybe the Popovs have valuable intel, Rafail. We should meet with them. Though, you might have to pry yourself away from your bride for a minute or two," he says, smirking.

I don't bother hiding my irritation. "Or we can have the meeting right here," I reply, my voice a low growl.

Anissa grins, a glimmer of mischief dancing in her eyes, softening her stance. "Or you could just tuck me into your pocket and take me along," she teases as if she's found a way to anchor me in place. I grunt. "Piggyback ride?" she suggests helpfully.

"Anissa..."

"You could fashion one of those children's wagons—"

"Woman!"

Her laughter is light and teasing, but there's something in her eyes—a spark of mischief, of freedom and hope—that unsettles me more than I'd like to admit.

She's joking now, but the thought lingers. *What if she wants to run again?*

"You're not going anywhere," I grunt, forcing a smile to hide the sudden tightness in my chest.

She arches a brow at me. "Who says I want to?"

But the truth is, I don't know. The flicker of doubt gnaws at me. Because right now, we're two strangers starting over. When her memories return... what if her reaction is something I can't predict? Something brute force and violence won't solve?

Something even I can't stop?

CHAPTER 16

"ANISSA"

I wake, feel for the warm reassurance of my husband, and snuggle closer. He's asleep, but does he ever *really* sleep?

Even when he sleeps, there's tension in his shoulders and the lines of his handsome, rugged features.

As weeks pass, I hate that I still have no more idea of who I was than before. Only bits and fragments poke through. So I've done what the doctor said, even though it's hard to do—gave my mind a rest.

I've resigned myself to what I do know: I belong here. I'm Anissa Kopolov. I'm the wife of the Kopolov *Pakhan* and sister-turned-mother figure to his band of siblings because now that I'm here, the missing link of a mother figure has become woefully apparent.

We have dinner every night, like clockwork, but instead of "business as usual," or the few quiet nights where no one talks, it's a little more lighthearted now. At least, that's what they tell me. I might not have much to offer, but it seems that bringing a touch of humanity to Rafail's rigid, uncompromising ways isn't entirely unwelcome.

His family grew up with a sense of duty and toughness and, honestly, a healthy dose of fear for their older brother. But all of them were children when they lost their parents, and one of them is a child still. They lacked a soft touch in their daily lives, and I aim to bring that to them now in my own way.

I wish he could relax, but he still carries the weight of the world on his shoulders. Even though it still bothers me to know that I ran away from him because I didn't know who I was, I'm making peace with it.

I mean. I think I am.

When I'm alone, and it's quiet like this after a dream, I remember... a little.

I know I have—*had*?—brothers. What troubles me is that my husband says I don't, and there's no indication he's lying when he talks to me. Sometimes, he seems evasive, but my instincts say he's telling the truth when it comes to my past. And yet... it doesn't ring true. He swears I only have a father, so why do I remember people calling me their sister?

And that woman in my dream, she was my mother. At one point, anyway. I know that now. I've seen her more than once.

That's one thing that doesn't make sense to me at all.

I don't believe he's completely lying to me. He seems confident in what he's telling me, but occasionally... just every once in a while... there's a tiny blip. Whether it's in his expression or the way I feel, I start to fear that something is wrong. And I need to know why.

Why am I here? Who am I? How do I get back to knowing who I am?

"Are you all right, baby?" His hand comes to the small of my back. I love the way he touches me like this, as if he and I are the only two people in this whole world.

My heart beats faster at the sleepy-husky sexiness of his voice when he wakes. I roll over and let myself bask in the heat that radiates off him like a furnace, the heaviness of his arm on my back, the comfort of knowing that he's my knight, willing to defend my castle.

How can it be that my past is shrouded in mystery, yet it feels like I've been his forever? Because there's a sureness between us, an honesty, that makes me cleave to him.

"Yeah, you know how it is," I say softly. "When I wake up like this, everything's all muddled. You should sleep, Rafail. I swear you're like a cat."

He shrugs his big shoulder but doesn't deny it.

It's familiar to me now, the way he's so protective. When we were attacked, and he pushed me beneath him, shielding me with his very own body, I knew then that he would take a bullet for me.

And that's not the only thing he protects me from.

In the quiet of night, when I wake trembling, fragmented dreams still lingering, he holds me until my breathing slows, and I can go back to sleep. When we make love, I crave the weight of his body pressing into mine, my wrists wrapped in his grip. There's freedom in the surrender. Quiet. And in the still, waking hours before sunrise, when my dreams leave me doubtful and confused, the sturdy feel of his strong arms around me brings me calm.

"I just wish I could remember."

He threads his fingers through mine. "Remember what?"

There's a note of edginess in his voice. Have I exhausted his patience?

"Who I am," I say softly. He should know that by now.

Rafail turns to me, bracing himself on his elbow as his eyes roam lazily over my body. "I told you," he says in a low growl. "You're my wife. Do you need me to help you remember that?"

"Rafail," I try, but once he sets his mind on something, there is no turning him away. Laser-focused on me, I know what's coming: a reminder of who I am.

The next thing I know, I'm pinned underneath him. His lips ghost my cheek, my jaw, my collarbone, trailing lower still to my breasts. My nipples furl. He licks one, then the other, as his thick, rough fingers lazily push my thighs apart. He grips one of my thighs in his strong palm and squeezes.

"I'm sleepy," I lie in protest, which earns me a sharp slap of his palm on my thigh.

"Allow me to wake you up, Mrs. Kopolov."

I sigh as he flicks one nipple with his finger and slaps the underside of my breast. Hard to believe he was just asleep, and now he's on *fire.* Morning sex has become a ritual.

"Rafail." I squirm because when I protest a little, he bears down harder, and I love that. This man is not tame. He may play nice for me on occasion—very rarely—but then the savage in him's unleashed.

Here, though, in the privacy of our bedroom, where we make love, he lets his guard down.

Whatever I wrestle with comes to a raging halt as his lips claim mine and his fingers spread me wide.

He's *mine*. Mine—every damn inch of his masculine, bossy, grumpy self.

I playfully roll him over on his back, which I honestly wouldn't be able to do if he didn't allow it. He smirks as he arranges me on top of him, giving me the momentary delusion that I was the one who pushed him over. He's much bigger than I am, stronger. I couldn't push him over if I tried. And believe me, I've tried.

Sadly, cowgirl style is a bit out of the realm of possibility with this cast, though I'm healing and hardly need crutches anymore. Still, I can awkwardly hold my leg at an angle and appreciate him, submissive for the flash of a second beneath me.

With a gentle nudge, he arranges my leg so that it's comfortable. *Ooh. I like.* My fingers splay across the expanse of his warm, bare chest, heat warming my palms as I trace the hard planes of muscle. His chest rises and falls in a steady beat beneath my hands, his thick cock at my slick entrance. His body pulses with restrained power.

"I like this view," he says in a husky whisper, his voice rough and sexy, the way his eyes rove over my body a testament to sincerity. He *does* like this view. He likes what he sees. My smaller, pale body is in such sharp contrast to his it's almost comical.

"Will our babies look like you? It's a crapshoot. I do think your genes are more... dominant," I say with a wink.

I bend and brush my lips to his. For the first time, the thought of having his children doesn't scare me. It seems... natural. He's already the father figure of the Kopolov family. The patriarch. I've already assumed the role of big sister-mother. Having children now seems only natural.

"I would love it if our children looked like you," he says earnestly, reaching forward to grasp my hips tightly in his strong, powerful hands. I don't wear much of anything to bed, so he easily finds my bare entrance.

My breathing hitches. "Would you, now?"

"Of course," he says, his own breath catching at the first thrust. I'm so full; my head falls back, his hot cock throbbing in my center. He glides almost fully out before sliding in me again with a brutal, delicious thrust. My eyes flutter closed as bliss floods me. "A chance to remind me of you? Yes. Every day. A reminder of my beautiful wife? I'd like nothing better." His gaze bores into mine with such fire and possession, my heart turns over in my chest. *"Ty—moya, navsyegda, Nikto i nikogda ne smo-zhet otnyat tebya u menya."*

You are mine forever. No one can ever take you away from me.

Another thrust sends pleasure coursing down my spine. I *love* riding him, the feeling of connection. Power. I love the feel of his hands anchored on my hips as I grind against him, fuller than ever before, damn near *fused* to my husband.

"Come here," he says, his hand sliding the length of my back to pull me closer. I bend toward him, and his mouth finds my breast, capturing a nipple between his teeth. I gasp when he laves my nipples one at a time, a touch of teeth and wet heat pushing me to the brink of climax, pulling me closer to the edge of control.

"Turn around," he says, pulling out of me. "I'll help you. Face forward. I need to taste you. I want you to come on my mouth before I take you completely."

I whine a little in protest because maybe I'm a bit spoiled and needy, and I wish I could sit on his face *and* have him *in* me at the same time, but Rafail doesn't suffer disobedience. When I don't immediately comply, his gaze darkens.

"Are you disobeying me, my little swan?" he asks, his gaze on me, half daring me to defy him, to give him a chance to punish me. He lives for this.

Fuck it, so do I.

"Maybe," I say with a pout and a whisper. Eager to hear what he'll do about that but scared to outright defy him. Rafail can be terrifying.

"On my face," he says with a low growl, his fingers on my side branding me. "You're in trouble already. Here's your one chance to be a good girl."

Oh god.

I can't exactly rush to obey with my clumsy cast, but with practiced ease, he arranges me in front of him. His thick cock in front of me, I bend and drag my tongue along the veined length. Wet heat floods me at the sound of his moan just before his hand, as thick and heavy as a paddle, slams against my ass.

I hiss in a breath, but that doesn't stop him. He spanks my ass again and again, punishing, sharp smacks before he spreads my legs wide and buries his face in my pussy. I'm still panting from the brief but painful spanking before that first stroke of his tongue on my clit.

He pulls off long enough to whisper hotly against my thigh, "I want to eat you out, then fuck you hard. You put your mouth anywhere near me, I'll fucking come in your mouth, and I want to own your pussy this morning."

Another sharp slap has me nearly climbing out of my skin, a swift reminder of who he is and what he expects, before he grabs my hips and pulls me closer to him. I'm lost to sensation, my hips undulating as the pleasure courses through me. He reaches for my nipples hanging in front of him and pinches and kneads them between his rough, hot fingers before he suckles my clit again and strokes my wet heat with his tongue.

His hot breath warms my inner thighs as he growls, "Good girls know how to listen, love. Are you a good girl?"

Over and over again, he licks me until it feels like his branding touch is on every inch of my skin—rough fingers in my core, pulsing, spreading my wetness over my ass and pussy, his tongue on my clit, tasting and easing me to climax, the fiery skin of my spanked ass turning me on until I feel like I'm going to scream.

"Beg me," he growls against my thigh. I bite my lip and don't respond because I fucking love when he gets just on the edge of growly with me. I scream when his teeth sink into my inner thigh. "*Beg me*, or I'll tie you to this bed and take that pussy all day long without letting you come."

Oh god. That sounds... torturous?

What will happen if I push him?

I'm on the cusp of begging, on the cusp of asking, when a sharp knock sounds at the door.

"Unless someone's about to bomb our house or die, get the fuck out of here," he bellows. Footsteps run away.

"Rafail," I plead. "You should be nicer. Really."

He stills beneath me. Uh-oh. Now I've done it. My heartbeat races, and my pussy throbs in need.

"Nicer?" he says in a dark whisper. "You want me to be nicer, do you?" Shaking his head, he reaches for my pussy and gives me one—just one—tiny, little press of his tongue. I move my hips closer to him, but he pulls his mouth away. "You're a naughty little girl, Anissa. You think you can tell me what to do?"

Fuck.

"I'm sorry," I begin, even as I know it's too little too late. I can't ever forget that while I might be Belle, trapped in a home with a monster, my husband is still the beast who will *never* fully transform back into a man. And he loves it when I give him an opportunity to punish me.

"You want me to be nicer," he says, almost thoughtfully.

Warningly. He buries his face in my pussy as if savoring the musky scent of my arousal before he pushes me aside.

Nooo.

"RAFAIL," I beg. "Please, please, please, don't do it." I hardly know what I'm begging for.

"Do what?" he asks, his eyes as dark as coal, his erection hard as steel between us. "Teach my wife to obey me?"

Without jostling my cast, he somehow miraculously manages to place me face down on the bed, not on my knees but propped up on pillows. What is he *doing*?

"Come here," he says, sliding down the edge of the bed and bringing me with him. He drags me down beneath him, his hand fisted in my hair. "You really want to push me, don't you? You were the one who decided to tell me what to do."

I open my mouth to beg him—to plead with him to let me come and I'll behave—when the little vixen who loves being dominated by her growly beast of a husband comes squeaking out of my mouth. I'm shaking.

"You're not the boss of me."

What?

His stillness is terrifying. I went too far. I said too much. I shouldn't push him like this, not when I know—

His punishing palm meets my ass with a force that makes my skin ignite and my clit *throb*.

Oh god.

Another sharp smack of his palm on the exact same spot makes me beg for mercy. "Ow! Oh god, please! I'll be good!" I beg, even as my pussy clenches, half begging for more.

"You're damn right you'll be good," he grates in my ear. "We have a lot of work to do today. You know that. Maybe a good reminder of who you belong to is in order." Holding me against the bed, his flank pressed up against mine, I feel him fumbling in the drawer beside me. "You're practically begging for me to punish you, to teach you a lesson."

Oh no. I know the shit he keeps in that drawer, all the instruments of torture he likes to surprise me with. My mouth is open in a silent gasp when he takes something out I can't see, but a second later, wetness trickles down my ass.

"Rafail!"

His only response is to spread lubricant down between my cheeks.

"I can't do this." I breathe, my heart pounding so hard I'm a little faint. "Wait! I've never done this before."

"You can," he says with certainty. "And you will. You don't tell your husband no, little swan, not when he's punishing you. Do you need a reminder of what happens when you misbehave?" Leaning in, he bites my shoulder. I scream and push, but I can't get away. Heat thrums in my veins, my body taut, arousal licking at every sensitive part of me with such intensity I can't breathe.

"Thank you."

I gasp. "For… what?"

"I'm going to enjoy every *second* of making you behave."

I know this is a game we play, a dance that we love, but a part of me wonders where he ends and I begin. If I begged him to stop, would he?

But my body's telling him a different story. My arousal trickles down my leg, my clit painfully hard and throbbing. I'm so turned on that even the teasing touch of his tongue would send me flying into orgasm right now.

My eyes squeeze shut as warmth and heat flood my senses. I want this. I *do*. I love walking the line of fear and arousal, terror and excitement, never knowing what he's going to do next. There's something about the unabashed way he claims my body with his that makes me feel like I'm the center of his whole *world*.

Bending so that his mouth is to my ear and his warm, hot body fully encompasses mine, he whispers, "Breathe, baby. *Breathe*."

On instinct, I obey, and with the next breath, he glides into me. Slowly. Easing. It isn't painful like I expect, but it feels so wrong, and my cheeks flame. "You kinky son of a bitch." I gasp around a wicked grin. His rare, deep chuckle makes me smile as he thrusts inside me.

"Are you going to come?" he asks.

Am I? I feel so full, so aroused, but on edge. "I need a minute."

"Good," he says with dark approval. "Because you're not allowed to until I tell you. If you do, you'll regret it, Anissa."

He glides into me again, and my clit throbs. Again, and my mouth falls open. I start to beg him to let me come when he pulls out. I mewl at the loss of him and slam the bed in frustration.

"Rafail!"

"You know the rule," he says with a grunt, stroking himself behind me. "Bend over. Take me. I want to mark you before we leave this room."

I throw myself over the edge of the bed, half-blind with arousal, when he grunts and moans. His hot seed spills on my back and glides over my ass as he comes hard and fast.

"THAT'S IT, ANGEL," he says as he strokes himself again. "That's what I want to remember when you sit by me today. You, wearing my mark."

"Rafail," I moan. "Oh my *god*."

I'm still on the edge of coming, so aroused I can hardly think of anything else.

"I'll let you come after you show me what a good girl you are." He bends and kisses my cheek. "And I promise you, it'll be worth the wait." He leaves me on the bed, and I contemplate what he will do if I make myself come.

Yeah. Not worth it.

Fuck.

WHEN HE COMES BACK, he has a folded towel in his hand. I scowl at him.

"No pouting, baby," he says with a self-satisfied smile. It's so rare for him to smile that when he does, it feels like the sun shining down after a long winter. "I promise it'll be worth it."

He wipes me off before he presses his hand to my lower back. "I'll dress you. Stay right here." He bends down and whispers in my ear. "And if you touch yourself without permission, you've broken a cardinal rule. Don't test me, Anissa."

"What rule is that?" I yell at his retreating back when he goes to fetch my clothes.

And all of it, damn near all of it, is almost worth the torture when he turns back to stare at me, his fiery gaze sparking. "No one touches what's mine."

I stare at him. I think I love him. I've fallen for this veritable beast of a man, every grumpy, growly inch of him. I've fallen, and I've fallen hard.

And I'm not the only one.

My mind whirs with this realization while he gets clothes from the closet and dresses me. I hardly even notice until I look down to see I'm wearing a dress.

"A dress?" I ask.

"I love seeing you wear a dress." His rough lips graze my cheek. "Better access. Now. We're heading downstairs. Rodion and Zoya need help with a few things, and then you and I are heading into town."

My jaw drops. He's letting me out of the house again?

Still wearing his *cum*?

"Rafail," I whisper. "Are you serious?"

"Of course."

"*Why*?" I whine.

"I have a business meeting, and it's in my family's best interest if you join me." He gives me a wicked smile. Tipping his head to the side, he clucks his tongue. "Surely, you don't have any plans on disobeying your husband in public, do you?"

I blink and shake my head wordlessly.

"Good," he says, satisfied. "Because I'm very much looking forward to your reward."

CHAPTER 17

RAFAIL

Turns out it was Rodion risking his life by interrupting us when she was sitting on my face.

Years later, Rodion sometimes still needs the fear of god put in him. As a boy, he'd tested the patience of saints and devils alike. These days, I've eased up on him a bit; he's managed to avoid the staggering amount of trouble he once found himself in.

My wife is pouting and trying to pretend she isn't. I spoiled her at first. I couldn't help it. She was so eager for anything and everything in the bedroom—she was putty in my hands.

But she loves when I tease her. She loves being edged. She'll come like she never has before, even if I have to torture her a little to get there.

And she *will* learn to yield to my authority. I won't ever back down and *will* insist. She has no choice. It's the only real way I can keep her safe.

"Now, Rafail," she says, holding onto my arm as we go downstairs. "You can't forget it's Rodion's birthday."

Shit. I *did* forget.

"You forgot, didn't you?" she says, her lips twitching. Anissa's been able to forego her crutches and walk on her cast, but she still needs a little assistance.

I shrug.

"Did you have birthday celebrations for them growing up?"

"Um."

"*Rafail,*" she says reproachfully. How can I tell her I had more important things to tend to? I was holding together an empire, finding my way as a man, and maintaining my family's legacy. And my parents never made too big of a deal of birthday celebrations.

"We did," she says with a smile before her words catch up with her. She pauses, gripping the railing for support. "We did. I know we did. I had a mother. Brothers. She made a big deal of birthdays. She made sure we had our favorite food and cake and lavished us with gifts. I can... I can still see a room decorated in pink and gold and a huge pile of gifts waiting for me." Turning to me, she looks distrustful and confused. "But you said I didn't have brothers."

She didn't. I don't know why she keeps bringing this up

"I promise you, Anissa, you had no brothers." Jesus, if she did, I'd have a lot more to worry about than I do. "Listen, I know you remember brothers, but maybe you had a large extended family? I don't know. Cousins? I have a few myself."

"I know," she says quietly, her normally placid brow troubled. "But... I don't think they were cousins."

"Alright."

"Anyway," she says, shaking her head. "That doesn't matter. What does matter is that you wish Rodion a happy birthday, you partake in the birthday festivities, and tonight, we have dinner with your whole family."

I nod. "Fair enough." I scratch at my chin. "So what did we get him for his birthday?"

I gave her a credit card last week and carte blanche to buy what she wanted. I thought she might be too timid at first to use it, but it seems another package or three turn up at the doorstep every day. "Pillows for the bedroom," she said. "You need more color in the office," or, "I really do need some more yoga pants."

I don't care. She can buy anything she wants. She's prettied up our bedroom with her signature touch. It's more feminine, and I like it.

"I got him one of those traditional Russian daggers."

My brows rise in mild surprise. "Kinjal?"

"Mmm. It's beautiful and well-crafted. A ceremonial one for his collection. He's older now, you know. Semyon suggested it."

"Alright," I say, my hands in my pocket. "But no more weapons without asking me first."

She looks like she's going to roll her eyes but thinks better of it.

I knew making her learn to yield would come, eventually.

"He's headstrong, Anissa."

"Yes, but he's come a long way. You said so yourself."

He has. It took a firm hand and a long time, but he's getting there.

"What else?"

"Oh, a nice watch. Something masculine, something he can really rely on. It's a good one, not too extravagant but practical and mature and has all these smartwatch capabilities."

"Nice."

"Got him some fancy sneakers, special edition."

I raise a brow at her.

"They're cool. He doesn't always wear all black and boots or suits, like *someone* I know."

I scratch my chin. "You want me to wear sneakers?"

She swallows and licks her lips, her voice husky. "I'd get on my knees and do whatever you asked just to see you wearing sneakers and a baseball cap on backward." Wordlessly, she flexes her fingers over my bicep.

I stare at her so long that she finally giggles. "Are you serious?" I ask her.

She breathes out a sigh and leans on the railing. "*Dead* serious."

Alright, then. Strange, but that's fine. She's so damn adorable leaning against the rail I can't help but crook a finger at her. "Come here."

She's in my arms in two steps. I kiss her cheek and run my hand along the back of her neck. She breathes into me, a half sigh, half moan. "You're such a good girl looking after everyone." I whisper in her ear, "Now I'm going to look after *you*. Touch yourself."

Her eyes grow wide. "Here? Rafail, are you serious?"

I feel my lips curve into a frown. "Do I look like I'm joking?"

"No one's here," I whisper. "Zoya and Rodion are downstairs. I checked the cameras before we left the room. I wanted to see who knocked on the door."

I hold her to me, bracing her, as she obediently slides a hand under her dress and tugs her panties down. Her mouth drops open, and her eyes go half-lidded as she strokes her pussy. "Good girl," I whisper, shoving my hand beside hers and taking over. I stroke until her back arches, and she's breathing heavily. "Remember that." I pull my hand aside. "Behave, and you'll see how well I'll reward you."

"Rafail," she moans, slumping against me. "You're *killing* me."

"So dramatic," I say, giving her a sharp but playful slap to the ass. "Now go downstairs."

Turns out she didn't just get him fancy, expensive sneakers he fairly drools over, a new watch, and a knife. He has packages in a tower so high they wobble before he opens them. She went all out—new clothes, some kind of motorcycle helmet for when he rides, luxury headphones, and new boxing gloves. Tickets to a concert and to get his car detailed. Her eyes dance as he opens one gift at a time.

Zoya watches with a smile on her face as she prepares waffles and bacon, his favorite.

"You spoiled him," I say, shaking my head, though I'm not really disapproving.

"It's alright to be spoiled on your birthday."

When he's opened everything, Rodion stands and reaches for Anissa. He bends down to engulf her in a big hug. "Thank you."

"Of course."

When they pull away, tears shine in her eyes. Fuck.

She's the missing link to the family I didn't know we needed.

I didn't realize how badly *I* needed her.

She's softened something in me. And for a minute, while I see my bride seamlessly blended into my family, my brother's shining eyes and my sister's smile, it feels like I can have it all—my family, my family's stability... and her.

She watches as we set the table, her eyes dancing with warmth. For someone who's lost everything and been forced into a situation she didn't choose, she's shown so much resilience. Damn, I admire that.

The whole house feels lighter with her here, and the usual tension that weighs on me is nearly... gone.

There's a strange sense in my chest so foreign I almost don't recognize it... *peace.* It's peace. Maybe, just maybe, I can have *her,* my beautiful little swan, and everything else. I can still hold onto the control I need to keep the people I love safe and still have *her*.

My world.

As I glance at her, my hand over hers, she smiles at me. Trusting. Warm. I pull her into me, onto my lap. My beautiful wife. The more time I spend with her, the more I hope she feels what I do, but I know... the moment is perfect. Too perfect, even. Peace isn't lasting in our world. I might as well enjoy these stolen moments while I can.

A knock sounds at the door.

"Don't open it," I snap to Rodion, his hand on the knob.

"Just us," my uncle yells on the other side.

Anissa frowns. "We should refuse to open and make them come in the way you've asked them to." Her arms cross over her chest, and she says in a haughty tone, "I don't like them disobeying you."

I don't either. I turn to the door. "This one's locked. Go to the front," I snap.

They curse, and I can hear the sound of retreating footsteps, but they do what I say. Anissa fairly gloats.

I send Rodion to let them in, and when the door to the kitchen opens, my uncle and aunt make themselves at home.

I don't like the way my aunt looks at Anissa. "I'm taking Anissa out. We have business in town." My business involves taking her on a bit of a spending spree before we meet the rest of the family for dinner.

"My, my, my, aren't we spoiled," my aunt says with a sour look, staring at the table with strewn wrapping paper and gifts.

"You got your son a *Maserati* for his sixteenth birthday," Zoya says, her eyes narrowed. "Rodion got a summons to court for his eighteenth. Seems fair enough he can be spoiled every once in a while."

Anissa nearly chokes on her tea. My aunt glares at Zoya and opens her mouth to snap back, when Anissa jumps in. No one will be rude to Zoya on her watch. "Excuse me," she says in her clear, confident voice. "Thank you for coming in the way you were asked. My husband has rules for security purposes." She smiles sweetly. "Please don't make that mistake again. I'd hate to see you shot by accident."

My aunt opens her mouth to protest, but Anissa is not done. "It's very important that you do what my husband says. He *is* the one in charge here."

My uncle stares but nods.

By the time we get to the car, I'm determined to reward her. She snuggles onto my lap.

"You were a good girl in there. Defending your husband."

She gives me a haughty shrug with her chin in the air. "That bitch will not put down your family and disrespect you. No *way*."

I smile into her hair, breathing her in. "Good girl," I whisper against the shell of her ear. "I think you've earned a reward."

"Ooooh," she hums.

"Spread your legs, baby doll. *Now.*"

She doesn't need to be asked twice. I slide my hand up her calf, her dress pooling around my wrist, and find the damp warmth of her pussy. "*Jesus,* woman. You're so fucking wet."

"You've been edging me for *years,*" she moans. "My god, Rafail, *please.*"

"Do you want my mouth or my hands?" I croon in her ear, stroking her swollen clit.

Her voice nearly breaks on a sob. "*Yes.*"

The interior of the car's filled with her pleas and my dark chuckle as I guide her down onto the leather seat, my grip firm yet measured as I spread her thighs and position her right where I want her. It feels intimate in the small enclosure.

I lean down, my breath hot against her skin, teasing her before I press my mouth to her throbbing, wet core. My tongue slides over her slick, hot folds, and she whimpers into a deep sigh of contentment. "Please, Rafail. I'll do anything you tell me. I'm sorry I didn't beg before. I want you. I want your mouth on me. I want to come on your tongue. Please, *please.*"

I growl in approval and slide my fingers in her core. She shivers and stabs her fingers into my hair. I hold her thighs as I taste her with deliberate, measured strokes. Every flick of my tongue draws a soft moan from her; the wet sound of my tongue working her to climax mingles with the hum of the engine outside.

She anchors onto my hair as if to hold her in place while my tongue circles and delves deeper, relentless, demanding. "Who owns this cunt?" I growl at her.

"You. *You*, Rafail," she says easily, choking on a half sob. "You own all of me. *All of me*. I'm yours."

I stroke her again and plunge into her center as her body arches toward me.

"Who's the one you yield to, little swan?"

"*You*. You, Rafail. Always."

"Good girl." I reward her with another swipe of my tongue and another until she moans. "Come on my mouth, angel. Come for me," I breathe out before I stroke her clit again. Her head falls back, and she screams, her body arching into mine.

The walls of her pussy tighten around my fingers as the first wave of pleasure echoes through her body. I hold her hips down forcefully so she doesn't fly away as she screams my name and comes so hard she's nearly hoarse. My cock throbs at the sound of her moans, at the way she comes with abandon as though the entire world outside of this car ceases to exist, and all that matters is getting lost in blissful pleasure.

I give her one parting lick of my tongue, and her hips jerk. She whimpers, her eyes closed. I drag her onto my lap as she pants, spent and exhausted.

"Was it worth it?" I say with a dark chuckle.

"I'll never forgive myself for this," she replies in a hoarse whisper. "But yes."

I'm still chuckling when my phone rings. "Goddamn it, they have a knack for interrupting at the worst times."

"To be fair," she says in a breathy voice, her eyes still closed. "We have a lot of times we, um... don't like to be interrupted. Maybe this is why they talk so much at mealtimes."

True.

I look down at the phone. It's Semyon.

"Yeah?"

"I've got strange news, brother."

"Yeah?" She sighs against my chest, oblivious to the call.

"Someone's said the Romanovs are in town."

Why does that make the hair on the back of my neck stand on end? I hardly know them. We're not enemies, but we're definitely not friends. I have nothing to fear from them.

"Yeah?"

"Something's fishy," Semyon says. "There's talk of them fleeing from the cartel, but the association's complicated. Some of their family have married into the cartel, but it appears they made enemies. That isn't the complicated part though."

"What is it?" I hate when people take a long time to get to the point.

"They're looking for their missing sister, Rafail. Her name is Polina."

CHAPTER 18

"ANISSA"

It's not uncommon for Rafail to look angry, but right now, he looks murderous. I'm half drowsy after what he put me through, but as he talks to his brother, I look down at the phone Rafail finally gave me. Yana had a question about tonight, and it's best I stay out of whatever has caused that look on his face today. I'm halfway through replying to her when Rafail's voice cuts me off mid-thought.

"Polina? That sounds familiar, but I don't know why. I hardly know them."

My phone drops into my lap. I stare at him. *Polina.* The name from my dream. I've heard it more than once now, and it still rings with a familiarity that makes my heart ache.

Polina.

A memory comes to me so suddenly I'm breathless. I'm standing in a room that's familiar to me because I've seen it in my dreams. A living room? The gray-haired woman looks with concern, and a man—*Mikhail. His name is Mikhail.*

I blink. I know his name. And not just his name. He's my brother. Mikhail. Aleksandr. They are my brothers.

I close my eyes. Remembering.

He's telling me to flee, that I'm in grave danger. And my mother promises that we'll be safe if we go to Moscow.

Moscow. I'm near Moscow now.

What happened?

"Polina?" I whisper, staring at Rafail. "The name from my dream." I sit up. I push away from him.

Rafail's look grows cloudy, his gaze concerned. "You may have met her at one point? Maybe you knew her. She's the Romanov sister."

Romanov.

"Romanov?" I whisper. "That's my name, Rafail."

I stare at Rafail. I feel as if I'd know if he was lying, but there's nothing but earnest sincerity in his gaze. Shaking his head, he snakes his arm around my back. "It isn't, love. You were never a Romanov. I know that for a fact. Your name is Anissa Kopolov now. Everything I've told you is true."

But that's when he looks away.

Everything I've told you is true.

Something in my mind begins to stir. Questioning. I feel confused and uneasy as flashes of memory start to surface that don't align with what I've been told. I can hear snatches of conversation, see visions of places that feel familiar, see faces of men and women that I know are... family.

I shake my head and close my eyes, trying to make sense of it all. He isn't lying, and yet... he's totally lying.

Could it be that he doesn't know the truth?

Or has he completely hoodwinked me?

I'm still half-drunk with pleasure, so the thought of him actually lying to me sounds atrocious. I hate the idea of my trust in him... wavering.

And yet...

I feel safe with him. I even began to think that despite my lack of memory, I could build a future with him. I love his sisters and brothers, and I feel like I belong here.

But... something isn't right.

"What is it?" he asks, his brows furrowed in concern.

"I just... well. I'm afraid that... my memories are coming back, and they're confusing me."

His scowl doesn't alleviate my concerns.

What is he hiding?

Why does this name trigger so much familiarity for me?

We pull up to the stores, and Rafail leans in and kisses my cheek. "I'm sorry for the confusion, my love. Remember, the doctor said that you could have false memories too. Give it time. Let it go for now, and just let things surface as they should."

False memories.

No... no, these aren't false memories. I can see the garden outside the home I grew up in. I can see a huge, muscular man with a big smile on his face. His name was... Viktor. He was my brother. When I was little, he'd walk around with me on his shoulders because he was big, even as a child.

He's my brother too. I had lots of brothers. Did I have sisters? I don't know if I remember sisters, but I know some of my brothers were... married. Yes. Like me.

Why don't I remember my wedding day?

I close my eyes and try to relax my brain.

Please, just let me remember. Please.

I paint a picture in my mind, but no matter how hard I try, I can't remember.

"Anissa," Rafail says gently. "Let's go. You're going to hurt yourself if you push too hard, baby. Don't. It'll be okay, I promise." He pulls me to him and holds me tight, his big arms wrapped around me as he kisses my forehead. "It'll be fine, Anissa. You'll see." He kisses my cheek again. "I love you." His voice drops. "We all do."

I swallow the lump in my throat. Because up until ten minutes ago, I would've thought I felt the same.

CHAPTER 19

RAFAIL

Polina Romanova.

I watch my wife retreat.

I watch her hear me, listen to the words I whisper to her without responding. Something's changed. I can't counteract the growing doubt she seems to feel as her memories begin to surface.

We're at a pivotal moment, and I don't know how to stop this from happening. The more she remembers, the more I feel like I need to anchor her to me so she doesn't leave.

It unsettles me. It's then that I realize my feelings for her have put me in a place I fucking promised myself I would never be.

Vulnerable.

Weak.

At the mercy of someone else.

I clench my fist and shake my head. No, I promised myself I wouldn't do this, and yet here I am, as vulnerable as I was the day she jilted me at the altar.

No. I won't let it happen.

She's mine, my bride, my wife... my everything. And I'll do everything in my power to keep her safe. *Everything.*

No matter the cost.

I know I should reassure her. I should maybe convince her that everything's as it should be, that nothing in our past is afoul. But the more I think about her growing doubt... the more my fear of being dangerously vulnerable surfaces.

"Rafail?" Anissa asks, her hand on my shoulder. And just like every time she touches me that way, my anger melts like snow under the blazing sun. I breathe more deeply. I feel... lighter.

I kiss her fingertips. "Yes?"

Her baby-blue eyes bore into mine with concern as she cups my jaw. "I think we're both confused," she says softly. She swallows hard before she continues. "Let's make a pact."

I nod, a lump rising in my throat. I didn't know I could love anyone as much as I love my family.

I was wrong.

This woman has swept into my life—no, I forced her into my life and by my side—and yet, here she is, fitting in with the rest of us as naturally as could be. She belongs here. She *is* one of us.

"What's that?" I ask, my voice strangely husky.

"We won't talk about the past today. Not with your family at dinner. We talk about the future, but let's make a pact that we don't drag up the past." She laughs, and something in my chest loosens a little. I love the sound of her laugh. I love everything about her. "Not that you can rely on my memory of the past anyway."

I haven't cried since the night my parents died, and even then, not until I held the small, sobbing frame of my baby sister in my arms—mourning the loss of her parents—to bring me to tears. But now... Christ, I'm two blinks away from losing my shit.

I kiss her forehead softly and hold her to me.

"Yeah. Alright, then. Agreed. It's a pact."

She lays her head on my chest as we approach the shops. Suddenly, I don't want to be here with her, not out in the open. Every instinct inside me's telling me this is the wrong thing to do.

I should run.

"We should go home," I tell her. "We aren't safe here."

Her eyes twinkle mischievously. "Your aunt is at the house. We're not safe there either."

I playfully tug a lock of her hair as she leans in to kiss my cheek. "I feel safe with you," she says simply.

And that's all the convincing I need.

Even as my mind is occupied with thoughts about what

could happen when she discovers the truth of our union… I can't help it.

I spoil the shit out of her.

First, we head to the dress shop. She winks at me as she tries on dress after dress. I choose a selection of different styles—some elegant ones for dinners with the family and more seductive ones for dinner with *me.* "These are gorgeous," she says, running her hand down the length of a few of them. I bought out the fucking dressing room so I could have her alone. "You seem to like the ones with slits."

I shrug a shoulder and wink. I love the way it makes her blush because she knows exactly why I chose them.

Next, the jewelry store. "Your aunt will have a conniption," she says with a giggle.

I growl at her. "My aunt can go fuck herself."

"*Rafail,*" she says half-reproachfully as she laughs out loud. "You're always telling *me* to behave."

I shrug. "It's good advice. Now get your ass in that store. I have money burning a hole in my pocket."

She grins at me and walks in with her head held high. That's my girl. She walks with the elegance of a queen. Royalty.

Because she is.

"I don't even know where to begin in a place like this," she says, tucking herself under my arm almost bashfully. She stares at the enameled jewelry, some of Moscow's most famous. They're vibrant and expressive, and Yana assures me that they are the most sought-after jewelry in Moscow. Looks like miniature pieces of artwork to me, which suits me just fine because I'd like to see my wife wearing something unique.

"May I help you?" A petite young woman with light brown hair gives me a winning smile, looking right past Anissa.

"Yes, I'd like to pick out a signature set for my wife."

Her face falls. *Jesus.* I can tell Anissa notices the saleswoman's chagrin when her eyes narrow. I tug a lock of her hair to remind her to behave.

"Your wife?" she asks, giving Anissa a not-too-subtle once-over. "What's the occasion?"

"For behaving herself and being a good girl for me," I answer, meeting Anissa's eyes.

Her cheeks flush, but the brightness in her eyes tells me she likes that answer. Unfortunately, so does the sales girl. She giggles like a little girl and goes to the back of the room, bringing out a case that locks with a key. I lean in and whisper in her ear, "*Ya dam tebe nagradu za to, chto ty vela sebya khorosho.*"

I'll give you a reward for behaving so well.

"Then, in this case, perhaps something from our regal collection. We call these pieces our regal collection because they're befitting a queen." But she's still looking at me.

She opens the case with a flourish. Anissa gasps. "Those are gorgeous," she breathes out, taking in the intricate works of art. "You say they're enamel?"

"Mmm," the salesperson says with a frown. "But wouldn't you know? You've been here before."

Anissa flushes. "I'm sorry, I don't—I don't remember," she stammers.

"But it was only last week. You were with another man," she says, her head tipped to the side. "Does that trigger your memory?"

Rage tears through me. "That's impossible," I seethe, glaring at her. "We were married last week." I turn Anissa away from the counter. "We're all set, thank you."

"But sir!" she calls after us, but we're halfway out the door.

I'm breathing too heavily. Anissa's holding onto my arm but hobbling because she can't walk straight. Wordlessly, I lead us down the street. I don't even know where I'm going.

"It's alright," she says softly after we've walked a block. "Really, Rafail. Remember what I said. It'll turn right in the end."

I blow out a breath. "I'm sorry," I say, shaking my head. "You deserved one of those gorgeous pieces."

She laughs and waves a hand at me. "Whatever. It doesn't matter, not really. They were gorgeous, but she wanted to sink her claws into you, so I'm happy she missed that sale. Too bad," she says with a petty little upturn of her chin. "Could've made good commission on that and maybe invested in some etiquette school. God, what is it like?"

I give her my elbow and slow my walk before I open the door to a coffee shop and hold it for her.

She shakes her head. "Looking so much like a god that people treat you like one."

I roll my eyes at her. "Exaggerating doesn't become you, Anissa."

Her giggle is worth the whole damn trip into town.

I order us coffees and pour cream into hers and take the paper bag over to where she sits, waiting, her hands folded in her lap with a look of unadulterated bliss on her face.

Jesus, I wish I could keep her there. Right there, unperturbed and at ease, without a care in the world.

"You got me a cupcake," she says, clapping her hands together.

"Of course. You told Zoya they looked delicious when you saw it on that cooking show the other night."

Her eyes twinkle as she takes a large bite, painting her upper lip with icing and licking the crumbs from her lips. "I didn't think you were paying attention. You were too busy lecturing Rodion on not ignoring your curfew rules."

I grunt and take a sip of my coffee. "I still paid attention. I'm so used to lecturing him on my curfew rules I can multi-task at this point."

She snorts. "He really does push your buttons."

I shrug. "More when he was younger. He does a lot better now."

We lean back in our chairs. "You've done a good job, you know. I don't know if anyone's told you that often enough, Rafail. You're hard on them but protective, and I don't know how anyone would've handled what you did better. They're close. Resilient."

My chest tightens. She's right. No one's told me that at all.

"Thank you. But it's far from over." I sip my coffee thoughtfully.

Anissa's eyes grow a little misty as she sips her mug in turn. "And that feels familiar too. What *doesn't* feel familiar is knowing who I'm meeting tonight. You've got your Aunt Irma and Uncle Eduard, who, unfortunately, I know all too well..."

I nod. "The six of us. Vadka, who you've met. My cousin Gleb and his brother Matvei."

"Are they Eduard and Irma's boys?"

"Mmm."

Anissa frowns. "Your grandfather?"

I nod. "My grandfather, yes. Maybe a few other cousins."

"Good. I love your grandfather, even if he wipes the floor with me every time we play chess, and one day, I *will* convince him there's more to the world of music than Tchaikovsky and Prokofiev. One day, I'll introduce him to composers who aren't Russian—and he might even like it." Her eyes twinkle before she sighs. "There's so much to remember," she says. "How will I keep track?"

I lean forward and squeeze her hand. "As long as you remember what's most important, baby."

She winks at me as I settle the tab, oblivious, her back turned to the door. It's always my way—situated to see everything, to make sure nothing slips by me.

But then the door opens, and every alarm bell in me clangs. I sit as still as possible and watch.

Three men. I recognize them from somewhere, though I can't quite place it. The first is tall and stern, his skin golden, his light brown hair slicked back with military precision. The second is a shadow to his light—dressed the same but even taller, with dark hair and a sharpness in his gaze that cuts straight to me. And the third, looming behind them like a storm, is all muscle, so massive he nearly fills the entire doorway.

Everything in me tenses. They're not here by accident.

I don't know who they are. I've never seen them before in my life. But for some reason, every instinct in me tells me to hide Anissa because other patrons in this place know exactly who they are. They give the trio a wide berth, and as the men approach the counter, the owner comes to the front, wiping his hands on a tea towel.

"Let's go," I tell Anissa, leading her to the door. I open it for her, my heart beating faster. I can't understand what the fuck is going on, but every hair on the back of my neck stands up as one of the men growls something in Russian to the owner.

"I'm sorry, I haven't worked the counter. I haven't seen anyone who looks like that. Have you?" In my peripheral vision, I see the barista scrutinizing a cell phone the man holds up, presumably with a picture on it.

"I... wasn't she just here?"

The door shuts behind us.

CHAPTER 20

"ANISSA"

Our car is waiting for us, and as the door shuts, I hear a commotion where we just left. Voices shout, and I swear... the voices are vaguely familiar.

My husband looks as if he's seen a ghost.

"What was that?" I ask Rafail.

"I have no idea." He shakes his head. "Trouble."

But he doesn't meet my eyes. The feeling that he's hiding something from me intensifies as memories of my past that don't resonate with what he's told me leave me feeling confused and bewildered.

"Rafail—" I don't know how to continue. I don't know what to say.

Leaning in closer to me, he wraps his arm around my shoulders. "Maybe it was too much, taking you out like this, especially when we're meeting up with my family."

But no. It isn't. I don't like being sheltered and made to feel like I'm too fragile to handle whatever happens. I hate it, and there's something about it that triggers a similar memory.

"What is it?" he asks. "You're pulling away from me."

I am, in more ways than one. I know I am.

"I'm just... confused. And a little scared," I tell him truthfully.

I love being with him. I love how protective and strong he is. I'm in a place where I'm wildly vulnerable and unsure of who I can trust. His strength brings me security when I waffle. Even his power and control call to me on a deep, primal level. But beneath his stern, unyielding, even angry exterior—I see the vulnerability he hides. Behind his implacable façade is a deep well of pain, the scars of past betrayal and loss of those he loved. And I love that so much it makes my heart ache.

"That's alright." The heavy weight of his arms around my shoulders, the surety of his words and the comfort of his presence make me feel as if he truly does understand. "It will become easier. You'll see. Trust me to take care of you, and as you say... it will come alright in the end."

Maybe I've imagined anything less? Maybe my confusion led me to believe the one person I can trust above all?

Because from the moment I first met him—or woke, anyway, as if it *were* our first meeting—there was an undeniable pull between us. Even when I've been unsure of who I am or who he is, what his motives are or where my place is, the primal attraction between us is undeniable. He's dangerous and powerful and utterly, madly devoted to... *me*.

I rest my hand atop his as we drive through the city streets. Rafail's alert, as always, even as he holds and comforts me. I can't help but love this about him too—his intense, commanding nature. It fascinates me how he commands not only his empire and family but the very space around him.

Maybe I have a thing for "alpha male in control" because, goddamn, it's intoxicating. The power play between us thrums hot and electric, cutting through my fears and uncertainties. Even when my past is an enigma and my future a blank slate, there's a dark, twisted freedom with him—a freedom from societal expectations and empty conventions, from the illusion of safety. With him, I can forge a new future, a new identity, even as we're deeply entrenched in this criminal world of his... No, of *ours*.

"Sometimes, I swear to fuck, I can feel your mind whirring like a machine," he says, reaching for my hand to bring my fingers to his lips. I shiver with the warmth of his lips on my skin before he places the flat of my palm on his chest. His heart beats madly beneath my touch. I swallow hard.

"Yeah. I wish I could stop it. I really do, but the past weeks have felt like speed dating or something." I shake my head.

"The fuck is speed dating?" I stifle a giggle at the look of consternation, biting my lip to keep from laughing.

"It's like a fast-paced version of the real thing. You remove the fluff and dive right into the actual meat. It's intentional, with the purpose of meeting multiple people in a single evening instead of stretching it out over weeks." I poke at his chest. "Maybe consider it for Zoya."

I expect him to growl in response, and I'm not disappointed. "The hell I will. She's not dating."

Outside the tinted window of the car, the view begins to slow. We're approaching our destination.

"Rafail, you can't keep her locked up in your tower forever."

He grunts, frowning. "Why not?"

I sigh. "Yana's married though?"

His eyes cloud over, and he looks away. "That was to keep her safe. It was her choice, and I allowed it."

Even though I know he's being facetious, to an extent, I... I know this argument. *No one's good enough.* I close my eyes at another rush of memories.

I'm standing with the woman I now know to be my mother. My brother—one of them—is arguing with her. It's prom night in high school, and I want to go on a date.

No one is good enough for her.

They said it was too dangerous, too risky for me to go alone without one of them with me. I remember I finally went with a group of girls, as any of the guys in my school wouldn't come anywhere near me, not with all those dangerous brothers on the periphery.

I remember...

I remember...

I wore a light blue gown with glitter accents and silvery heels. My long blonde hair was piled on my head in loops and swirls. I felt like Cinderella waiting for Prince Charming; only my enchanted pumpkin was a luxury town car, and the guards who accompanied me were three of my oldest brothers.

My god.

I remember.

"We're here," Rafail says. I blink as if waking from a memory. It feels as if my amnesia's begun to unravel as fragmented memories surface. Bits of my past swim in front of me, but I have no time to dwell.

I'm not sure I want to.

The car comes to a halt outside a restaurant. I half expect uniformed valets, but this is a more casual affair. The people entering the restaurant are dressed informally and hardly look at us as we pass. I like it this way. The last thing I want to do is be noticed by anyone.

When we get inside, however, the hostess's eyes go wide behind her glasses as she sees us. "Mr. Kopolov."

Rafail nods to me. "And Mrs. Kopolov, yes."

My heart does a little flip in my chest. I love when he calls me that when he claims me. And the way his fingers lace into mine, at once a reminder that I'm his... I tell myself I shouldn't fret so much about what I don't know and hold on instead to what I *do*. Maybe my identity as *Anissa Kopolov* is all that matters.

Rafail Kopolov—stern, unyielding, powerful, and sometimes angry... passionate and devoted, fearless and brave—loves me. *Me.*

I hold his hand, feeling a bit shy, as she leads us to a back room. Before we even enter, we can hear chatter and laughter.

I'll know some people here, anyway, and I'm thankful when I see the familiar faces of Zoya and Yana. Zoya waves at us and beckons us to come over to her, but Rafail is still saying hello to a few people.

"Ah, there's the happy couple." His grandfather is small and frail, but his eyes remind me of Rafail's, and beneath his calm demeanor lies undeniable strength. His warm eyes and soft voice don't bely the power he holds. "Welcome. Come, come. Have a seat. Have some wine."

He gestures to the two vacant seats next to Zoya's, but Rafail's still scouting the room. He nods to his friend Vadka and to Semyon, Rodion, and a few other unfamiliar faces I don't recognize. He introduces me to a few cousins.

"Matvei, Gleb, meet my wife Anissa."

"Oh," I say with a smile. "We didn't meet at the wedding?"

The two men look sharply at Rafail, who only shakes his head. "I'm sorry, she's forgotten a lot, but her memory's slowly coming back." My cheeks flush. Is he embarrassed by me?

"I'm-I'm sorry," I stammer.

"You're fine," Matvei says, extending his hand. He's a large guy like the others, with broad shoulders and a quiet intensity. Even though he's not as outwardly threatening as Rafail, his presence alone commands respect.

Noted.

"Your husband is like an older brother to me," Matvei says with a smile. "We grew up together, and I look up to him. I'm pleased to meet you."

I smile at him. "He's everyone's older brother, isn't he?" I hold onto his arm, his bicep taut beneath my hand.

Leaning in, he brushes his lips to my cheek.

"Not everyone's," his other cousin says with a smirk that makes me feel a little uneasy. "Gleb." Gleb is more slender than his brother, with sharp features and a charming smile I can't trust. It doesn't quite reach his eyes, and I'm immediately on edge. "So you're the woman who finally got Rafail to settle down. Must be quite the story."

I glance at Rafail. Settle down?

Why has it never occurred to me that there were other women before me? *Settle down*? How many women were there before me?

"Oh, I guess you could say that." I laugh.

Gleb winks at me. Rafail's muscles tighten under my hand, but his face remains placid. "We'll have to hear all about it sometime. I bet with my cousin here, it isn't all candlelit dinners and diamonds."

"Oh," I say lightly with a lame attempt at a laugh. "He's pretty damn good with those candlelit dinners and diamonds if I say so myself."

Rafail stifles a low growl. "Good girl," he says softly. "Let's keep the questions to a minimum, Gleb. I'd much rather hear about your adventures in America. You spent some time in New York, didn't you?"

America. My heart aches for reasons I can't quite understand.

Rafail pulls out the chair next to Zoya, who leans in and whispers in my ear, "Now, don't worry about him at all. Gleb's a jerk. Matvei's alright, though, you'll see."

But his cousin isn't finished. "It's not every day we get to meet the new Mrs. Kopolov."

Rafail grimaces at Semyon. "Did you let Gleb get into the wine again? We talked about that."

Gleb's eyes flash at Rafail so quickly that I think I may have imagined it. "Just be careful around him. Life with Rafail can be..." He leans forward. "Intense."

I smile. "Oh, I've noticed. I happen to like intense. Life isn't all fun and games, you know?" I give him a wink back and take the glass of water Rafail offers me.

Rafail's warm, firm hand on my thigh sends a shiver down my spine, somehow both approval and a warning to behave. I half flirt with the idea of pushing, just to see what he'll do, but the memory of this morning's still fresh in my mind.

So, while they talk about business and football and the American version of vodka, which they all seem to despise, I talk with Zoya about which dress she should wear to her upcoming semi-formal.

"Have you asked your brother about that yet?" I whisper to her.

"Oh no," she says with a little smile that's part grimace. "I was, uh, sort of hoping you would."

I nod. "Of course I will." When he's drunk on sex and half-asleep, I think.

I don't have to remind myself that I'm in the presence of criminals. That my husband runs a powerful empire, but that none of these people here, not one, not even sweet little Zoya, is innocent.

The way Rafail constantly scans the room, continually vigilant. The glint of metal on Semyon's hip when he stands to welcome another cousin and aunt. The waitstaff's furtive glances and rush to immediately make sure the food is served promptly and our glasses are constantly filled.

Uncle Eduard smiles at me as he helps himself to yet another glass of wine. "You've married right into a ready family, Anissa," he says while Rafail is busy talking to Gleb and Matvei. "He's been a father to these hoodlums for years now. Should make it easy to start a family of your own, you think?"

I blink, startled at the directness of his comment. "Well, when the time is right," I say with a shrug, though my heart races at the thought. "And even though he's their older brother, it seems—"

Matvei cuts in with a grin. "Seems he's already had plenty of practice raising a family, huh?"

Rafail gives a half-hearted smile, but when I look at him, he winks at me. My tummy flips.

"Rafail is too humble to tell you, but he was on his way to college when... when the accident happened," his grandfather says. "I bought him a suitcase, and he was ready." His voice grows softer. "Ready to fly away, weren't you, son?"

I look at Rafail in surprise. For some reason, it never occurred to me that he'd ever wanted anything more than what he has, right here, with his family.

"My flight was supposed to leave that night," Rafail says, a note of wistfulness in his voice. "When I got the call."

My heart hurts for the man he had to become so quickly, so unexpectedly. "And you had to cancel everything?"

"Of course," he says with a smirk. "It took every second of my time keeping these hoodlums in line."

Semyon snorts, and their grandfather shakes his head, his worn, leathery face all creases as he smiles. "If *that* isn't the understatement of the year. I tried to help, but I couldn't keep up with them. There was a time they were *wild*, and my days of reining in terrors were past."

Matvei snorts and shakes his head. "*Jesus*, do you remember that time Rodion decided to 'borrow' Rafail's car for a joyride? What were we, sixteen?"

Rodion's smile is a little pained as he rubs the back of his neck and gives Rafail a sheepish smile.

"I remember it well," Rafail says with a pointed look. He doesn't appear quite as amused as the rest of them, but even his serious eyes spark with a hint of humor.

"We were *fourteen*," Rodion admits, shaking his head. "And we had fun, didn't we? Until, uh... until Rafail caught us."

Rafail growls next to me. "Yeah, nearly driving yourself straight into a river sounds like excellent fun."

"Oof," I say with a grimace. "You two! Did you really?"

"Oh," Rafail says, shaking his head. "They did. *Once*, anyway."

"You got that right," Matvei says, his eyes bright with laughter. "He dragged us out of that car so fast, my head was spinning. And the look on his face? I thought he was going to kill us right there."

"I thought about it," Rafail says dryly, making everyone laugh.

"No, instead of killing us, he made sure we *wished* we were dead," Rodion adds with a grin. "Good enough, right?"

Matvei shakes his head. "Yeah, that was kind of a turning point, I think. Didn't pull *that* shit again."

My chest tightens as I take in their words. The man who had dreams and hopes beyond the city of Moscow and the confines of family had to give it all up. He had to step into the role of protector, laying aside what he wanted to keep what he already had.

Right then, I feel the weight of responsibility alongside him. I want to help him shoulder it. He might be grumpy and intense and so bossy it sometimes makes me want to scream, but I feel it—an undeniable pull to the boy he left behind.

I want to give him back some of the freedom he surrendered.

I reach for his hand and give it a squeeze. In response, he nestles my one hand in both of his as the waitstaff clears our dishes and brings out large platters of dessert plates with shimmering pudding and layered cake.

"Ooooh," Zoya says, her eyes dancing. "Their chocolate cake is *epic*, Anissa."

I nod along with her. "I might not remember everything, but I can say with absolute certainty that I *love* chocolate cake."

Suddenly, another memory surfaces, like a snapshot from another life I once lived. Honest to god, if I didn't believe in reincarnation before this, I sure as hell do now.

My brothers—I remember a few names now.

Mikhail. Viktor. Lev.

My heart aches.

Their laughter echoes around me as I reach for a slice of chocolate layer cake. My mother, her gentle smile lighting up her wrinkled face, cuts me a piece and tugs my hair. "Had them make your favorite," she says, leaning in to kiss my cheek. "Happy birthday, sweetheart."

I blink, and the memory slips away like a fading dream.

"Anissa?" Zoya looks at me with concern. "Would you like a piece?"

I nod, not trusting my voice. If I talk, I'm going to cry. Rafail's intense gaze sweeps over mine. Wordlessly, he brushes a thumb across the top of my hand. Reassuring me. Leaning in, his breath is hot at my ear. "Do we need to go?"

I swallow the lump in my throat and force a smile. "Not until I have that cake, please."

A commotion sounds out the window, and like they did at home, in the kitchen, every damn one of them comes to immediate attention. Rodion is the first to get up, pushing away from the table so fast his chair hits the floor. I stare, my fork suspended over the cake, as Rafail snaps into commander mode. Even his uncle and grandfather look immediately to him.

"Semyon, guard the door. Matvei, go with Rodion. Gleb, you stay here. Yana, scan the outer perimeter on surveillance and see what the fuck is going on out there."

As everyone runs to obey, he leans in close to me and slides an index finger under my chin, bringing my eyes to his. "You do *exactly* what I say."

I nod, both terrified of whatever's happening and confident he'll take care of me. Of all of us.

"Could be anything," his grandfather says to me, leaning in to take a sip of his coffee. "Someone cut someone else off. They had heated words. Some idiot hit another guy for flirting with his girl. People do dumb things all the time." He doesn't need to supply the rest of his sentence because I already know. They don't have the luxury of assumptions.

And yet... this all feels familiar, just like it did before. The shift from lighthearted memories to being on guard, ready to protect each other, doesn't exactly catch me off guard. It's second nature now and hints at a past I can't remember in detail, but one that's not very dissimilar to the present.

Yana speaks first. "They're here for us, Rafail." She's on her feet, her phone in her hand. "The Popov family is here for you." Her eyes go straight to his. "And they're looking for you."

CHAPTER 21

RAFAIL

My first step is to make sure Anissa's safe. She follows me with wide eyes, but she doesn't look surprised or anxious. No. A sudden turn of events isn't outside her experience at all. She's ready for my command, which could range from anything to duck for cover under the table or catch the Glock 19 that I bought her midair and take a stance at the door.

She knows.

There's more to Anissa than I've thought, and I aim to find out what.

The door to the small room we're renting flies open, Rodion and Semyon in the lead. Behind them, Popov walks in alone. He stands tall with a lean, athletic build and an air of authority that makes most men cower. *Most* men. Not me.

He meets my gaze. "I need a word, Kopolov," he snarls as if he's barely holding onto his temper. He's cold and merciless, a force to be reckoned with in the Russian underworld. Anissa's eyes are comically wide as she stares, hidden behind me.

I grin at him and clap him on the back. "Jesus, it's good to see you, brother."

Popov grins back at me. "As it is you. I've heard you have someone to introduce me to."

I pull Anissa out from behind me proudly, my hand on her lower back. "Anissa, meet Roman Popov, eldest of the Popov family just north of Moscow. He likes to make a dramatic entrance."

"So it's true," he says as if to himself. "I needed to see it with my own eyes." Popov is well schooled in the art of a poker face, but even he can't help the brief look of shock he quickly hides. His lips brush Anissa's knuckles so briefly, I almost keep my temper fully in check when his wicked eyes glint at me.

"Welcome, Anissa. It would take a strong woman to withstand the likes of this motherfucker."

I grunt at him and pull out a chair. "Join us? We were about to have dessert."

Rodion and Semyon stand guard by the door. "He didn't come alone, brother," Semyon says quietly.

"I didn't," Popov continues as he declines my invitation to sit. "I came directly to you with news that will impact all of us. May I speak with you in private? I'm sorry for the drama." He blows out a breath. "It cannot wait."

Everyone's eyes are on me. "Of course," I say, reluctant to leave Anissa, but before I can say a word, both Rodion and Semyon step to the table. I meet both of their eyes and know what they vow—protection for all, no matter the cost.

"We are safe for a little while," Popov says. For a split second, I swear his eyes go to my sisters—but it's Zoya who flushes pink and turns away. "You have my word; your family is safe, even your sisters... for now."

I don't miss the ominous tone as we step into a vacant hallway between the dining rooms and the restrooms.

"What is it?"

He doesn't waste any time. "Manuel Soloto, head of a cartel organization in Colombia. He's after a woman by the name of Polina Romanova." Popov's eyes hold mine. "Does that name mean anything to you?"

Again, a feeling of dread builds in my stomach. I shake my head. "All I know is she's the missing sister of the Romanov family."

"Yes. And when I heard the news, I thought nothing of it. Not until I went to get a cup of coffee and met the Romanov brothers in person." He shakes his head. "There are a few things you need to know. First, the Romanov brothers are a force of nature—six men, well-armed and ruthless, each one prepared to fight to the death." I shake my head. What does this have to do with me?

Popov continues. "Second, they're here because they sent their sister to Moscow in an effort to protect her from Soloto. Soloto has an axe to grind, and she's on his radar."

I listen, my heart beating faster before I even hear the rest of what he has to say. "Third..." He swallows hard. "Your new wife has an *uncanny* resemblance to the Romanov sister, Polina."

I stare, disbelieving. It can't be true... can it? *How*?

"Show me." My voice is hoarse as he pulls out his phone and shows me a picture.

I stare at the woman in front of me—pale, porcelain skin. Eyes as blue as a spring day. Blonde, nearly white hair that hangs to her waist, and a ready smile I know all too well because I carry it with me wherever I go.

"It can't be," I whisper, shaking my head. "That... how?"

He pushes his phone in his back pocket and shakes his head. "I have no idea, but we have questions that need answers. As soon as I saw her picture, I came to find you. There's no question your wife will be mistaken for the Romanov princess. The question is, who will come first?" He pauses, the weight behind his gaze pinning me in place. "Soloto or the Romanovs?"

Jesus.

"Get her to safety, brother. Lock them all down. And find the answers that you need."

My voice is low and guarded. "I will. Who else knows this?"

He glances around the room. "There's no telling. If I were you, I would flee. You have people in Naples and Cape Town. Take your pick."

I shake my head. "I don't run, Popov, you know that. I never have and never will."

He blows out a breath with a grimace. "I know it all too well. I was afraid you'd say that." With a nod, he stands taller. "Which is why, in that case, I'll offer you the strength of my brotherhood to aid you. Say the word, and I'll help."

Help from the Popovs will come at a cost—that much is true. But right now, to keep my bride safe, there's no price too high to pay. It's in his best interest to keep on my good side, and he knows, as well as any other leader of this city, that alliances in the underworld are more valuable than any riches.

I nod. "Thank you."

He stands up straighter. "Retreat. Secure your family. And find answers, brother. My men will lead yours blindfolded. No one, not even you, will be able to see the location of our refuge." He jerks his head to the table. "If I were you, brother, I'd skip that cake."

I have to take a leap of faith. I know I could be leading my family into greater danger, but my gut instinct says I have to trust him. The weight of responsibility feels crushing, when I look over at Anissa and see her blue, blue eyes focused on mine. She smiles and nods, a silent vote of confidence.

I know what I have to do.

CHAPTER 22

"ANISSA"

When Rafail returns, he looks as if he's encountered a ghost. I've never seen him so pale, even as his eyes are blazing and his thunderous voice booms across the restaurant.

"We're in danger. More danger than you realize," he says, his gaze flicking to mine with warning. "I can't explain—not yet. You'll have to trust me. I want all of you—every last one of you to go where I tell you."

Grandfather is the first to get to his feet, his hand gripping his cane, serious eyes on Rafail. Uncle Eduard stares at him, but when he opens his mouth to ask questions, Rafail shakes his head. "Not now. You and your wife are free to do what you please, but since your sons have vowed themselves to me, they'll go where I tell them."

Gleb and Matvei follow wordlessly. It is a seamless execution, as no one questions Rafail's instructions. Semyon, his cold, calculating eyes laser-focused on making sure we evacuate promptly, is shoulder to shoulder with Rodion, who looks as if he's ready to toss a hand grenade or launch himself headfirst into an oncoming cavalcade.

Rafail doesn't leave my side. Zoya, however, has gone white as a sheet.

"Where are we going, Raf?" she asks, her wide eyes troubled. She grips the back of the chair as though it's grounding her in place. It isn't the first time she's faced fear like this, I know.

It isn't the first time *I* have.

But when Rafail leans close to her, he drapes his arm around her and holds her. "You have to trust me, Zoya. I won't let anyone hurt you—not ever. As long as I'm here, I'll make sure you're safe." He pushes a stray lock of hair behind her ear, gentling his voice while the rest leave quickly, wordlessly. He's taken a moment in the midst of chaos to soothe his sister's fears. God, I love him for that. "Can you do that for me?"

She nods. "Of course I can, yes," she says.

I reach for her hand. "Stay with me. You'll be alright, sweetheart. I have it on good authority your brother bought me a new pressie, and for some reason, I have a feeling I'm an *excellent* shot."

She smiles at me, even as her lower lip trembles. Rafail pays the waitstaff with a flourish of bills, then leads the evacuation. At the exit, a team of sleek, gunmetal gray cars purr at the curb, uniformed men waiting for us. Zoya and I look to Rafail at the same time.

"Go," he says quietly. "Trust me."

If I have to trust him, then why doesn't he meet my eyes?

Is he hiding something? It feels as if I have more questions than answers, and I don't like it. He wants us to trust him blindly when I've never felt more confused.

"This way," Rafail says, leading me to a car. Zoya gets into a car with her sister and brothers. I hardly see the others as everyone's quickly leaving. "We'll see them in a bit."

Blindfolds rest ominously on the car seats, vivid reminders of our need to trust without question. "We're going to the Popov safe house," Rafail explains, his voice calm and controlled as always. "Even I don't know where it is. We're all blindfolded, no exceptions."

My heart beats faster when he places the blindfold around my eyes. "I could have a lot of fun with this, Mrs. Kopolov," he whispers in my ear, trying to keep things light.

I only swallow and shrug. Something tells me we're on the cusp of a shift in our relationship. Something's coming, and it will be big. Maybe even... catastrophic.

"What did he tell you, Rafail?"

Voices sound near us. "Wait. They're checking to see if our blindfolds are in place. We'll be recorded on the way in so no one peeks."

I nod. My mouth is dry.

"And no, Anissa. I can't tell you what he said, not yet. Please, just trust me."

I want to trust him. But now, I have no choice. "Alright. Can you give me a hint?"

I hear the depth of his sigh in the silence before his hand reaches for me. Our fingers entwine. "All I can tell you is that we're in grave danger... all of us. I have questions that need answers before I give you any more details." The wheels of the car purr beneath us. I can't see out the window, but I know we're driving at a breakneck speed. My back is pressed to the seat, my feet glued to the floor.

I nod. "Okay."

"Tell me this, Anissa." I feel the reassuring warmth and weight of his hand on my thigh before he continues. "What can you remember? Tell me everything."

My pulse races. I swallow hard. "Everything?" I ask him.

But what if what I tell him threatens... us? I don't want it to.

What if I'm... *happy* being Anissa Kopolov?

And then he's drawing me to him. In the dark, both of us blindfolded, we find each other's hands. "Trust me. Please," he whispers. "What you know could impact your safety, baby. Please, just trust me."

Tears wet my blindfold as we careen toward whatever hideout we'll be in next.

"I know my name's not Anissa," I begin in a whisper. "It's Polina. I know it is. I can hear it loud and clear, and it isn't just a dream anymore, Rafail. I had... *have*... brothers. Lots of them. And they were so good to me." I blink and sniffle. His hand caressing my shoulder slows. "They were protective, yes, like you are with your sisters, but they loved me. I don't know how I ended up here, and I can't remember much more about my past. And I… I don't know who Anissa is." I shake my head. "But I'm not her."

"What else?" he asks hoarsely. "I need to know."

"But the doctor said that I can hurt my brain if I push—"

"You *must* push. You have to. There's no other way forward."

My hands are shaking when he holds me tighter.

"I know that I came to Moscow because I was in danger. I remember running from you, and I know that… when I ran from you, I didn't know you. But here's the thing, I…" My voice trails off. I'm afraid of giving voice to my fears.

"What? Say it." His voice is a harsh whisper.

"I don't know if what I remember is real or not. I can't tell the difference. Because sometimes, I imagine I worked in a hospital, and sometimes, I imagine I know how to shoot a gun. Sometimes, I think I do have sisters, but when memories from my childhood come back, I'm the only daughter."

I close my eyes, the blindfold soaked. "I remember being a little girl, alone, and I remember a kind woman. And I know that she's my mother."

It's absolutely brutal, telling him all this without being able to *look* at him.

"I want to see your eyes," I say with a big sniff. "*Please*, Rafail."

"You can't," he says in a harsh whisper. "If you take off your blindfold, they'll shoot you. Then I'll have to murder them, and we'll start a war in Moscow. The streets will be flooded with their blood, Anissa."

He calls me that by habit now. I've adopted it as my name.

"Well, then. I guess I won't take my blindfold off."

He holds me in the quiet, stroking my shoulder with ease. "Tell me what else you know." With a gentleness that belies the tight timbre of his voice, he kisses my cheek.

"I know that you love me," I whisper. "I know that you'll do anything for me. I know that you'll protect me from whatever comes next, even if neither one of us knows what that is."

"Yes," he says simply. "*Yes.*"

I swallow the lump in my throat and sniffle. "Now it's your turn."

"My turn?"

"Yes," I whisper vehemently, my need to know the truth choking me. "Tell me what *you* know. *Please.*"

But he's silent for long moments, so long, I wonder if something happened. I reach for his hand, but he's warm and strong beside me.

"I can't do that," he finally says. "I can't tell you anything. Not yet."

My jaw drops open in shock. "That's not fair. I told you everything, even the things I didn't want to. You can't refuse to do the same for me!"

"I can and will," he snarls. I coil away from him. My nose tingles.

"Rafail," I say reproachfully.

"You heard me," he snaps. "We're here. Remember to do exactly what I say. Exactly."

"You demand my trust and obedience but won't give me any answers in return. How is that fair, Rafail? What kind of love is this?" My hands are balled into fists.

"You were mafia, Anissa. You ought to know this. All's never fair in love and war, especially if you're raised in organized crime. Now behave yourself. Believe me when I tell you... you do *not* want to cross me right now."

The air in here feels hot and stuffy. My nose is running, my eyes are swollen, and I've given myself a headache. And we've only just begun.

"Very nice," I mutter. "Threatening your wife."

"Eto ne byla ugroza!"

That was not a threat.

We come to a screeching halt. The door opens, and hands reach for me before there's the sound of fists slamming on flesh. "Touch her and fucking die."

Then it's only Rafail. His familiar, rough but firm touch guiding me out of the car. The blindfold comes off, and I stare in front of me. We're underground. I can tell by how cold it is here. The floor is concrete, the walls made of stone. Armed guards, standing in military formation holding loaded weapons, watch us with stony faces.

They all give Rafail a wide berth.

We march in silence together. I feel... *betrayed.* Yes, betrayed by his sudden withdrawal and cold words. I know he's concerned, but it isn't right that he expects me to tell him everything with no expectation of him giving me the same courtesy.

But I can't think of that now, as we're moving together, his siblings nearby and cousins behind us.

"Blindfolds off. Watch your step."

I blink in the dim light but quickly find Rafail beside me. I'm pissed at him, and I *will* demand answers, but I still take no small solace in knowing he'll protect me... protect *all* of us.

I quickly observe our surroundings. There isn't one safe house, but several—a network of brightly lit interconnected rooms. Hidden beneath the city, the entrance is concealed with something up above, but none of us are able to see. The air is cold and damp down here and slightly musty, but it's swept clean.

Two armed guards in front of us open the door for us. "Entry in or out must be approved by Mr. Popov," a young, masked guard says. "Only accessible with biometric scanners. Anyone who tries to leave without explicit permission to do so will be immediately executed."

The door swings open, and he gives us a sardonic smile. "Enjoy your stay."

CHAPTER 23

RAFAIL

Popov doesn't fuck around.

Each safe house feels like a fortress, this place with low, arched ceilings with impenetrable walls of reinforced concrete and steel. The walls are lined with soundproof panels, and the rooms are surprisingly well furnished. The more I look at it, I realize... this isn't just a hideout but a cage. A cage we could be trapped in for a lot longer than we're prepared for.

Jesus, I hope we're not here long-term.

The rooms are windowless but brightly lit, furnished with beds nestled in steel frames and a series of locks on the door.

"Oh, there *is* a window," Zoya says excitedly when Rodion shakes his head with a snort.

"That's one of those panels that looks like a window, but it's only digital."

Her face falls, and she stifles a sigh.

"It doesn't matter," Semyon says, ever pragmatic. "We're safe."

There's a common area where all the rooms converge, and surveillance cameras are mounted on one wall. It's furnished with upholstered chairs with a large network of plugs and outlets. Though this place is designed primarily for safety, there's an undercurrent of luxury. I poke around a bit more. Leave it to Popov to have a well-stocked liquor cabinet, high-quality beds and bedding, and a wall of luxurious soaps and amenities in the bathroom. There's even a tiny but functional workout room with a weight bench and a cable system.

I check in to prepare to lock everyone down. Matvei and Gleb are in the largest room with Grandfather. Eduard and Irma in another. My sisters share a room, my brothers share another, and Anissa and I share the main room.

She hasn't spoken to me since we exited the car. I know she wants answers, but what she doesn't know is how dangerous it is for me to give them to her.

I need more information before I risk... fucking *everything*.

How could she be Polina Romanova? I saw the pictures of Anissa. I read her file. She saw me and fled when I went to chase her, obviously guilty. It makes no sense to me that the woman who fled our vows isn't the woman who I—fuck it all to hell. *The woman I've fallen in love with.*

She has to be Polina. She has memories that don't resonate with her identity as *Anissa*. She can't possibly remember having brothers, as Anissa had none.

And if she is Polina... the worst part of all is that I have no claim on her and never did. And doing what I've done... kidnapping her, taking her as mine, *fucking* her, will bring down the wrath of the entire family of Romanovs.

If the fucking cartel doesn't get here first.

I need answers.

"Rafail?"

"What?" I turn to her, barely paying attention, as my phone is buzzing with messages from Popov, and I don't want to miss anything important.

"Put your phone down, please." There's steel in her voice, and her hands are anchored on her hips. I frown at her.

"I know, I know," she says with a shake of her head. "You're not used to being told what to do."

I quirk a brow at her. Now? She chooses now to challenge my authority? With my family in the same vicinity?

"Don't test me, Anissa."

"Stop calling me that," she whispers. "You know as well as I do that isn't my name."

I turn away from her so she doesn't see the fury in my gaze. It isn't directed at her. It isn't her fault we're in this situation. I grit my teeth.

I turn to face her again. "We don't know what the hell is going on."

She shakes her head. "Oh, no, we won't play that game either."

I shut the door behind me with a bang as a call comes into my phone from Popov. "I have to take this."

She brushes past me to get to the door, but I grab her arm before she escapes. "You stay right here until I—"

"Or what?" she snaps, spinning around to glare at me, defiance blazing in her eyes. "You'll tie me up then demand answers for things and refuse to give any yourself? You think you can keep me chained up and make me bend to your will?"

I take her by both arms and barely avoid giving her the teeth-rattling shaking I want to. I fucking hate this situation. If she tries to fucking leave, the last thread of humanity I'm holding onto will fucking snap.

"Yes," I growl. "Go ahead. I dare you to defy me now." I shake my head.

With a sharp cry, she swings her hand back and slaps me across the face. The second her palm connects with my cheek, my vision blurs with rage. Fury surges through my veins, begging to be unleashed, but I can't hurt her. I fucking *won't*. It would be so easy, so damn easy, to hurt her.

My chest heaves with pent-up frustration as we glare at each other. I pace back and forth, needing the anger to leech out of me before I do something I regret. I'm not new to this. I don't give in to my anger. Instead, I clamp it down like I've learned to. Years of raising these damn hellions have given me plenty of experience.

I pull her into my arms, my grip firm and unyielding, wrapping around her like iron. "Don't you ever fucking raise your hand to me again." My voice is thick with anger.

"Let me *go*," she hisses, pushing against my arms, but she might as well try to move a mountain. It brings me no small amount of pleasure to keep her restrained as I put my mouth to her ear. "*No*."

I feel her shiver against me as my words hang in the air between us.

Every struggle, every push, only stokes the need growing in me.

My anger morphs into something darker. Dangerous. Primal. My dick throbs against her, my hand itches to spank her ass and tame the fire in her wild, defiant eyes.

"You like this, don't you?" I whisper in her ear, my voice low and dangerous.

Her breath catches, but she doesn't answer at first. Her lack of protest is all the confirmation I need. I press her harder against me, grinding against her ass as I lower my hand and squeeze it roughly. She barely stifles a moan.

I have to take the call from Popov. I have to make sure everyone here's safe and on the same page. I have to—I have to fuck my wife into submission and make her remember who she belongs to before everything goes to hell.

"Tell me the truth," I whisper as my hand roams down the length of her hot, sultry body, sliding under her clothes, desperately seeking her warm, pliant skin. Her body arches into mine, tension snapping between us like live wires. When she gasps, I spin her to me and cup her face roughly in my palm.

"I hate you," she whispers, but the shimmer in her eyes and waver in her voice betray her.

"You little liar. You hate me?" My fingers delve between her thighs. I chuckle low and dark when I easily glide through her slick folds. "You hate me, do you? *Prove it.*"

She whimpers even as she glares at me, her eyes dancing with challenge but riddled with need and hunger. Her lips part, her breathing heavy as she grabs the back of my head and yanks my mouth to hers. I plunder her mouth, claiming her with my tongue as her nails scrape my back. This is no surrender but a fucking *dare.*

I crush my mouth to hers, tasting her fear, her need, the desire she wishes she could hate. A flare of shock hits my chest when she bites back without warning. My hand trails down to her ass. I grab her leg, wrap it around me, and spank her ass hard.

She moans into my mouth, and I swallow every ounce of her need, her anger, her desire and frustration. My tongue licks hers. My teeth graze her lips and tug them into my mouth. My cock aches to fill her.

She's a challenge and a dream, and I need to own every inch of her. I fucking will. I don't care who she is, where she came from, what her name is, or what her history is. This woman is *mine.* Mine. I'll scream it from the rooftops and brand it on her body. I'll annihilate her enemies and erase all memories of her past until all she cares about is *us.*

She. Is. Mine.

And whatever or whoever wants to stop us will rue the fucking day they tried to pull us apart.

Fuck the cartel.

Fuck the Romanovs.

Fuck history and alliances and enemies and war.

Fuck it all to hell.

"You belong to me," I growl against her skin, my mouth tracing the line of her neck to her collarbone. I lift my palm and brand her ass again with another searing slap. "*Mine.*"

I rake my fingers through her hair and yank her head back. Her mouth parts, red and puffy, her eyes on fire with that passion and heat that makes me half-mad for her. "Do you understand me?"

Every part of her is a challenge I'm more than ready to meet. I tear off her clothes, my movements rough, unrestrained. We have no fucking time, and I won't wait another second. She's under me, her tattered clothing around us, as I unzip my pants and yank my cock out.

When she reaches for me, guiding me to her core, it's all the permission I need. She wants this, wants *us,* every bit as much as I do.

"You say I'm yours?" she whispers, her fingers digging into my back. "Fucking prove it." Her challenge echoes mine.

Her hands find my cock. Our fingers brush. I line myself up against the wet heat of her pussy, and plunge into her.

Her head falls back with a whimper, and her eyes flutter closed

. This is no lazy lovemaking on an early morning, tangled in sheets, with sweet words and caresses. This is no curious exploration, getting to know each other and wondering how to make sense of it all. No. This is nothing but pure, unadulterated claiming, fucking, as I surge into her and own the walls of her pussy.

I build a fast, heated rhythm as her legs wrap around mine, and her hands scramble for purchase around my neck.

"Tell me you belong to me," I order, lifting my hips so I can surge in her again and again until she's breathless and half-drunk on the first spasm of pleasure I can feel echoed in my own body. "Tell me, or I'll pull out right now and leave you tied to the bed." I kiss her damp cheek. Is she crying? "You know what that's like, don't you?"

"I'm yours, Rafail," she whispers. Blinking, another tear rolls down her cheek. "Yours." She shakes her head as if she hates admitting the truth. "And you're mine."

I roar in release as her head falls back. We rock each other's bodies—hers, naked and submissive beneath me. I'm still fully clothed and barely reining in the need to fuck her until it hurts. My hot cum spurts into her, the walls of her pussy tight around me. I ride my release with hers as if grasping for the last thread that can hold us together so we don't fall apart.

I want to hold her close, whisper in her ear that she's everything, that I'll love her until my last breath. But I can't, not yet, not until I have answers. I'll protect her, even if I can't give her the words she needs.

So, I go back to what I know.

I pull out of her and hastily wipe her clean with her

shredded clothes. Bend my head to hers and hold her gaze with mine.

"Stay right fucking there until I take this call. We are *not* done yet."

I stab at my phone and return the missed call from Popov.

CHAPTER 24

"ANISSA"

I STARE at the back of my... husband?

Is he? Or has this all been a lie?

My pussy still throbs in the aftermath of climax. I can still feel the ache on my scalp where he pulled my hair, the fullness of my lips where he bit me, the branding smack of his palm on my bare ass.

I still feel the remnants of our lovemaking slick between my thighs, a reminder that I'm no longer the girl I used to be. I'm someone else now—someone who craves him, who feels alive when held in his arms, even when everything around me feels like it's crumbling.

What is going on here?

I remember vestiges of my past that don't resonate with my present, but it's like looking at a puzzle that's only partially assembled—a few more pieces need to fall in place before I get the whole picture.

I'm scared I'm trapped in a relationship built on a house of cards. Deception. But even in the darkness, shrouded in fear and uncertainty, there's one thing I can't doubt: he loves me.

It's written in his kiss, in the way his control slips when we're together... like I'm the only one who has the key to his vulnerability. I'm the only one who can undo him. It's not something he says, but something I feel in the way he touches me, the way he looks at me.

I see it in the way his brow furrows when he's watching me as if I'm an enigma he needs to solve. He carries the weight of the world on his shoulders and, in his own way, has done his level best to carry mine. I feel it in the steady beat of his heart against mine, the grounding pressure of his palm on my back when I'm in trouble, a silent reminder that I'm not alone.

I feel it when he tucks my hair behind my ear and places a tender kiss on my forehead. The way he tucks the blanket around me in the middle of the night and wordlessly holds me when I wake, shaking and panting, from another dream.

He loves with the fierce protection of a warrior, and I'm his victory prize.

But is it... is it enough?

Can it be?

Can I love a man who thrives on control, who makes me feel like both a prisoner and a queen? Can I love a man whose every touch makes me feel owned, even if I don't truly belong to him?

Can I love a man who's lied to me?

Has he?

Rafail ends the call and shoves his phone in his pocket. I've been so wrapped up in my thoughts and fears that I didn't hear a word of the call. I'm not sure it would've made much of a difference if I had.

I still have no idea what's going on.

"And?" I ask, hoping for a shred of light on what's happening, even though I know he probably won't tell me anything.

He only shakes his head, his shoulders drooping. "We need to meet with my family. With everyone."

"Um, about that..." I gesture to the bed. He looks over his shoulder at me and realizes with a grimace he's destroyed my clothing.

"Fuck." He runs his fingers through his hair. "Popov had a fucking liquor cabinet, you think he has clothes here?"

I shrug, still wrapped in the sheets. "I have no idea." I go to push myself out of bed to explore the room but Rafail shakes his head, his voice firm. "Stay there. I'll look."

I don't protest. This is very much a *pick-your-battles* situation.

He rummages through the closet and dresser, muttering to himself and making a few low hums of approval.

"Good. Here we go," he says, tossing a generic pair of gray sweats and a white tee at me. They'll be too big, but they'll do. When I pull them on, the clothes hang awkwardly on my frame, the waistband sliding down my hips, and the shirt wears like a sack. They're not just too big, either, but scratchy and uncomfortable.

Rafail notices me tugging and fidgeting, his eyes narrowed on me as he watches me try to make it work. Stepping toward me, his gaze softens for a fraction of a second before he curses under his breath again.

"Those aren't going to work," he growls before he tugs his own black tee over his head. "Take those off."

Before I can argue, he's pulling his soft, worn, comfortable tee over my head. It falls past my hips but feels better. Familiar. I inhale deeply, enveloped in his rugged, masculine scent. He eyes me for a second, then tugs the other backup clothes on.

"There," he says with a nod of satisfaction. "That's better. Not that you're going out *there* like that until I find something more suitable for you, but it'll do for now."

I sit up in bed and cross my arms on my chest. "You think I'm going to sit in this bed while you and the rest of your family have a meeting, or eat dinner, or whatever the hell you're planning on doing?"

I glare at him, fully aware that my threatening look is about as effective as a miniature Chihuahua growling at a Great Dane. But still, I try.

Shaking his head, he levels me with a look, reminding me that he isn't just my husband. He's the head of the Kopolov family dynasty and very likely one of Moscow's most feared. I should hate how naturally he takes control. But even as the weight of his power bears down on me, a part of me *craves* it. Craves *him.* I should be running from him, not aching for him.

"Do you think *I'm* allowing my cousins, brothers, and uncle to see my wife's body, barely covered by my tee?"

Yeah, so I'm not going to win this one.

I sigh.

Cupping my jaw, his troubled eyes grow gentle. "I promise I'll find something more suitable," he says.

I know I'm not the only one deeply conflicted, but I can almost see it in his eyes—the moment he pulls away.

We haven't resolved *anything.*

I draw my knees to my chest and nod at him, not even entirely sure what I'm agreeing with. I have no choice but to retreat, as he has. When all else fails, self-preservation seems my only option.

When he leaves the room, I can see the shadows of others outside. I want to be with them. I want to check on Zoya and see if Yana's okay. I want to make sure Rodion hasn't done something reckless and crazy, and Semyon hasn't buckled under a torrent of whatever Rafail throws at him.

I want to make sure Irma isn't bullying the girls, and Eduard isn't taking advantage of the boys. I want to get to know the cousins and see what makes them tick. Matvei seems fine enough, but I don't trust Gleb. The fact that these two are Irma and Eduard's sons is not a point in their favor.

And I want... I want my husband. I don't like the distance between us... emotional or otherwise. But the space between us isn't just physical—there's a chasm that grows with every secret, and I don't know how to cross it.

It's hard to table my need for answers, but there's no use screaming at the universe to tell me anything when we have more pressing needs to tend to and no answers are coming just yet.

So I wait.

I scroll through my phone and look up Polina Romanova, but it's just what I suspect—if she has any social media, they're well hidden. None of the Kopolovs have social media accounts either. Rafail would have a conniption because privacy is their greatest ally when it comes to cyber protection.

But then, as I scroll through seemingly irrelevant links and pictures, something catches my attention. An old photo, grainy and poorly lit, surfaces on an obscure blog site. It's a group picture but obviously from a while ago, at a—charity gala?

I know that blonde hair, pale skin, and striking blue eyes. They're definitely... mine. That's me.

I close my eyes when I'm assaulted by memories.

My mother and me, planning our yearly gala, the one time of year my brothers played nice for everyone because it was in their best interest to gain alliances and the good graces of their community. Art auctions... We did an art auction every year. I can even remember when I bought the dress I wore in that photo because I wanted the one that showed my cleavage, and my father forbade it.

That was a few years before he died.

I blink back tears. Would I remember them if I saw them?

Are they looking for me?

Out there, somewhere, is there a family desperate to find me? Or is my home here with the Kopolovs for now? Will I ever know?

Will the truth be enough?

I stare back at the photo, my memories coming back now the way fire licks at wood. Slowly at first, but as it builds... *all-consuming.*

There's Viktor, my enormous brute of a brother, beside Aleks, the thinner, muscled one with piercing blue eyes people used to say mirrored my own. We were all adopted—I remember that now, a collection of family members pieced together over the years.

I see Lev, my younger brother, the fierce look in his eyes so familiar to me, and Ollie, loyal to the core but dangerous as hell. Mikhail, the eldest, in some ways not unlike my husband—protective and stern and utterly devoted to the safety of his family.

And my mother. My beautiful, elegant mother, with her mane of silver hair and dancing eyes.

But who's the other person standing beside us? He isn't *in* the pictures, but the blogger managed to capture him in the same shot. I blink, staring, because he's familiar.

My breath catches in my throat, but what makes a chill snake down my spine is when I recognize him... because today I ate lunch with someone with that exact sharp jawline and cold, calculating eyes.

Gleb.

Why is Rafail's cousin in my family photo?

My breath catches in my throat, and my heart pounds. How did I get here? Did Gleb orchestrate all of this? The walls feel like they're closing in as I try to make sense of it all. Was it all a lie from the beginning?

I try to swallow the lump in my throat, to no avail.

How did I get here, and what did he have to do with it?

CHAPTER 25

RAFAIL

Zoya and Yana sit on the comfortable couches as I leave the room. Popov didn't have much to offer except a promise to destroy us if we break anything, do anything stupid or dangerous, or leave. None of that's in the plan, so I let it go.

Zoya looks at me questioningly, but I don't give her more than she needs to know. "Anissa's resting," I say, my voice firm to brook no argument. What Anissa and I shared is ours. She's mine, and I'll protect her privacy—just like I'll protect her from everything else.

Yana frowns toward the bedroom, her gaze more calculating than Zoya's. She's so fierce, I almost take a step back. "What did you do to her? I swear to god, Rafail—"

"She's fine," I snap at her. "She's my wife. What the hell do you *think* I'd do?"

She blows out a breath and shakes her head as Irma and

Eduard come into the room, followed by Matvei. Rodion and Semyon are the last to join.

Rodion leans back, glancing around the room with a grin. "Gotta hand it to Popov, this place is *slick.* Low profile, secure as hell, but it's got that... what's the word? *Ambiance. Grit.*" He gestures toward the brick walls and industrial lighting. "Feels real. Someone could drop an atomic bomb, and we'd be safe."

"Yeah," I mutter. "Let's not test that theory."

Rodion shrugs, his gaze flicking to the sleek shelves stocked with high-end bottles of whiskey and vodka, but I don't miss the way his fingers twitch, looking for a distraction. "And the booze? His taste is impeccable. Look at this stuff. Top-shelf, man. A single sip could take off the edge."

I level him with a look, and he squirms. "Go ahead, drink up," I say, my voice low with warning. I cross my arms over my chest. "Lose control. That sounds like an excellent idea when everything's at stake." I lean forward. "Touch any of that shit, and you'll regret it."

Rodion sighs but lifts his hands in surrender. "Point taken, big brother. I'll admire it from afar."

I grunt and turn to Matvei, who's watching us both with a grin, his large frame hunched over on the couch beside Rodion. "Where's Gleb?"

"Using the bathroom." He shakes his head. "He takes a while. I swear to fuck, he falls in."

"Checking in on his—" Semyon's eyes shoot to Irma and Eduard before he looks back to me. "Investments."

I'd bet my ass said *investments* are illegal and dangerous, but I don't have time to deal with that.

I shake my head and sit on the edge of an ottoman.

"I want to check in with everyone. We need to make sure accommodations are alright."

"It's fine," Eduard says, while Irma looks like she's bitten into a lemon. "Are you going to tell us why we're here?"

I nod. "You all know that I trust the Popovs. And what he told me makes sense. We're all in danger."

I fill them in as best I can.

"Polina Romanova," Zoya says, shaking her head. "Are you sure?"

I nod. She looks at the bedroom. "And is she..."

"I don't know," I say. I feel like a prick when she flinches as if I struck her. I shake my head. "I need more answers, but I don't have them, not yet. For now, we believe we may be targeted—perhaps wrongly—by the Romanovs *and* the cartel."

"So, how long do we have to stay here?" Irma says with a frown.

"Until I know we're safe."

Eduard leans back in his chair and slides his arm over Irma's neck, but she flinches and pushes him away. He goes on as if she didn't just disrespect him in front of all of us.

"This place is outfitted for long-term stay, Rafail."

I nod. "It is, which is reassuring if we need it. We also have secure routers for Wi-Fi, so all of us can continue to work as usual. But I don't think we'll need to stay here beyond a few days."

"Days!" Irma is on her feet. "I can't stay here for days. I have social commitments and appointments."

"Sit down, Irma," Eduard says, fruitlessly of course.

She spins around and glares at him, her eyes masked with thick, false lashes, her bright-red lips pursed. "It's cramped in here, and the ventilation's terrible. I suspect the water's hard, which will absolutely *wreck* my hair, and I cannot sleep on a bed that hard."

"The bed's fine," I say through gritted teeth. "And you can keep your appointments as soon as we know it's safe."

She frowns at me but talks to her husband. "And why do I have to do what *he* says? He's a child."

I hold her gaze. I haven't been a child in over a decade, and she knows it. "You'll do what I say because I'm *pakhan* of this family, and if you challenge me, Irma, I'll remind you exactly what that means." My tone is sharp, unyielding, and I see fear flicker in her eyes.

Her jaw drops. "You wouldn't *dare*."

"Sit *down*, Irma," Eduard snaps at the same time Matvei shakes his head and frowns at her.

"He *is* in charge, and he's also right."

She opens her mouth and stares before she finally flounces down on the sofa like a spoiled child. "They'd better have decent food," she mutters, then thankfully clams up.

"Oh, they do," Zoya says eagerly. "I've inventoried the kitchen. It's excellent. I'll be able to keep us well-fed for as long as needed. There's a fully stocked pantry, and the freezer's full of meats and fish."

"Thank you," I tell her with a little smile. "You won't be the only one cooking."

I ignore the others' groans. No one ever died from burnt toast and overcooked eggs.

"Really, Rafail, the accommodations are fine," Yana says. "It's honestly way more comfortable than I expected. Very nice." Her face is pinched, and I know exactly why. There was no time to take her husband with us. I reach for her hand and give it a squeeze. "I promise we'll leave as soon as we can."

Semyon nods in approval. "Not bad at all. We should take notes."

I nod. "I am."

Rodion agrees. "You know I like it."

Matvei shrugs. "My only complaint is having to share a room with Gleb like we're kids again, but having to deal with him is a small price to pay for security."

I look back to their door. "Speaking of Gleb. Go check on him, Mat."

We make a brief plan for who's cooking what and when with the help of Zoya before she and Rodion head to the kitchen to get dinner started when Matvei finally comes back in. His face is pale, but his eyes are fire when he returns.

"He fell asleep."

I nod, trying to consider whether or not we should wake him up. I want him present. We all should be. There's plenty of time to sleep. But in the end, I decide to let it go.

Zoya and Rodion prep dinner, and when I return to the bedroom, Anissa's resting as well.

"It's almost dinnertime," I tell her.

Her back is to me, but I can hear her loud and clear. "I'm not hungry," she says in a pouty voice.

Sighing, I sit beside her. "You need to eat."

"I ate plenty earlier."

I stroke her back, but my mind's already ten steps ahead. The unknown looms in front of me, and I fucking hate it. This waiting, this powerlessness, is driving me mad.

I continue to rub her back. It seems to soothe me as much as it does her while I fill her in on the meeting.

"Rafail?"

"Yeah."

"What did Gleb say?"

She rolls over and looks at me, her brow furrowed.

"About what?"

"About what you've said tonight."

"Nothing. He wasn't there."

She sits up straighter in bed, her eyes wide as she clutches the sheets. What the hell?

"Where is he?"

"Relax, he was sleeping. What's going on?"

Wordlessly, she shows me a picture on her phone. "This was from a few years ago."

I look it over. Cold dread tightens my chest when I see her—my bride, Polina Romanova—smack dab in the center of the Romanov family.

"Do you see him?"

"Who?" She has lots of brothers.

Fuck.

"Look," she says, stabbing at the screen. I didn't even notice the smaller boy in the corner of the frame. I squint my eyes before realization hits.

"Is that—Jesus, that looks like Gleb. It's hard to tell; this is an older photo, and the quality's shit. But if it is him... why's he in this picture?"

"I don't know," she says, shaking her head. "I don't remember him at all. I know that we had galas and auctions; it was an annual event with my family. Can you ask Gleb if he remembers anything?"

I nod. "Yeah, and I'll ask my uncle too. Did you find any more clothes?"

She points to a small pile on the dresser.

"I did." Folding her arms over her chest, she gives me a curious look.

"And? Are you going to get changed so you can join us, or what?"

"I told you," she says stubbornly, her eyes hard. "I'm not coming."

I step toward her, my voice deep and commanding. My patience is at an all-time low. I thought I already made it very clear that this bullshit won't fly with me. I take a step closer, my voice dropping to a growl. "You're coming with me, Anissa. This isn't a negotiation." Her defiance burns in her eyes, that fire I crave and want to crush. She straightens, challenging me. God, I fucking love that about her even as I want to shake her.

"No, I'm not."

I let out a slow breath, moving closer. "This isn't a debate. You get dressed and get your ass out there for dinner before I carry you there myself."

I don't have time for this.

Her eyes flare, but I see her hesitate. She knows I don't bluff, and it matters to her to save face. "You can't just—"

"I can and will," I growl, my hand brushing her arm as I lean in. "If you think I'm going to let you sit here alone while god knows what happens, you're wrong. You're a part of this family now."

She's infuriating.

When she opens her mouth to argue, I cut her off. "If you don't get changed, I swear to god I'll put you over my knee and make sure you regret it. Or," I lower my voice, the edge softening but still unyielding, "you can get dressed, come with me, and we'll handle this together. Your choice."

Her defiance wavers, her eyes searching mine. Finally, she blows out a frustrated breath. "You really *are* the beast with all his bluster."

I shrug, unapologetic. "If the shoe fits."

"Fine," she mutters, turning toward the dresser, strategically placing distance between me and her.

I can't force her into compliance. I can't force her to like me. Hell, I don't need her to. But I'll make damn sure she stays safe, even if she hates me for it. I'll protect her with everything I have because as much as I want to control her, I'm terrified of losing her.

"You'll stay with me when I question my uncle and cousin."

CHAPTER 26

"ANISSA"

Dinner is a tense affair. After showing Rafail the picture, I braced myself for questions. For something. But all I got was confusion... no answers. The look he gave me when he saw me with my brothers though... like I'd betrayed him... like something vital had died between us. I hate that look. I hate that it feels like I'm falling apart.

Still, despite the tension between us, we do our best to pretend things are fine for the sake of appearances. We exchange polite words and smiles.

"This looks delicious," I tell Zoya.

"Believe it or not, Rodion made the rice," she says, looking as surprised as I am.

"Hey," he says. "I know how to cook."

We share a look behind his back. Grandfather pronounces it the best meal he's ever had in confinement, and while the rest of them laugh, I can't help but wonder when else he's been confined. Is he joking?

Still, it's strained between Rafail and me, and, I don't know, the tension is palpable.

"Is Gleb still sleeping?" Rafail hasn't broached any questions, but I suspect he's waiting until we eat first. This could get ugly. For once, I'm happy to follow his lead on something.

A part of me doesn't want to know the truth, and I hate that.

As the others chat, the tension between Rafail and me simmers, unspoken. I'm hyperaware of his presence, yet I feel like we're worlds apart.

Zoya seems to notice that something's off. The little furrow between her brow deepens, and she looks from me to Rafail, but she keeps quiet. Rodion, on the other hand, isn't so demure. His gaze goes from me to Rafail and back again.

"What's going on?" he asks bluntly. "Something's wrong with you two. Spill."

Oh, for crying out loud—

I bite down hard, trying to swallow the rush of panic, and grip my fork, trying to appear normal. I don't want to get into it. If he keeps pushing, I might have to admit what I don't want to—I'm totally in over my head.

"Drop it, Rodion," I warn, my words sharper than I intended.

Naturally, he doesn't take the hint. "Seriously, what's going on? You're both acting like someone died." He leans back and pushes harder. "You're like parents trying to pretend they didn't have a fight in front of their kids."

Argh.

I want to shake him. I open my mouth to retort when Rafail leans in close, his voice lowering. "She said *drop* it." Yikes. It's not good when he lowers his voice.

Rafail's voice cuts like a whip, his tone one you don't argue with. Silence falls immediately as everyone else stops breathing. I gulp a sip of water.

Rodion raises his hands in surrender, and I let out a breath.

"Easy, brother," Rodion says, shaking his head, but he clamps his mouth shut when he catches Rafail's gaze. "I'm sorry."

For once, I'm glad they do what Rafail tells them. I blow out a breath of relief as the others talk among themselves.

As we're finishing, Rafail and Semyon start clearing the table. "Where's Gleb? We need to talk."

Eduard looks sharply at him.

My stomach clenches. Either I'm going to get some answers or more evasion.

"I'll get him." Matvei pushes away from the table and marches over to the door, pounding on it. "Dude, get up. We need to talk."

There's no answer. Rafail opens and loads the dishwasher as Matvei knocks again. Eduard and Irma are busy over by the liquor cabinet.

I sit at the table, not wanting to push my luck. Rafail's like a ticking time bomb. I'm not far behind him.

Matvei knocks again, and once more, I'm thankful for Rafail's bossy ways because my own patience is wearing thin. He levels a look at Matvei. "Open the fucking door before I do."

Matvei turns the handle hard.

Rafail looks at me, his dark eyes focused on me as if I'm the only person in this room. I swallow hard.

I want to make up.

I want to tell him I love him.

I want to throw my arms around him and tell him that I love him, but more than anything... I want the truth.

And something tells me Gleb's the next step in that direction.

"Rafail!" Matvei yells from the room. We all go still as Rafail crosses the kitchen and heads to their bedroom as Matvei comes to the door. His face is red with rage, his hands clenched into fists. "He's gone. That fucking bastard's gone."

A glass crashes to the floor. I look to see Eduard hastily cleaning up the drink Irma dropped while Rafail curses and asks questions.

"He was here when we were talking. I went over to Rodion and Semyon's room before dinner, and I haven't gone back in, so he had to have left between then and now."

"Did you see him?" Rafail asks Grandfather.

"I haven't. I was in the kitchen helping prepare dinner. There are so many of us here, in and out of the rooms, I didn't take note."

"How could he have gotten out?" I ask, shaking my head. "That's not possible. We have guards outside this door." My stomach aches.

He shakes his head as he pulls out his phone. "The rest of you, check every room in this place thoroughly."

"Mine's been locked since I left it," Yana whispers. Matvei pushes past his parents and enters their room. He comes back a few seconds later and shakes his head.

"Our room is clear," Rodion says, his jaw tight and weapon drawn. "He's not here. That motherfucking son of a bitch... I'll fucking kill him."

Irma glares at him, but I've never been prouder.

Rafail shakes his head and makes a call. He puts it on speaker.

"We have a problem."

"What is it?" Popov's voice is as tight and angry as Rafail's as he fills him in.

"Permission to open the door and speak to your men?" Rafail asks. I can tell it takes a lot for him to ask someone for permission.

"Granted."

Rafail gestures for all of us to stand back. Everyone is quick to obey before he opens the door. On cue, the Popov guards raise their weapons in perfect sync, the clicks echoing like the clicking of a grenade. But Rafail doesn't flinch. He stands tall, still commanding the space around him as though daring them to make a move. He's the one in control here, and everyone knows it.

My heart slams against my ribs, every beat a reminder of how close we are to unraveling. Zoya stifles a gasp beside me, but I can't tear my eyes from Rafail. He's deadly still. I reach wordlessly for Zoya's hand and give it a gentle squeeze.

A phone rings, and one of the guards holds up a hand to the others.

"*Nam prikazano otstupit*," he snarls. *We've been ordered to stand down.*

Rafail stands fearlessly in their midst, the call to Popov still on speaker.

"One of our party is no longer here. Check your ranks." His words are a sharp command that can't be ignored. No hesitation, no weakness—Rafail's in control, and anyone who dares challenge him will regret it.

The guards stare at each other and quickly do what he says. Popov and Rafail talk to each other quietly until the first guard comes back to him.

"Sir," he says to Popov. "We're down a man."

Rafail goes deadly still. "So one of your men was in league with my cousin," he begins. "We need to find everything we can."

"Here! Look!" Yana stands in front of one of the surveillance cameras.

Rafail swivels to the armed men, eyes blazing. "Popov, call them off," he growls.

Popov gives the command, and the guards lower their weapons.

Yana stares, her eyes wide, until Rafail nods to her. "Go on."

"I saw him with his cell phone a few minutes before we were cooking. There's no footage of how he got out, but I was able to zoom in on his phone."

Rafail walks to her, his eyes glued to the screen.

He reads quickly, cursing under his breath. "He's betrayed us."

CHAPTER 27

"ANISSA"

"No," Irma says, shaking her head. "It can't be. He did not!" She points an irate finger at Rafail, aimed like a dagger. Her voice shakes. "*You* were the one who made us come here. *You* were the one who got us in this trouble to begin with, you and your stupid bride. Don't you dare blame my son!"

My blood boils. How dare she? I grit my teeth, my fists clenching. *No one* insults my husband, not while I'm standing.

We all know what it means for Gleb. He's a dead man walking.

"Keep her under control," Rodion snaps to Eduard. "Unless we know otherwise, we're assuming Gleb betrayed us and escaped."

"No!" Irma shouts, starting toward Rafail. I know the look

of a crazed woman about to lose her mind. "You're a fool!" she snarls.

I'm still hobbling on my cast, but that doesn't stop me from stepping between the two of them. "Stand *down,* he said."

Irma's eyes flash to me, irritation boiling. She surges forward, trying to shove me aside, but the moment her hand reaches out, my body moves without thought.

Instinct.

Training.

My body reacts before my mind does. I grab her wrist, pivot on my good foot, and twist her arm with just enough force to tip her off balance. I don't want to hurt her... unless I have to. No one, *no one,* touches my husband. The thought sends a surge of something primal through me. Love. Fear. Fury.

Stumbling, her eyes widen as I step forward, forcing her retreat.

"Don't," I warn, my voice low. "You heard my husband. We're wasting time. He betrayed us, and the longer we chat, the more danger we're in."

Zoya stares at me with something like awe in her features, and Yana flat-out grins.

Irma hesitates, thrown off. I may not remember everything, but my muscles know exactly how to disarm a threat, even before I do.

Yana speaks up. "The evidence is right in front of you. Look at the text. Not only did he leave with one of the guards, but he also set us up. He set *all* of us up."

"I won't believe it!" Irma says, but she doesn't come at Rafail again.

Rafail's icy gaze snaps to his uncle's. "Get her out of here." Eduard has the good sense to listen as Yana reads the texts out loud.

He's onto her being the Romanova woman

Soloto is in the city

We have to move

Ice pulses through my veins. Zoya stares at me. "The Romanova woman?" she asks, shaking her head. "Who?"

I look to Rafail. I don't know how to tell them this. I don't know what to say. I don't know who to believe.

For once, I'm thankful Rafail is so decisive. "We'll tell you more when we know more." He turns to Semyon. "You were the one who led me to the city."

Semyon runs a hand through his damp hair as he shakes his head. "I ran the files. I checked her location. I matched her pictures to the ones we were given and confirmed it was her."

Rafail clenches his jaw. "How? Gleb's texts reveal that he knew Anissa's identity."

Yana's sitting on a sofa, her phone in hand. "I think I know how."

"Brother, with all due respect—" Rodion interrupts.

Rafail yanks his gaze to his. Rodion swallows but continues.

"If Gleb and the Popov guard know our location and they're working with Soloto, we need to *move*. We aren't safe here."

Rafail curses under his breath and grits his teeth.

Semyon interjects. "It might be too late," he says, shaking his head. "If they're in the city, we don't have time to retreat. We'll have to arm ourselves."

"No." Rafail shakes his head. "We aren't safe here, but we aren't safe if we leave. We need to arm ourselves and come up with a plan."

Grandfather raises a hand, his worn, wrinkled face placid, but his eyes narrowed in concern. "Rafail?"

Rafail looks to him. Grandfather holds a tablet in his hand and flicks it on. "Popov left the specifications for all exits and points of retreat in the event of an attack. I studied them while I was in the kitchen before dinner." He shrugs. "Keeps an old man busy."

He turns the tablet around and points to a few marked places on a map of the network of rooms. "There are secondary exits. We have two choices, then. We could create a diversion if they attack and exit the main door, or we can use a secondary exit." He frowns. "That said, the rooms are impenetrable. Once someone enters them, and they double lock the door from the inside, nothing can get in —not smoke or gunfire, even a flood."

Rafail nods. I can almost see his mind whirring as he snaps into commander mode, humble enough to take advice from his family but confident enough to decide what to do. "The larger our party as we exit, the more vulnerable we become. Matvei, you'll stay with your parents." He shakes his head.

"It will calm them and make you less of a target if we encounter Gleb."

Matvei scowls but nods. No one has a choice but to obey. He continues.

"Grandfather, I want you here as well. I promise we'll come for you as soon as possible."

Grandfather nods and hands the tablet to Rafail. "I trust you," is all he says, but I swear Rafail stands taller.

"Zoya and Yana—" he begins.

"We're coming with you," Yana says, staring Rafail down. "We are *not* staying behind."

"No fucking way." Fury simmers in Rafail's eyes. "I will not allow my sisters—"

"You promised!" Zoya's little voice wavers, and when Rafail's fiery gaze comes to her, she blanches, but she keeps her eyes trained on him. "When Mom and Dad died, you said *one family, one fight—never apart.* I-I won't go. I'm with Yana. We go with you."

He clenches his fists and growls, but I place a hand on his shoulder and whisper in his ear, "I am trained, Rafail. I can protect them. We all can."

"They're trained too," he whispers back. "You think I only made them learn how to cook?"

Pride surges in my chest. "Then let's arm ourselves. We have no time to waste. I know you're afraid of what you can lose, but... we're stronger together. All of us. A chain-link fence is stronger the more links you add."

"Fine," he grits out. I don't miss the way little Zoya does a tiny fist pump. "Our family comes. All of us. The rest of you, in the rooms, *now*. Once you lock those doors, you do not open for *anyone*."

Everyone runs to obey.

He looks down at my leg. "Don't even think about it, Rafail."

His dark brows snap together, and he growls, "Think about what?"

"Leaving me behind. Just because I have this stupid cast doesn't mean—"

"Leave you behind? Hell no. I was trying to decide if I should put you on my back or carry you out of here."

Something melts a little in my chest, but there's no time to dwell.

"Oooh, yeah," Rodion says with utter glee. "Come to Papa, baby." We turn to find him standing in front of a panel concealed behind a hinged painting on the wall.

"How did you *find* that?" Yana asks, advancing toward him.

"Easy," Rodion says with a snort. "Look at this place. Does Popov look like the *Water Lilies* type? Hell no. It had to be hiding something. Locked as fuck, but those don't hold me back."

"Good to know," Rafail mutters. "I'll hand them out. Touch them, and I'll fucking break your hand."

"Alright, alright, no need to get violent," Rodion says, raising his hands in surrender.

"There's absolutely a need to get violent," Rafail snaps as he assesses the weapons we have. "Here." With the precision of a lieutenant and with absolute efficiency, he distributes weapons.

I look at the gun in my hand and grin to myself. It's no Desert Eagle, but it's gorgeous... a Wilson Combat X-TAC Elite 1911 Compact. I don't know where he got this, but I'm definitely keeping it.

"I'm gonna owe Popov my fucking life for—"

A faint hiss interrupts him. My head snaps up, my eyes catching the small, round canisters rolling on the floor, spewing thick smoke into the room.

In seconds, the air turns dense and choking.

"They're smoking us out," Rafail snarls. "All of you, do what I tell you. Move!"

He grabs my arm and reaches for the hidden compartment in the wall, pulling out masks and thrusting them at us. "Put them on and follow me. We have to evacuate. The rest of them are safe in their rooms."

I cough, trying to suck in clean air before I slide the mask on. Rafail's eyes are narrowed as he quickly scans the tablet Grandfather gave him, every muscle in his body as tense as a bowstring, ready to snap.

It's hard to breathe in this thing, but I have to stay calm.

"Stay low and stay close," Rafail says with a harsh cough.

I tug on his mask and gesture wildly for *him* to put his on. He nods and motions for everyone to follow him as he puts his on.

An explosion makes the walls around us tremble, followed by the unmistakable sound of gunfire.

We're running out of time.

I blink, my eyes burning from the smoke, when Rafail yanks open a hidden panel in the floor. *There it is.* A trapdoor.

Rodion leads the way. Semyon takes Yana's hand, I take Zoya's, and Rafail stands sentry at the back.

Even though Rafail can't talk, his gestures are unmistakable as he stabs a finger in the direction ahead. He shoves me in before sliding in behind us. We crawl quickly. The door leads to a tunnel barely wide enough for Rafail. Smoke follows us, but it's lighter and less dense the further we go.

We exit into a narrow passage behind the house, a set of steep, brick stairs ahead of us. Here, the air is clear and cold, a welcome relief.

We rip off our masks, gasping for fresh air. Rafail's voice is steady, unwavering, a lifeline in the chaos. "When we get to the top of those stairs, there's no telling what we'll find." He pauses, his dark eyes meeting each of ours. "But we'll face it together. *All* of us."

My heart beats madly. I turn to Rafail. "And if there's no way out—"

His eyes meet mine. "We'll make one."

We both hold each other's gaze.

We aren't just talking about an escape route.

If there's no way out... we'll make one.

The screech of tires warns us that we won't be alone for long.

Soloto's here.

He knows where the safe house is.

I remember now with vivid clarity why I came to Moscow. Why Mikhail sent me. I balked at him and protested, but my god, he was right—Soloto's merciless and he's come. Behind us, the smoke is getting thicker.

"We have to go," Rodion says, fearless and brave. "Move!" I swallow the fear rising in my throat. Now isn't the time for doubt or second-guessing. Now's the time for survival. I'm ready to fight.

He takes the steps two at a time. Rafail opens his mouth as if to protest, then closes it and shakes his head. It's time. Time for Rodion to earn his spurs.

"Go," Rafail says, his voice hoarse. "Follow him."

We quickly climb in single file, Semyon at the lead. One by one, we emerge onto a dark, vacant street. I have no idea where we are.

The sound of approaching tires comes closer and closer. We stand shoulder to shoulder, ready for whatever comes, when the night *explodes*.

Oh god. Black-clad figures move with deadly precision. "Get cover!" Rafail urges. "Behind the cars."

I move as quickly as I can.

We're surrounded though. There are easily twenty in their number, armed and ready. They shoot, gunshots pinging off the cars. We hold them off. I manage to get one straight behind the eyes, and Semyon's a veritable cherry picker, taking each of them one at a time.

They keep coming.

"Fucking bulletproof vests," Rodion snarls. "Keep going. Zoya?"

It's then that I notice Zoya's fisting hand grenades. She tosses one to Rodion, who pulls out a pin, rears back, and whips it as far as he can ahead of us. The explosion is deafening. Bodies fall to the ground in a torrent of smoke.

And still they come.

My heart sinks. We can't do it. We don't have the sheer manpower to help.

"Fuck this," Rafail says. "I'll create a diversion. *Run.*"

He stands, his gun shooting fire as he pulls the trigger in rapid succession.

But no. I won't leave him. *I can't.* Not now, not ever.

The sound of a heavy car approaching comes again. Oh god. Oh no. We can't survive another attack—we *won't.* If they bring more people in—

A huge, armored vehicle screeches to a halt, the doors swinging open. My heart clenches, instinct kicking in before I see them, hope battling with fear rising in my chest.

They're here.

CHAPTER 28

POLINA

My brothers.

Every single one of them, larger than life, furious, formidable, weapons drawn. Relief floods my veins as love and loyalty shake me to my core.

My brothers have come for me.

I know them.

My god, I know them. All of them. That's Mikhail, the eldest, with his golden skin and light brown hair, his eyes little pools of red-hot fury as he points his weapon.

Aleksandr, tall and muscular with an expression of utter fury on his face. Lev, my younger brother, his gun trained in front of him as he pulls the trigger relentlessly, spitting fire and devastation. Ollie, his vivid green eyes as placid as a field of grass, totally in his element as he slides a knife out of his boot with ruthless efficiency, kneels, and slices the neck of a man who's down.

Nikko, our fierce protector, his jaw set and weapon readied.

And Viktor. *Huge.* A human tank. Some of Soloto's men try to flee at the sight of him, but Ollie and Lev suffer no escapes. Lev shoots, and Ollie finishes them off. My brothers have caged them in.

With a scream of rage, Semyon charges, tearing through the enemy ranks, his face a mask of cold fury. Rodion, ever the wild card, follows behind, dual pistols blazing. His manic grin sends shivers down my spine as he mows down the enemies in his path, seemingly taking great delight in the chaos and bloodshed. He's wild and unpredictable but deadly accurate.

Rafail, ever calm and unperturbed, picks off stragglers with chilling efficiency. When I see a bloodied body rise and point his gun at him, I scream and pull the trigger. I hit him straight between the eyes.

"Good girl," Rafail mutters before he pulls the trigger again. Each shot is deliberate, clean, with no room for error.

My breath catches as I watch my brothers—*my brothers*, my protectors, alongside the Kopolovs, absolutely decimate Soloto's men.

"Gleb!" Rodion screams. "Don't let him fucking get away!"

Semyon barrel-rolls into the crowd without hesitation as Zoya, little Zoya, plants her feet and covers him, gun raised. She screams before each shot but hits with deadly precision.

"Gleb," Semyon snarls, launching to his feet and advancing with a deadly gleam in his eyes. "You're not running away again. Take one more step, and I'll shoot out your kneecaps."

Gleb, the utter fool, decides to call his bluff. I scream when Semyon pulls the trigger, and Gleb's left kneecap explodes. With a holler of pain, he falls. Yana, as athletic as a ballerina, soars through the air and reaches him first. She kneels beside him, a blade pressed to his neck and fists his hair.

"You son of a bitch. I hated you since the first time you tried to blackmail me when I was a kid."

The look of shock on Rafail's face tells me that's news to him. If Gleb wasn't dead before, he's a dead man walking now.

Semyon steps forward, his voice low and dangerous. "Where's Soloto?"

The human shield of my brothers surrounds them, menacing and unyielding.

They're on a mission to decimate Soloto, and then—and then what?

Nikko has a gun trained on Rafail.

I open my mouth to protest but realize we need this information from Gleb. I choke on a sob.

"I-I don't know," Gleb stammers. "Please!"

Viktor towers over everyone, casting a shadow over the prone form of Gleb in Yana's grip.

"You're with him," Viktor growls at Semyon, gun raised.

"No!" I scream. "Don't shoot them! Please, no!"

Viktor swivels to me, his eyes wide. "Polina?"

Something in me breaks when I hear my brother call my name. I heave a sob, desperate and terrified. "It's me," I sniffle. "Please, Viktor. Don't hurt them."

Rafail steps forward, deliberately putting himself in the line of fire. He's calm, determined, and fearless. "That's my wife. Put your gun *down*."

As huge as he is, he's nowhere near as big as Viktor, and still fearlessly faces him unarmed.

"Rafail!" I scream. "That's my brother! Viktor, don't shoot!"

Surprise flares in Rafail's eyes. Mikhail curses softly behind me.

"His *wife*?"

Viktor jerks his head at Semyon. "Interrogate him," he growls. "Or I will."

Gleb cowers and whimpers. "I don't know where he is," he sobs. "He's gone, but I can find out where he is, I can!"

Rafail steps forward, his hands up in a gesture of surrender to my brothers. Viktor gives him a subtle nod, his eyes narrowed. "Go." My heart pounds. It's a temporary boon.

Rafail's gaze sharpens, his presence darkening as he turns the full weight of his authority on Gleb. The shift in the air is palpable—predatory. Lethal. Gleb shrinks back, shaking under the force of Rafail's ruthless stare, and it's in that moment I fully understand. The man I thought I knew... the one I've *fallen in love with,* has been holding himself back all along. The softness I've seen, the restraint, was only evidence of his self-control.

Because now, before me? This is the real Rafail. A man whose eyes sear with promises of violence. My heart stutters as the reality hits me: this man will stop at nothing. There are no limits, no lines he won't cross for the people he loves.

His voice is low and calm as raw power radiates from him. "We'll find Soloto," he says with deadly intent. "Popov's man led us straight to him. Now, the truth from you."

I shiver when he says with deadly calm, "You broke trust. You manipulated our family." He spits on the ground. "You *betrayed* us all."

Each syllable is a threat and a promise that he has no intention of stopping until he knows everything. If I ever had a sliver of doubt before, I don't now—I'm hopelessly in love with a man who will stop at nothing to protect what's his.

"The-the truth?" Gleb stutters, staring at Rafail in wide-eyed terror.

"The truth!" Rafail bellows. We all watch in stoic silence. "Tell us. Tell us in front of her brothers. Tell us how Anissa came to be here, how you manipulated all of us."

Yana's grip on his hair tightens.

I stare, my heart pounding, torn between the violence before me and the fear of whatever he'll say, wrapped in undeniable relief that finally, *finally*, I'll be able to clear some of the fog.

Zoya squeezes my hand. Rafail walks in front of me, facing my brothers head-on.

As my brothers close in, Rafail's voice cuts through the silence. "I want answers. He's *mine.*"

Shit. Gleb is going to rue the day he was born. I shiver.

"I worked with Soloto," Gleb confesses, his face a mask of terror. Between the Kopolovs and my brothers, he's facing a firing squad from the depths of hell.

"When I saw the picture of Anissa, it triggered a memory."

Yana shakes him. "You accessed the files before Rafail planned to marry."

"Yes," he admits. "She looked so familiar it was uncanny. So I investigated and knew that she looked almost identical to Polina Romanova."

Mikhail and Rafail share a look. "We are all adopted," Mikhail says, his jaw tight. "We'll need to bring my mother into this conversation."

Nikko lowers the gun trained on Rafail. I release a breath with a gasp. Zoya gently squeezes my hand, and the lump in my throat dissolves. Hot, fat tears silently roll down my cheeks.

Rafail nods before returning his attention to Gleb. "Go on."

My mind, however, is reeling.

She looked almost identical to Polina Romanova.

We were all adopted.

Does that mean…? Anissa… somewhere out there, I have *a sister?*

"When I heard Polina was coming to Moscow, I knew."

"You," Rafail snarls. "You were responsible for Anissa leaving, weren't you?"

Gleb stares at him, the whites of his eyes bright in the dark night. His silence condemns him.

"It was your chance to bring the fire of hell from the cartel to both the Romanovs *and* the Kopolovs," Semyon concludes, shaking his head. "You motherfucking son of a *bitch.*"

"Semyon," Rafail says so low you can hardly hear him. A warning to keep his shit together. Semyon clamps his lips together, simmering.

Gleb doesn't answer.

Rafail's gaze hardens, his jaw taut as he turns to Mikhail. "We have family obligations, but make no mistake—this is not over." His gaze shifts from Mikhail to Gleb, his eyes flashing in a way I know all too well. "Gleb will face swift punishment. And believe me, it will be as merciless as he deserves."

Rafail's gaze darkens as he turns to me, his expression cold and intense. Unreadable.

What does this mean for us?

We were never married.

He lied to me.

He took me as his own and had no right to.

Shifting his gaze to Mikhail, his voice is low and controlled. "You and I will discuss Polina." His eyes lock onto mine again, but this time, they're burning with pain and frustration but also a barely restrained fire. "I know I don't have a claim on her," he says, his voice tightening. "But that doesn't mean I'm willing to let her go without a fight."

CHAPTER 29

RAFAIL

I'll never, as long as I live, forget the look of betrayal on my wife's face.

No.

Not my wife.

The truth hits me as hard as it did the day I found out my parents died. She was never mine.

I've fallen in love with a woman I have no claim to.

The Romanov brothers might kill me still, and I half wonder if I wouldn't welcome death, but I said what I meant: I will fight. I will fight for her.

I get a call from Popov. I look to Mikhail, and he gives me permission with a stern nod. I defer to no one, but in this moment, it feels right to allow him permission to call his shots. Hell, if one of them had kidnapped one of my sisters, I know exactly what I'd do.

"Yes."

"We have Soloto's associates in our sights."

I fill him in as quickly as I can before one of Anissa—no, Polina's brothers interjects. "Popov. Nikko Romanov here. We met six months ago. Your uncle knows my wife."

I have no idea what the connection is, but the fact that Popov and the Romanovs aren't rivals will prove to be useful.

Polina stares at me as words are exchanged, plans are made, and Popov promises to give us updates as they close in on Soloto's men. Popov's men pour into the street and surround us. They're young, strapping men he's recruited from the Armed Forces, a tactic he's well known for. In a few short words, I introduce them to the Romanovs. We don't need any more bloodshed.

"We must ensure the rest of my family is safe," I tell Mikhail and Popov. I quickly explain the situation.

"Go," he says with a nod. "Polina comes with us."

Polina's jaw drops open, and she stares, half-torn between allegiance to her family and mine, when little Zoya speaks up, her timid voice clear as day. "Only if I go with her."

"Zoya—"

She holds up a hand to me. "No, Rafail. I'm going with her." Bright blue eyes meet mine. "I have to."

One of the Popov men stares in open admiration. Zoya notices and flushes as bright as an apple. I narrow my eyes at him, and he looks away.

Jesus. She isn't a kid anymore. When did that happen? I want to lift her in my arms and squeeze her tight, my brave little sister. I want to shake her and give her a stern talking-to for putting herself in danger.

"Agreed," Polina says, holding her chin up high.

Christ.

"And me," Yana says, pushing herself to stand. She shakes her head. "Not sure any of you have noticed, but there's a severe shortage of women in these families." With a sound of disgust, she rolls her eyes. "And we need to stick together."

Popov has the nerve to chuckle on the phone. "Go. Get your family out of there."

"We'll talk about reparations and what I owe you."

Popov clears his throat. "Oh, we will."

Polina's brother Nikko smirks as a car pulls up to the curb.

"This is ours, sir," one of Popov's men explains. "This way, please."

"Semyon, Rodion, you come with me to evacuate the others." I turn to Mikhail Romanov. "Is your mother here in Moscow?"

"Yes. I'll have her brought to your home."

"You know where it is?"

Mikhail's lips hint at smiling. "Kopolov, within the past twenty-four hours, you've become my most intimate acquaintance."

Jesus. Of course. I'd expect nothing less.

The evacuation is seamless. Irma bitches and moans and, thankfully, doesn't know about her son's betrayal and the brutal punishment that awaits him. I take Matvei aside. I feel for the man. "I'm sorry," I tell him. "But you know what has to happen."

Matvei's eyes blaze into mine. "My allegiance is with you. His betrayal cuts deeper than death. All I ask is that it not be me who carries out the execution."

I nod. "Keep your mother under control, and I'll grant you that."

I fill Grandfather in briefly. When I'm done, he puts a heavy hand on my shoulder. "You've done well, son. Keep forging forward. You know what has to happen." His voice doesn't waver. "You know what you want. Call Vadka and bring him in."

Grandfather knows that while I've held the weight of responsibility on my shoulders, my best friend has been my rock. I swallow and nod. I'm ready for all of this to be over.

I text Vadka.

> Need you back at the house. I'll fill you in before you get there.

His response comes swiftly

> See you soon, brother.

When my family's been evacuated, everyone on the way

back to the house, I get into the car Popov provides, Semyon and Rodion with me.

Rodion fumes and rages the entire way. I let him. It's almost cathartic.

"Of all the fucking ways to betray us. Jesus, Rafail, I hope to god you let me take a turn."

I lean back in my seat and blow out a breath. "Yeah. We all will."

"How long has he been working with Soloto? Do we have any idea?"

I shake my head. "I don't know."

I should be more concerned with the betrayal. I should be planning Gleb's execution and how I'll make an example of him to every other man of the Kopolov Bratva who's pledged allegiance to my family. But all I can think about is... Polina. She isn't technically mine, and I know that. But I've fallen deeply, madly in love with the woman, and I meant what I said. I'll fight the Romanovs if I have to. I'll fight them to the death.

It isn't just about control anymore. My need for her transcends that.

"I lied to her," I tell Semyon, shaking my head. "I had her believe we'd been married."

"And it was the only lie you told her." He stares at me, his eyes hard. "You did what you thought was right. You believed her to be someone else, someone who betrayed your family and threatened our safety. You did believe she belonged to you, by all intents and purposes, Rafail."

I nod and blow out a breath. I did, I know, but will she see it that way?

"I'd have done the same," Rodion says. "You know I would. Take her as mine. Teach her who's the man of the house. Tied her to my bed and—"

"*Enough.*"

Rodion's eyes dance as he shuts up. He still means every word.

Good. I raised him right.

"What's your plan?" Semyon asks as we pull up to the house.

I blow out a breath and straighten my shoulders. "Tell the truth. Be as transparent as I possibly can. Fight to work with the Romanovs so we can forge a partnership that benefits us both." I lower my voice. "But I meant what I said about not letting her go without a fight."

Semyon straightens. "Damn right."

Rodion pats his holster. "We fight with you."

A car pulls up as we do, and in short time, a regal but older woman with silver hair pinned in a bun, dressed in slim-fitting jeans and a pale-pink sweater, exits the car.

It's the woman I saw the first time I laid eyes on Polina.

I extend my hand to her. "Rafail Kopolov. Welcome to my home, Mrs. Romanova."

She takes my hand and shakes it firmly. "Ekaterina Romanova." She sighs, and her eyes grow sad. "I believe I owe you all an explanation."

CHAPTER 30

POLINA

Little Zoya does her best to bring ease to the tension in the room. "May I bring some tea and refreshments?" she asks Rafail, who begrudgingly allows her with a nod. She's at home in the kitchen and wants to play the part of hostess.

He has his work cut out for him, and I know this. We also have unresolved conflict we need to deal with. Still, I don't know what to do first. I look around the room, half-bewildered, as Rafail issues commands and makes calls as my brothers' cars pull up to the curb.

"It'll be alright." I look to see Grandfather sitting in one of the upholstered chairs, his gnarled hand gripping the top of his cane. "Stay strong."

I nod and lift my head. I will.

When my brothers enter the room, however, I move without thinking. I run to them. For once, I feel like a little girl again

—safe, loved, and protected. These are my brothers, my flesh and blood.

How will I ever choose between the family who raised me and the one I've come to love here?

Mikhail's arms are wide as I launch into his bear-like hug. My oldest brother, my protector. We have always been close, even when we fought like cats and dogs as kids. Now, in his arms, I feel like a part of me that was missing has returned.

"God, we were so scared," he says in my ear. "I felt so guilty for allowing you to come here and then knowing you were gone. Polina, I can't tell you how good it is to see you're alright." He holds me in front of him. "You'll tell us the truth about how he treated you?"

I nod. "I am. Oh god, I've missed you all so much."

I'm crying freely by the time Lev hugs me. Ollie comes in to join us, and in seconds, I'm a blubbering mess, and we all try to talk at once. Viktor can practically put his arms around all of us, but it's a crying, messy, sniffy reunion. We're all talking at once.

"I couldn't remember you," I sniff, swiping at my eyes. "I didn't know who I was, and they told me I'd remember you, but—"

"—couldn't find you. Looked everywhere. Scoured Russia until—"

"—beside ourselves."

"Are you *sure* you're alright?" It's Mikhail, who's pried the others off me and now holds me at arm's length, his eyes boring into mine. Speaking in a low tone, he leans in close. "We don't have much time, Polina. Did he hurt you?"

Did he hurt me?

How do I answer that question?

Did he tie me to his bed and lie to me, telling me I was his wife and I'd taken vows?

Yes.

Did he dominate me, force obedience from me, and make good on punishing me when I pushed back?

He did.

I swallow hard.

Did he show me he loved me? Did he prove himself to be authentic and real and so absolutely devoted he'd burn the world for me?

He did.

So I give Mikhail a watery smile. "Hurt me? It was nothing I couldn't handle." And when Mikhail's eyes narrow on me, I state the argument he can't defeat. "He did nothing you wouldn't have done, Mikhail. Nothing *any* of you wouldn't have done."

Mikhail, my fierce and protective warrior of a brother, who tethered his own wife to him as a form of punishment for hacking into the Bratva of The Cove. Aleksandr, madly in love and father to the children of his own wife, promised to him in a loveless union of an arranged marriage. I could go on because each one of them could tell a similar story of an unlikely union, family loyalty, and love despite the odds.

My mother enters the room. She stares at me for a few seconds as if she can't believe her eyes before she rushes to me. The familiar warmth of her embrace makes something deep inside me unravel.

Mom.

I fit here. I belong here. It's as familiar to me as my own two hands being held by her.

Mom.

"I'm sorry," she whispers in my ear. "I'm partly to blame for all this, and I hope you find it in your heart to forgive me."

I wipe at my eyes. "I think there's a lot of forgiveness that will have to be granted."

But how is she possibly to blame?

The tension in the room is palpable, but we're closer to the truth than we've ever been.

"Sit down, everyone, please," Zoya says softly in her child-like voice as she enters the room carrying a large tray of tea and cups. "I find it's easier to have a pleasant conversation when we're sitting."

I love her so. Rafail takes the tray from her despite her protests and slides it onto the coffee table. "Semyon. Get the vodka for those of us who need something stronger than tea."

"You're wise, Zoya," Grandfather says, his eyes twinkling at her. "You have more than your parents to thank for that."

She's so cute when she blushes.

Yana sits up straight, her eyes never leaving Rafail. "Where's Gleb?"

"In holding."

Yana nods and turns her focus straight to Ekaterina. "As I said to the others, there's a shortage of women in these two families, so we must stand together. Allow me to make some introductions."

I barely hear her. My gaze is trained on Rafail, who paces behind the sofa despite Zoya's request. His friend Vadka has joined us.

"Before we begin," my mother starts. She places her teacup down on a saucer, her hands trembling. "I'm afraid that some of this... is my fault." Her eyes shimmering with tears, she turns to me. "I... I wanted a daughter, Polina. So badly."

I stare at her, bewildered. I knew I was adopted, but I never knew the terms of the adoption.

"I begged your father for a daughter, and after years of waiting, he finally granted my wish. He was reluctant, you know —daughters hold a different meaning in our world. Sons bring strength, alliances, power. That's why we have six of them. All adopted, yet all bound by loyalty. Then, one day, he brought me you." She smiles, but her eyes reflect a sadness from long ago.

My throat feels tight, and my nose tingles, but I listen as calmly as I can.

"I didn't know until ten years later that you had a sister. That you were separated in infancy. Another family adopted Anissa and took her as their own. It was a closed adoption, and they made it clear they wanted no one to ever contact them again." She shakes her head. "But I knew your father was powerful and above all that. I knew he could've found out what he needed to."

I stare, trying to process what she's telling me. I haven't had time to truly dwell on this since Gleb mentioned someone who looked just like me, and now my own mother is admitting as much.

I have a sister.

A sister who was supposed to marry the man who I'm in love with.

A sister who looks just like me and is presumably alive if she ran from him not that long ago. Who is she? Does she remember me? I don't remember her, but my heart aches thinking there's someone out there I'm related to who I've never met.

Jesus, I'm gonna need some therapy after all of this shit.

Zoya meets my eyes and swallows hard before giving me a tentative smile. This sweet girl has lost both her parents, was raised into near adulthood by her brother, and knows her family lives on a razor's edge. And still, she hasn't forgotten how to smile.

She's inspiring.

We all listen in rapt silence. Even Mikhail looks shocked. He didn't know.

She clears her throat. "So I never told you, Polina. I feared you'd want to find her, and I feared the wrath of her family if you did." Sighing, she continues. "I let fear guide my decisions, and for that, I'm so sorry and ask your forgiveness."

My god. What other secrets is she hiding?

With a sigh, she continues. "And our family was weakened. With the divide that tore us apart after your father's death, Mikhail was on a mission to strengthen us. We made strategic choices. I never imagined that bringing you to Moscow would have put you in danger. I was trying to do the very opposite."

Rafail watches in stony silence, his gaze fixed on my mother. I feel the rift between us as painfully as I felt the ache in my bones after the accident. I close my eyes and remind myself I overcame that then. I can overcome this now.

Zoya hands me a cup of bracing hot tea. I nod in thanks, not trusting my voice, and take a sip.

It helps.

"And when I brought you here, I thought I could keep you safe. I have friends in Moscow," she explains to Rafail. "And I feared the attack of Soloto."

Nodding, he listens in stoic silence.

"And then... when I heard you were gone," she says in a voice that wavers, on the brink of breaking down. "Witnesses said you were hit by a car. I feared the worst. We thought—" She clasps a hand to her mouth.

"We thought one of our enemies killed you," Mikhail says with a deep sigh. I close my eyes, feeling the weight of their fear and worry. "But we had no evidence. No body. No witnesses who saw them bury you."

I can't imagine the pain they all went through, not knowing, fearing...

"But we kept hope," my mother continues. "We hoped you'd only been... taken." Her eyes flutter closed as I realize she's spent the last month battling her greatest fears: I'd either been killed, or I'd been stolen and used.

Rafail shakes his head. "I had no idea." His voice cracks. "I'm sorry."

Zoya nods, her eyes wide and fearful. "I can promise you, he's telling you the truth. He *didn't* know; he truly thought Polina was Anissa."

"The woman who betrayed us," Rodion clarifies with cold decision. "She jilted him at the altar after she was promised to him. When we found An—*Polina,* we truly thought she was someone else."

"Gleb wanted us to think that," Semyon says, shaking his head. "And when we found out she had amnesia, we thought..."

"No," Rafail cuts in. "When *I* found out she had amnesia. I won't let anyone else take responsibility for my decisions." He turns to me. "When I saw you that day, and you ran from me, I thought you were running from a man you knew. I had no idea I was a stranger to you." He curses under his breath, shaking his head.

My voice feels small but carries with confidence across the room. "When I woke up, and I was restrained, you thought I would try to get away... again." I face Mikhail. "I know this much is true because he told me bits of Anissa's story. That my father had given me to him in payment for a debt. That I ran from him. Anissa *did* run from him. And so did I."

I look at Rafail. As the veil of deceit falls the more we discuss what happened, the more vulnerable the two of us become.

"Forgive me, Polina," Rafail says, his voice hoarse. "Outside the safe house, I said I wouldn't let you go without a fight." His gaze locks onto mine. "But I won't hurt your family. I can't do that. This is me, fighting." He stands, all corded muscle and alpha-male power, bridled but pulsing with life and promise. He turns to Mikhail. "I love your sister. I love her with all of my heart. Though I lied to her and take responsibility for my part in this... when I called her my wife... I meant it. I treated her the way I'd treat my wife. I took her into this family with the promise to love and protect her, and I promised I would do that to my dying day. I won't stop fighting for her." He holds my gaze. "I love you, Polina."

My heart beats so fast I feel nearly faint.

He loves me.

And somehow, I already knew it, but hearing him confirm what I already knew is the reassurance I needed. I wipe at my eyes again.

He loves me.

Mikhail stares at him, unblinking. Rafail continues. "I would give her anything she wanted. Even her freedom, if that's what she asked for. And all I ask from you, Polina," he says as he faces me again. "Is your forgiveness."

Yana sniffs and wipes at her eyes. She won't look at me. Zoya sits beside her, consoling her. My heart feels wrenched as I see the people I love most in the world distraught and bereft.

I wish I could wave a magic wand and make everything right, but we have to wrestle through it. We can slay the dragons in our midst, but we still have to tend to the wounded... like me.

Mikhail clears his throat. "Thank you both for telling the truth. It took courage." He sighs. "It seems we've all been deceived in one way or another, and it's refreshing to see the truth come to light."

I take another sip of tea to prevent myself from losing my shit.

Forgiveness.

Can I forgive him? *How*?

I may have thought it impossible one time, that I'd never be able to look at him without seeing lies. But now I realize love is so much more complicated and imperfect.

He loves me, there's no question, but he... he loved me thinking I was someone else. He loved me, believing we were destined to be married. He loved me because he was loyal to his family and determined to make me pay.

"May I speak?" I don't even know who I'm asking, but Rafail and Mikhail both nod.

I think, mulling over my words before I say them, deliberating over what needs to be said. My thoughts swirl like a tempest, and it's hard to get them under control. I finally decide just to dive in and speak my heart.

"The time I've spent here has been challenging for me, and not because I wasn't welcomed by the Kopolov family. I want to make that clear, that the code here is as similar to our family's as could be."

Mikhail nods. Everyone waits for me.

But I'm also aware of little Zoya and Yana, looking to me as the big sister they never had. Of Rodion and Semyon, two men who've become like brothers to me in such a short time. My mother, who thought she lost me and sacrificed so much —who begged for a daughter and has always treated me like a gift she'd been granted. My brothers, who thought I was gone, who've scoured the city looking for me and were ready to do anything and everything to keep me safe.

But most of all... Rafail. The man I thought was my husband.

The man I've come to love.

I'm keenly aware of Rafail watching me, the heat of his gaze burning into me.

"What will happen, Rafail? Mikhail? If the two of our families did marry? Would it be wrong to assume it would be a mutually beneficial situation?"

Mikhail shakes his head. "Not at all."

Rafail nods wordlessly in agreement. It's then that I note tears shining in his eyes, something I never thought I'd see.

I look around the room, seeing so many of the people I love the most gathered in one space. While some of my memories are still foggy, they are coming back rapidly now. My brothers are married. I love their wives, all of them. I have nieces and nephews and friends I've forgotten, but I know now who they are.

I look at *these* people. My innermost circle. My brothers, who would do anything for me. My mother, who hid the truth to protect me, and Rafail, who lied to me yet loved me through everything. It's a lot to digest. But if there's anything I've learned, it's that love is messy, complicated, and beautiful. That it takes courage to love someone and courage still to let them love you back. That love comes in unexpected ways and sometimes when you least expect it.

"I won't lie to myself or you," I say to Rafail. "Any of you. You hurt me. You took my freedom away. You lied to me and made me believe something that wasn't true." My voice cracks. "But I also know it to be true that you love me. And that I... I love you."

Pain flickers in his eyes. He's afraid of losing me; I know this. Losing the people he loves is one of his greatest fears. "Polina, I won't make excuses for what I did. But I'll spend the rest of my life making it up to you." His gaze remains fixed on me. "Tell me what you want, no matter the cost... even if it's your freedom." His voice breaks. "Even if it means never seeing you again."

Mikhail watches us, his gaze harsh. "Asking her to forgive and forget, after everything she went through, is a big ask." I look at my brothers, stern and angry, and I'm not the only one who's noted the tension in the room. Semyon and Rodion stand at the ready, and Vadka is on standby.

"We're not fighting here," Zoya says in her quiet way. "If you guys have to fight it out, please go outside."

I shake my head. "That won't be necessary." I pin both Mikhail and Rafail with my gaze. "Will it, boys?"

Rafail shakes his head. Mikhail reluctantly does the same.

Uniting my family and his would be the right thing to do.

Forgiveness would bring peace.

So would marriage.

I draw in a deep breath, steadying myself. "I choose to forgive you, Rafail. It's the right thing to do." I continue, my voice tremulous. "Because I know you. And I love you too," I say softly. "I've seen who you are beneath all those layers. Below your armor." I reach for my cup and take another sip of tea, silently praying for courage and clarity.

I've seen the man behind the mask. I know how vulnerable and afraid he is behind that veil of coldness.

"While I would never call you... *soft*," I continue. Rodion snorts but stops with a predictable scowl from Rafail. "There are rare moments when I see you love, and you love deeply. Everything you've done was for good reason. I've seen you willing to sacrifice, to change, and even here today, be meek enough to admit wrongdoing and ask for forgiveness. And for that, and so much more, I love you."

I turn to Mikhail. "So I ask that you all give me the one thing I've never had and have begged from *both* you *and* Rafail."

"Yes?" Rafail says hoarsely.

I blow out a breath. "A choice."

A clock ticks on a distant wall. In the distance, a dog howls, and the wind beats at the windows as they wait for me.

"Of course," Mikhail says. "It's the least we can do after all you've been through."

Rafail nods. "Agreed."

"Good," I say, my heart beating rapidly with nerves and excitement. I'm shaking. "I want to stay. I... I belong here now. But I want to live here knowing that my family is welcome and that I'm welcome at home."

"After everything you've been through," Mikhail says, his face hard. "You're choosing him? Are you sure?" Though his voice is low and controlled, I can still see the storm brewing in his eyes.

"Yes, Mikhail," I say, my voice firm. "Because I love him. And because it's *my* choice."

He gives one last lingering look to Rafail before he finally nods. "I saw the way you defended her when we were attacked. I watched how you protected her." He nods. "It is your choice, but it's my job to make sure you're well cared for. And you believe he has the ability to do so?"

I nod, my throat tight.

He does.

"I want our families united. Together, we prove a more powerful entity that even Soloto and all his men couldn't destroy. I know this is putting a target on our backs though. I know we'll have to be ready for a fallout."

Rafail nods. "Agreed."

I smile at him. My heart feels lighter than it has since well before I came here.

I breathe out, the weight of my decision finally lifting from my chest. My family and Rafail's watch me with a mixture of relief and cautious hope. Finally, the tension begins to dissipate into something... lighter.

New.

Zoya claps her hands, her eyes sparking with excitement. "Then it's settled! We'll have a wedding!" Her infectious joy spreads, and for the first time in what feels like a long time... I smile.

"Since we're all in agreement, then," I say, turning to my mother. "I believe it's time to plan a *wedding*."

CHAPTER 31

POLINA

Rafail finally brings out the vodka. The tea was excellent, but it's time for something much stronger.

We drink shots and try to ease the tension in the room, but it's been a long, long day. Hell, it's been a long, long month. My eyes are heavy and my body exhausted.

Still, I sit with my mother and brothers, a part of my soul basking in the balm of our reunion until Rafail finally stands. "You need rest," he says, his eyes meeting mine across the room.

I swallow hard, and I'm suddenly very, very awake.

"We all do," Mikhail says, pushing to his feet. "The irony is we aren't very far from here."

He shakes hands with Rafail, and something passes between them in the rough palm-to-palm contact, their eyes locked on one another.

"Come for lunch." Rafail invites him in what sounds almost more like an invitation than a command, which tells me he's definitely trying. "My men will have more information in the morning."

"As will mine," Mikhail says with a nod. "We have connections in Colombia and will know more about the whereabouts of Soloto." I think all of us, even Zoya and Rodion and Grandfather, are aware of the tenuous hold these two have on peace.

But I'm the one aware of my position at the crux of it all. I'm the linchpin keeping the two families from an all-out feud.

So I walk over to them and place each of my hands on one of their shoulders. "Very good, gentleman," I say with a smile. "You're playing nice. Let's keep it that way, shall we?"

I know my family would love if I came back with them. If I let them take care of me and we could catch up on all that's transpired.

But I belong here now. It's more than a sense of duty or obligation... this is my home. This is my world now as much as it's his.

Mikhail gives me a begrudging smile, and as he opens his mouth to speak, I continue.

"I'll see you tomorrow." I look to Rafail. "And Rafail and I have much to discuss."

I need closure, and so does he. We've come to the end of a long battle, dust still rising in the air, our wounded not yet tended to. We have much to attend to.

Mikhail looks at Mom. She smiles sadly and nods, but the line between her brows has softened. I turn to her and squeeze her hand. "Tomorrow," I remind her gently.

After my family's gone, Rafail turns to me. "The rest of you get some sleep. Zoya, will you prepare lunch for us?"

"Absolutely," she says, her eyes shining. "I need to get some groceries."

"Make a list, and I'll make sure you have them." He reaches for me, almost tentatively, as if he's afraid if he moves too fast, I'll evaporate. Our fingers meet. It feels like home. I step closer to him as he goes over what he needs Rodion and Semyon to do. "I'm proud of you," he finishes. "I was proud to have you by my side."

I smile at both of them. "I was too. Thank you."

And then, finally... we're alone. Everyone's gone, and it's just the two of us. I stare at the man I thought was my husband, who soon will be.

"Come here." My heart pounds.

And then I'm gathered in his arms. He holds me to him so tightly I gasp for breath before he bends, swoops me up, and lifts me into the air.

Our faces hover inches from one another. He cups my face with one hand while holding me with the other. Pulling me against him, the first brush of his lips to mine makes heat pound in my veins and my breath come in a gasp. I can feel when his control snaps, and he pours every ounce of anger and frustration, need and desire, fear and wanting into that kiss. I'm so lost in his orbit that I barely know up from down or night from day. I'm fully lost in the power of silent forgiveness.

The weight of our decisions and the promise of tomorrow are held in the kiss that takes my breath away. I taste the salt of my tears mingled with his desperation for oneness. The tension in my body begins to seep out of me bit by bit until I'm boneless and pliant to his sturdy grip.

His fingers on my jaw brand me, his lips both soft and firm. I lay my hand on his and kiss him back.

We're breathless, panting, and wrecked when we pull away, gasping for air.

"I love you," he says in a shaky whisper. "And I'm sorry. I swear to god, I'll spend the rest of my life making it up to you if only you'll stay."

I slide my hand on the side of his face, cupping the rough scruff and holding his gaze. The man I once thought invincible has a vulnerable side. "I love you," I whisper. "And I already forgave you. But you're more than welcome to spend the rest of your life making it up to me." I wink at him.

His eyes dance at me, his lips quirk up, and he tosses me over his shoulder like I'm a sack of potatoes. I squeal when his palm slaps my ass affectionately.

Even with me draped over his shoulder like a trophy, he takes the steps two at a time. The door to our room slams shut, the sound of locks being thrown final.

The air is thick with barely resolved tension, the weight of truth, confessions, and revelations rocking our world, but not so much we aren't still *us*. He's desperate to earn forgiveness, while I'm desperate to find solid footing again. I have my family back. I know who I am.

Now I need to know who *we are.*

He tosses me onto the bed, the air around us charged with raw, desperate need. We've been through the wringer, both of us, and our battles are hardly over. I lie on the bed as he towers over me, his eyes like thunder. Heat emanates from him in waves. "I'll show you how much you mean to me," he says in a hoarse whisper.

I swallow hard. "You already have."

He kneels on one knee beside me, bracing himself with his palm on the bed. His gaze travels over me as if he's only just found me, or he's afraid I'll vanish. "I hurt you," he whispers. "It doesn't matter that I thought you were someone else. None of that matters now. I heard what you said, and I feel the weight of what I've done."

I swallow hard and lick my lips. My voice is soft but confident when I reply. "Love is messy. Both our families have proven that, haven't they? But I love you anyway, and for everything that you are. I've known from the first time I opened my eyes in your world that you weren't just any man. You're fierce and dangerous and flawed. But you love me, you love your family, you're steadfast, and it's why I love you. When you love someone, you forgive them."

I see the moment when his restraint breaks. His eyes burn like flames as he stabs his fingers in my hair, fisting it as he pulls me closer. Our lips clash desperately, his body pressed against mine, caging me beneath him. His kiss is urgent and demanding, and I sigh with relief at the familiarity. A deep well of longing is wrapped in that kiss, a need to find oneness and raw vulnerability.

His tongue licks mine, sending fire through my veins. My hips rise to meet him.

He growls against my lips, his voice thick and rough. "I'll put my baby in you. I want to make you mine in every way possible."

I give myself to him fully, without reserve, without regret. "Yes," I whisper, holding his gaze. "Make me yours. I want to hear you say my name."

Holding my gaze, he whispers the words I've longed to hear. "I love you, Polina."

Our hands are frantic and desperate as we tug off my clothes and his, fabric thrown on the floor until finally, our naked bodies press against each other. I sigh at the touch of his hot, rough palm on my body. My eyes flutter closed as he lowers his mouth to my neck and kisses a trail from my collarbone to my breasts. He takes his sweet time, bridling his urgency, as he cups each breast before he drags my nipple between his teeth and suckles.

My hips undulate, and wet heat pools between my legs. My mouth drops open in a gasp as he holds my body between his hands and continues to torture and worship my nipples. I sigh into him at the feel of his hot, hard erection pressed against my naked skin.

He smells like snow-capped mountains and a field of grass, earthy and clean. I savor the sight of his powerful, muscled body and tanned skin. His weight presses on me, and I feel as if I've been swallowed whole. Every moan he elicits is met with his own growl of need as we move together, two lovers who've been through hell and back and won't ever let each other go.

His lips meet mine as he parts my legs with one knee, his hungry gaze on my body making me feel wanted. I want him inside me so much I can hardly breathe.

I love the weight of him on me, his large hands exploring my naked skin with a branding touch. He kisses first one breast, then the other, before he pushes my legs apart. With unabashed hunger, he draws in a deep breath as if drinking in my scent. With a moan of pleasure, he laps my inner thigh. My pussy spasms, and he hasn't even gone there yet.

I'm breathless, my mouth dry, as he pins my arms by my side and growls something unintelligible, a command to keep them there. His fingers dig into my thighs, spreading me so wide apart it's indecent, his gaze on me wicked as he breathes hot air on my throbbing clit.

"Shh," he whispers. "Not a word, my little swan. I asked for your forgiveness. You granted that. Now let me taste you. I *need* you."

He tongues my slick thighs with a guttural groan. I moan out loud, desperate for the wet heat of his mouth on me, as he glides thick, hot fingers in my core and presses in deep, his second hand under my ass, lifting my pussy to his mouth.

"Fucking gorgeous," he growls. "*Ty moya, Polina.* I'll give you pleasure until you scream my name and forget how to breathe. I want you to feel me over every inch of your body."

His tongue flutters over my clit. My hips jerk. My hands go to grab him, but I remember his warning and holy hell, I am not doing the slightest thing that could earn me punishment, not now, when I'm at the very gates of heaven.

He licks me again and again. I writhe and moan as the first wave of pleasure arrests me. A second shudder rocks me to my core, even as pleasure continues to build—cresting, soaring, climbing, until utter, blinding, mindless bliss consumes me.

I scream, and he lets my hands go so he can grab my hips and hold me down on earth. I tremble and writhe, fist my hands in his hair, my knees graze his beard, and his tongue doesn't stop.

I can't breathe as every muscle in my body tenses, ensnared in utter, devastating bliss.

I collapse on the bed. I can't move. I am utterly paralyzed beneath him, yet still so wildly hungry for him inside me, I whisper a heated, desperate, "Please, Rafail."

His eyes on me are wild with passion as he pushes himself above me, grabs the thick length of his cock in his fist, and glides the tip to my core. My mouth is open in anticipation, my body trembling as his hands anchor on my hips and thrusts. My head hits the pillow as the echo of ecstasy electrifies me.

"Oh god," I half sob, half plead, as he thrusts again and again, hard and demanding, pleasure echoing through my body like the beating of a drum. My skin's on fire, and my breath is coming in gasps. I feel his hardened length in me, filling me, stretching, sending spasms of pleasure to every inch of me.

Bending his mouth to my neck, he kisses me, his eyes filled with nothing short of adulation, as if he's been searching for something his entire life and… it's me. He's found it.

"Rafail," I whisper in his ear as he thrusts again.

Baby.

I want to put my baby in you.

I'll make you mine in every way possible.

I'm still riding the wave of pleasure when a second orgasm echoes the first. I lock my fingers around his neck, our sweat-slicked chests pressed together. I shudder and moan, meeting his thrusts as he grips me in his arms and comes with a low growl of pleasure, so masculine, so raw and primal, it sends me straight into another orbit. I scream beneath him as he spills inside me, his forehead pressed to mine.

"I love you," he says in a hoarse whisper as pleasure pulls me under.

"I love you," I whisper back as my eyes flutter closed. I ride the waves of pleasure while he continues to thrust. I cherish the feel of his hot seed inside me, and I welcome the branding heat of his kiss on my forehead before he falls beside me.

We're still wrapped in each other's arms when the first hint of sleep washes over me. I'm blissed out. I never knew pleasure so perfect and full, and now I've got nothing left to give. He pulls out of me, rolls me over, and tucks me against him. I'm a mess, and so is he, but I don't care. I feel the warmth of his balled-up tee between my legs. The weight of his body behind me and the heft of his arm around me as he tucks me to his chest. His nose in my hair and mouth on my neck before I fall into a deep, blissful, restful sleep.

When I wake, I frantically check for him. I'm used to him up by now, working out, checking messages and updates on his phone, staring out at the sunrise while sipping a cup of coffee. But today, he's right beside me.

I know he's awake when he strokes my shoulder, the heat of his hand travels the length of my body, and his rough fingers splay across my belly. I don't know how one can feel completely consumed by another person, but he's gone and done it.

"Morning, beautiful," he says in that sleepy-sexy growl. "Are you alright?"

I turn to face him, tucking my head into the warm space of his neck. Here, I feel protected... but for the first time, I realize this is what I've been fighting for, this is what I've wanted. *To belong*. For someone to choose me as much as I choose them.

And I mean it. The weeks of confusion, pain, and uncertainty, even as I was falling in love with my would-be husband, were worth it, every damn second, so I could revel in the bliss of being reunited.

"Never been better."

His strong hand cups my ass as I nestle in. "I smell coffee."

"Mmm," I murmur with a sleepy sigh. "Sounds delicious, but... I don't want to see anyone right now."

"Hell no. Me neither. I'll get us some."

I sigh. "I'd rather skip morning coffee than have you leave right now."

His phone dings with a text. Without letting me go, he reaches over and checks it.

"Hot damn. Zoya brought us up breakfast and coffee. Thought we could use some alone time."

"You need to buy that girl a pony."

"A pony?"

"Yeah. Or like... I don't know. A Camaro. Private island? Something. She deserves it for putting up with you all these years, then pulling her weight like a boss when we were attacked, and just everything."

He kisses my cheek. I stare up at him.

"You have no idea how much it means to me that you love them too."

I think of my brothers and smile at him. "Actually, I think that I do. Once you and Mikhail get over your pissing matches, you might even find out you get along."

He smirks. God, I love it when he smirks. "We have no choice after the wedding, so that sounds like an excellent idea."

We eat a simple breakfast of warm, buttered muffins and strong, hot coffee. I wipe butter off his chin, and he nibbles a crumb off my lip. We kiss, and soon, we're tangled in the sheets all over again.

"We have to stop this," he says with a teasing smile. "We have work to do."

"Fine," I say with a belabored sigh. "Any word on Soloto?"

"He's been sighted on his way back to Colombia."

"Good riddance," I say with a shake of my head, but he quirks a brow at me.

"You really don't think we'd let him go unpunished? After all this? Hell, Polina, even if he hadn't done what he did, the fact that he came after you is enough to sign his death warrant."

I swallow hard.

We. He said we.

He means his family and my brothers.

And yes, we're talking about the undoubtedly painful and merciless death of a man, but Soloto is a tyrant who will stop at nothing, I reason. If we don't end him, he'll only set his sights on another vulnerable target or double his efforts to retaliate against us and the destruction we brought to his men.

I nod. "Yeah," I say softly. "I do know that." I lean back against the pillows, my belly and my heart full. "Do you have any preferences about wedding ceremonies?"

His eyes shine at me. "Yes, very much so."

"Oh?"

"I want you in my sights every second until we take our vows."

"Oh, is that all?"

"Nope," he says with a possessive growl that makes me giggle. "That's not all."

"What else?"

"I want you to have everything you want. Whatever flowers or cake, dances or favors, venue or songs. It doesn't matter to me. All that matters is that you have what *you* want."

"Why's that?" I ask teasingly, tracing my finger along his jaw.

Rafail leans in and kisses my cheek before pulling back and sliding his hand under my chin. "Because, my love. I want this to be a wedding that you never, *ever* forget."

EPILOGUE

Epilogue:

POLINA

I tap the floor nervously as the soft hum of music floats through the grand hall but I hardly notice it.

My heartbeat thrums in my chest, steady and sure, as I step into the aisle. At the far end, Rafail waits, his presence commanding, his dark suit fitting him perfectly, his expression calm yet unyielding. His eyes, though—those eyes—are fixed on me, holding a warmth that no one else sees.

He's all I see for long moments. I'm not used to seeing him fidgeting or looking nervous.

Beside me, my brother Mikhail stands solid as ever, his arm linked with mine. His reassuring strength boosters me. "You're ready, Polina?" he murmurs, his deep voice low.

I nod, my lips curving into a small smile. "I am."

We step forward together. The hall quiets as every gaze turns to us, but I barely notice. My focus is on Rafail.

My husband.

It's strange to think we'll make it official now.

My fingers tighten slightly around the bouquet of flowers as I move closer, closer, until the world narrows to just him. Mikhail places my hand in Rafail's with a sigh I'm not sure he means to release, and I feel the familiar steadiness of Rafail's touch. His fingers close around mine, warm and sure.

"You're beautiful," he murmurs, his voice low, meant only for me.

"And you look terrifying." I wink, my smile soft.

His lips twitch, almost a smile, but the tenderness in his expression is enough to send my heart racing.

The priest seems to be talking quickly, as if he wants this signed, sealed, and delivered. I guess that makes all of us.

I love taking my vows to him. I love the feel of my hand in his sure one. I love the way he holds my gaze, the Russian words of promise and forever written like indelible ink on my heart.

The weight of the vows we exchange feels like an unbreakable thread weaving us together. When Rafail slides the ring onto my finger, his thumb lingers against my knuckle, a fleeting, intimate gesture that steadies me.

When it's my turn, I take his hand, my fingers trembling slightly as I slide the band into place. "You're mine now," he whispers, his voice deep and possessive.

I look into his eyes and smile. "And you're *mine*."

Two can play at *this* game.

The kiss he pulls me into is far from ceremonial but intense, raw, and filled with promises only we understand.

The crowd cheers, but I hardly hear them. I'm dimly aware of tables filled with food and servers with bottles of champagne and vodka.

"Polina!" Zoya's bright voice cuts through the crowd as she bounds toward me, nearly knocking over a server in her enthusiasm. She throws her arms around me, her petite frame vibrating with joy. "You look like a queen! The most beautiful bride ever!"

I laugh, hugging her back tightly. "And you're my little star." Pulling back, I mock scold her. "Did your brother give you permission to drink champagne?"

She puts a finger to her lips as Rodion appears beside her, his ever-present smirk firmly in place. He raises a glass. "We're celebrating!"

I smile warmly at him as he leans in closer and kisses my cheek. "Congratulations, Polina. You've officially tamed the beast."

I grimace. "For *now*. Let's not get ahead of ourselves," I reply, glancing at Rafail across the room. He's deep in conversation with Semyon and Matvei, his presence still magnetic even at a distance. "He might hear you."

Rodion grins, tipping his glass toward me. "If anyone can keep him in line, it's you."

"I'll do my best, but make no promises." I really do mean it.

As the night deepens, the lights grow warmer, and the music shifts to something slower. I'm standing near the edge of the dance floor when Rafail finds me. He holds out a hand, his eyes fixed on mine.

"Dance with me."

My brothers watch on the sidelines, vigilant but reserved. It warms my heart to see them here, to see them chatting peacefully with Rafail.

But then the crowd fades as we walk to the center of the room. I love the warm feel of his hand on my waist. We move together.

Thank *god* that stupid cast is gone. Still, I'm a bit wobbly on my feet, and it feels good to lean into him.

"You're good at this," I murmur, tilting my head up to meet his gaze.

"I've had practice," he replies, his lips curving into a faint smirk.

His hand tightens slightly on my waist, drawing me closer as we turn. "You've always been stubborn," he says, his tone teasing.

"You've always been impossible," I shoot back, a soft laugh escaping me.

"And yet, here we are."

"Yes," I whisper, my chest tightening with emotion. "Here we are."

When the dance ends, he doesn't release me. Instead, he pulls me even closer, his forehead pressed against mine.

The crowd claps and cheers, but his next words are just for me.

"You're my everything, Polina."

My breath catches, and I press my hand to his chest, reassuring even myself with the steady beat of his heart.

"I love you, Rafail."

And for the first time... I feel the certainty of forever.

"You know," I say softly, my fingers entwined with his. I swallow hard, not sure exactly how to say what I need to tell him.

"What's that?" His dark eyes bore into mine. I don't know if I'll ever get used to his intensity.

"Maybe...nine months from now or so..." I let my voice trail off. I can't really speak. I'm all choked up, unsure of how to continue.

"Nine months *what,* Polina?" His hands frame my face, his gaze glued on mine.

I don't trust myself to speak above a whisper. "Maybe... we can well and truly marry the two families together by blood."

"Do you mean...?"

I laugh, even through unshed tears, as I nod. He raises his glass as if to cheer, then lowers it and pulls me to his chest.

"It's our little secret, for now. Let's keep something that's just ours, for this little while."

My heart swells. "I *love* that. Yes, please."

He kisses my cheek. "*Za novyye nachinaniya i schastlivyye kontsy,*" he whispers.

I kiss him back and smile. "To new beginnings and happy endings."

THE END

BONUS EPILOGUE

WANT TO READ MORE OF RAFAIL AND POLINA'S STORY? SCAN THE QR CODE BELOW TO GET THE FREE BONUS EPILOGUE FOR *UNLEASHED: A DARK ENEMIES TO LOVERS BRATVA ROMANCE*!

PREVIEW

UNTAMED: A DARK FORCED MARRIAGE BRATVA ROMANCE

SYNOPSIS

Be careful what you wish for…

I don't just dream about possessive anti-heroes, I crave them. The dark, dangerous ones dripping with Bratva energy, the ones who claim you with a single look and make the world kneel just to keep you safe.

"Touch her and I'll unalive you…"?

I live for it.

"My wife…"?

My ***favorite***.

It's all a harmless fantasy, right?

Until it's not.

Rodion Kopolev, the lethal masked hero thousands of social media followers fangirl over, doesn't just embody the dark anti-heroes I love…he *is* one.

And when his obsessive focus lands on me, I feel like the heroine in one of my books.

His possessive words claim me.

His dominant touch brands me.

And when I try to run, he chases...

But when the threats of my past creep closer and I need protection from a dangerous stalker, Rodion is the devil willing to give it to me... for a price.

Turns out, when the fantasy becomes reality, it's not so harmless after all...

CHAPTER ONE

RODION

The low thrum of dance music beats steadily, like the heartbeat of California's underbelly. Neon lights slash across the dance floor, throwing jagged shadows over the dancing forms of women. I lazily watch them. I love women of all shapes and sizes. I don't care about the color of their skin or their hair, if they're short or tall, curvy or slender, or if they have glasses or freckles or whatever. Women are god's gift to men, and fuck, I miss having one in my bed. It's been way too long.

I've tried to be good. Responsible. *Mature.*

God.

California might glitter, but I miss the familiarity of home. Here, under these neon lights, I feel untouchable and detached—like a tiger prowling, watching the world from behind the bars of a cage.

I want out.

I nurse my glass of the bar's sorry excuse for vodka—some cheap, local crap that doesn't hold a candle to what we drink at home for any excuse to cheer a victory—and glance at my hands.

Fuck. For a second, I swear I see flecks of blood from the job I wrapped up earlier. But no, it's just the lights messing with me. I washed my hands in the penthouse bathroom so many times under scalding water that they're half-scalded.

Not that it matters. Rafail, my oldest brother and the pakhan of our family, rules with an iron fist and expects every job to be wrapped up neat, tied with a bow. Me? I like the reminders of what I'm capable of.

Maybe it makes me a sociopath. I like to think it keeps me human.

Got one more job to do here.

A burst of laughter gets my attention. I look over to see a table of giggling women. I shift closer to the bar, slinking into the shadows so I can watch unnoticed. Six of them, dressed in low-cut tops and short skirts, sit at a table cluttered with empty glasses. A young brunette with waist-length glossy hair shoves her phone under the nose of another woman. The second one's wearing something across her shoulders. A sash?

I squint.

Bride to Be, the gold lettering reads. Ah. A bachelorette party.

How cute.

"I'm telling you, it's the possessive ones! Like, 'I own you' energy!" A blonde giggles over her drink. Her friend rolls her eyes but doesn't argue.

My ears perk up. *"I own you energy."* What are they talking about?

I've got better things to do than eavesdrop, but I'm bored as hell and need to get laid. Rafail would fucking kill me for not sticking to the plan.

I fucked up, big time, and he sent me here to lay low while he manages the fallout. Turned out I could utilize my skills while here for the greater good of my family, so I can't lose focus now.

I look away from them.

My phone buzzes with a text.

> **Rafail**
> Heads up. Semyon got fucked over... instead of wedding bells, looks like he'll be playing clean-up crew and teaching some lessons.

Shit. It's been a year since Rafail married his wife, Polina, which meant it was time for one of us to get married. We had to. Taking the position of leadership after my father's death, Rafail wasted no time in establishing himself as the married eldest because, in the old-fashioned, cutthroat world of the Russian Bratva, a married man had more power. Respect. A man like *me*—wild and free, untamed by the love of a woman—was unfettered but unpredictable... *and* wielded less power.

We don't have time to date casually and don't have the luxury of playing around. Marriage, children, the stability of vows are a must.

Semyon was ready to marry before the ink on Rafail and Polina's marriage certificate was still wet. He didn't have the time or patience for anything less.

What *was* it about our luck, anyway? Rafail's first attempt at marriage was an epic fail, and now Semyon...

> **Rafail**
> So maybe... if you happen to find a wife in California, make it happen. At least for now. The Romanov gala is in a month, and we need a show of strength when we attend

Of fucking course. Rafail didn't "joke." Semyon's fucked-up nuptials left us with few choices, and one of them was up to *me*.

God.

Find a wife, he says. Like it's that simple. I already play his enforcer, his pawn. Now he wants me to play groom too? God forbid I don't bow to the family legacy.

I roll my eyes and lift my hand, about to order another drink, but the bartender beats me to it, sliding a glass into my outstretched palm. "Here," she says, smiling. "This is better than the vodka here. Do me a favor? You seem like a decent guy."

Little does she know. Still, I flash her the grin that melts panties and throw in a wink. Her neck flushes with heat, but she schools her expression fast, tilting her head toward the end of the bar.

I take a sip of bourbon—strong, potent, now we're getting somewhere—and follow her gesture.

"I'm not supposed to intervene unless customers cross the line," she says, her voice low. "But that asshole's been buying drinks for that table of women, even though they're clearly trying to avoid him. I don't like it. You seem decent enough. Not my business, but that guy's bad news. Maybe just park yourself down there, yeah?"

I nod. Playing silent bodyguard for a stranger isn't on my agenda, but I push off the bar anyway, drink in hand, and head down the row.

The bar thrums with a low bass. The air reeks of expensive cologne, tequila, and cheap sex. I shake my head. I hate California. Too many rules, too many people who thought money made them untouchable.

But tonight isn't about me—it never is. I'm here for the Bratva, for my family. For Rafail's newly born son, so small he can't even hold his little head up yet. For my parents, who were buried way too young, with their lives still ahead of them.

I'm here because Rafail and family honor demanded it.

One target's an arrogant little bastard who thought he could cheat the Russian mafia and walk away. And I came here to remind him how far loyalty went when it was wrapped in barbed wire.

I know immediately who the bartender's talking about. I give the businessman in a wrinkled suit a once-over. He's got one of those comb-over hairstyles to mask his receding hairline and a gold chain around his neck. I glance at his hand, where the indentation on his finger indicates a wedding band recently removed.

Sigh. So predictable.

I'm not a hero. Hell, I'm barely human some days. But I know the lines a man doesn't cross. And when I see this guy crowding her, all I can think is *I've crossed too many lines already. This one? Not tonight.*

He leans across the table and pushes a drink to one of the women.

She shakes her head. "No, thank you."

"I bought it for you," the chubby douchebag says, pushing it over to her again. Oh, for the love of...Rafail would get on a plane just to throat punch me if he knew I was getting involved, but I can't help it.

There's nothing I like more than helping a damsel in distress. *And* it's gotten me laid more times than I can count.

My voice is low when I meet his eyes and push the drink back. "Hey, buddy. She said no. Drink it yourself. Better yet, why don't you leave her the fuck alone and don't come back?" I feel their eyes on me but focus on this guy and this guy alone.

Beady eyes narrow on me as he draws himself up to his full height. *Aww.* He thinks he can get away with it. I almost feel sorry for the poor bastard.

I'm easily a head taller than him, with one more tool in my kit he probably doesn't have: *I* don't care if I spill another man's blood tonight.

"Who the fuck asked you to get involved?" the businessman asshole says. "I bought her a drink. She wanted one."

"I did *not*!" I turn to look at her and narrowly miss getting cold-cocked by this asshole. I swivel, grab his wrist just in time, and shake my head with a little *tsk*.

"You really shouldn't have done that," I say in a whisper, twisting his hand back until pain dances in his eyes and he grits his teeth. "I promise you. You're going to regret that. Why don't we take a little walk."

Still gripping his wrist, I drag him toward me and discreetly shove him in front of me.

"I'm-I'm sorry," he begins, but I shake my head.

"Too late for apologies, my man," I say, my temper rising. "You disrespected a woman."

I follow few laws, but *never disrespect a woman* is one of them.

As we head toward the exit, I can hear the table of giggling bachelorettes.

"Oh my god, he's like one of the book guys."

"Did you see those muscles?"

"He looks like the video mafia queen posted!"

Mafia... what? I catch a glimpse at the screen. What the fuck is *that*? I try to take another look, but my friend, the predator, tries to use my distraction to his advantage and wheedle out of my grip.

Nah.

I wrap my hands around the back of his neck and help him focus on doing what the fuck I say. The neon *Exit* sign flashes in the center of the doorway above a dark hall.

"This is what you're gonna do," I tell him as we near the door. "You're gonna get the fuck out of here and pretend tonight never happened. You'll pretend we never talked, that you never tried to push yourself on a woman who said no."

Blood thrums in my veins, molten lava teeming with destruction.

"You can't—"

I lean in close. He's half a breath away from meeting my fist. "I have a knife in my pocket and a gun in a holster at my back. I can and will." I hold him in my right hand so I can discreetly flash the sign of the Bratva, a universal tat that every man of our family gets when he's sixteen years old.

I watch his eyes widen in recognition. Good. I kick open the door. "Good riddance," I mutter as I shove him out and slam the door behind him.

The bartender catches my attention and gives me a thumbs up. The women giggle and wave at me, but I only jerk my head and sit back down at the other end of the bar. I shoot my cousin Matvei a text.

Dude, you see these mafia posts these girls online are raving about? tf?

The response comes immediately.

Matvei
I was just gonna ask you the same thing. Got tagged in a post last night, man. This is amazing.

I smile, already relieved. His timing is impeccable. I don't know if I'd say it's *amazing,* but it's amusing, definitely.

I tap the screen as I sit back at the bar and drink. He sends a group text.

Jesus, Matvei. Leave Raf out of it. We leave him out of anything remotely fun.

Matvei
You guys see this shit online?

I roll my eyes and play dumb.

I'm swimming in shitbags in California. My brain is fried. Maybe I need to find one of those oxygen bars they have or something. The fuck are you talking about?

Matvei
All those girls online are drooling over mafia men.

Ice hits my teeth, and I shove the glass back on the bar while I glance at the girls who are whispering to each other and casting discreet glances my way.

Seymon
what the fuck are you going on about now?

Matvei
Social media, dumbass. Apparently they're drooling over dangerous, tattooed men who do dirty things to them and wife them up.

I pop an ice cube in my mouth like I'm eating a bowl of popcorn. This is entertaining, but I need real food that's not in the form of liquid and ninety proof. My gaze falls on the table of scantily clad, giggling women.

This time, I take a closer look.

It's some video with a masked man holding an ax. He's swinging it with force, cutting wood in the dead of winter. Bare-chested. Fuck. Who *does* that? Wear a coat, fuckwit. Even my nips ache just thinking about that frozen hellscape.

Americans romanticize the strangest shit.

My phone buzzes again, and I consider flushing it in the nearest bathroom when a video pops up from Matvei.

I click the triangle. I have to download a fucking app just to see the damn thing and immediately have to turn the volume down on my phone when some stupid dance music blares on the screen.

It's a girl—no, a woman—talking about her fantasies of dark, possessive mafia men. It should've been absurd, laughable. But there was something about the way she said it, her tone laced with teasing vulnerability. Like she wanted to be swept away but couldn't trust anyone enough to let it happen.

And she's... crying. I know it's staged. I know it's just for show, but something in me cracks at the sight of a woman in tears. My hands clench into fists.

Who do I need to punish?

Her caption reads:

> **"Who else dreams of being kidnapped and 'tortured' by a hot, billionaire, masked mafia man? Asking for a friend."**

My lips curve into a smirk. No tall order, lady. Though... I mean... I tick off all *those* boxes.

I just need a mask. That's easy enough.

Matvei
This shit's gone viral.

Semyon
Is this a bad joke?

Rafail
What the fuck is this shit?

Matvei
You guys need to listen up. There are MAFIA THIRST TRAPS. They want us. Like, really want us.

Rafail, you're not keeping him busy enough.

But just for the fuck of it, I click the link.

And I watch. A gorgeous blonde with wide blue eyes and

thick lashes licks her lips while the right side of her screen shows a masked man with tats and muscles.

I roll my eyes. He's fucking scrawny compared to *my* brothers, and did she really think those pecs were real? Nah. I can tell from here he used a filter like a goddamn fucking pussy.

I almost shut the thing and get another drink when she starts fanning herself with her phone—no, it wasn't a phone, it's much too big for a phone. I look closer. Is that an e-reader?

That's when I notice the wall of books behind her, like some sort of fucking shrine to a bookstore, but it isn't just any bookshelf. They're color-coordinated in a rainbow, twinkling pink lights entangled with greenery, making it look festive.

"This is all I want, girls," she says, wiping a fat tear from her cheek. "I work sixty-hour weeks at a thankless job, and when I come home? I want *this guy* waiting for me." She lowers her voice. "Is that too much to ask?"

Huh.

I scroll.

And I scroll.

And I scroll.

I feel my lips curve into a smirk, the kind that typically makes my enemies rethink their decisions.

They want... *us*?

They don't. No, they really, *really* don't.

They think they want us—the bloodstained hands, the barbed-wire promises, the wolves lurking just beyond the storybook light. But what they want is the illusion of us, not the raw, vicious truth. No woman wants my calloused, bloodstained hand in her hair—or, more accurately, wrapped around her throat, pinning her to my headboard, or—heh. Maybe that *was* a good drink.

I tap my finger against my jaw. I still have a job to do before I go back home, but January in Moscow is frigid as fuck, and if I'm honest, I might not want to move here, but this weather feels downright balmy. And it's nice not having to put up with the daily discerning eye and constant criticism of my eldest brother.

I look back over at the giggling party girls. They're glued to their screens, their expressions dreamy as they scroll thirst traps who make me cringe—tattoos, leather jackets, bare chests...

I can't help but snort when a few of the videos have *three* men, ropes in hand, masks hiding fuck knows what, with a low growl of a man's voice. *"We're coming for you. And when we find you, beware..."*

It's so damn *fake.*

Obviously, a real man didn't fucking *share.* This is the stupidest shit I ever—

My hand hovers over the *x* at the top of the page, ready to shut it down, when I see... *her.*

Fiery red hair tied back in a thick ponytail, a mischievous spark in her jade-green eyes.

She doesn't look like the typical influencer—no heavy filters, no plastic sheen, no puffy little microphone next to her glossy lips.

She looks... *real.* Strong. And even though she's wearing a plain white top and a pair of jeans, the girl fills them *out.* She has the body of a gymnast, tightly wound and powerful. My breath slows as I take her in—sparkling green eyes, a strength in her every movement that makes my fingers itch to touch her, to feel if she's as real as she looks.

"Girls," she says, shaking her head.

Girls? Was she completely unaware of the absolute magnetic pull a woman like her had on a man like me?

I'm instantly, irrationally filled with rage toward any other man who sets eyes on her. She's unlike anyone I've ever seen before.

"Stop what you're doing *right now* and read this book." She holds up a black and gold book with raised lettering, the edges sprayed gold, as she flips through it. "You've never heard of it before. No one has. It's unlike anything I've ever read before. And this book." She shakes her head and bites her lip.

Bites her lip.

That single motion her teeth grazing her lip—ignites something primal. It's the smallest tell, but it screams louder than any word: she wants to surrender, even if she doesn't know it yet. And I'd make damn sure she learned what that meant.

I swallow hard and watch.

She lowers her voice to a whisper. I hold my breath, mesmerized by her voice, the way she talks, even the way her fingers grip around the book in her hand. I imagine what it would be like to have those hands splayed over my body or pinned in one hand while I fisted her gorgeous hair in the other. I'd fuck her right against that bookshelf until she screamed for mercy... until she knew the difference between fiction and reality and never again fell for a goddamn book boyfriend when she belonged to *me*.

"This looks tame, doesn't it? A poor school teacher on holiday in the wild Scottish moors. A single father, mourning the loss of his wife while navigating the world alone..." Her voice drops. "Only *this* guy's in the mafia, and he'll stop at *nothing*..." Her voice drops even lower. "*Nothing* to claim her."

She shakes her head. I hold my breath. She fingers the golden edges, and my dick comes to *life*.

"When I tell you there's *no line this man won't cross for* her..." She shakes her head as if completely overcome with emotion. "Chases her in the woods... kidnaps her in the back of his car... fucks her blindfolded in an abandoned warehouse while suspending her from—"

She covers her mouth as if she's said too much.

"You'll have to take my word for it."

My mouth is dry. This woman is *completely* unaware of what she's playing with. She doesn't realize the line she's walking—romanticizing the very thing that could destroy her.

"Careful what you wish for," I mutter under my breath before I down the rest of my bourbon.

The bartender slides me another without being asked. I raise the glass in silent thanks before my gaze flicks back to my mark, the reason I'm here.

Still busy with the blonde, still oblivious.

All I have to do tonight is case him and confirm he's cheating on his wife before I blackmail the fuck out of him and extort him for ten times what he owes us.

Easy.

I exhale and stare back at my phone as if rewarding myself for a job well done. My mouth dry, I click the *follow* button at the top of the page and check the messages that have been buzzing in my pocket like an angry swarm of bees.

> **Rafail**
> I don't know what stupid nonsense you're spending your time watching, but if you don't do what I fucking tell you, I'll show you exactly where I'll shove your goddamn phone

Rafail is impatient on a good day. Sleep-deprived, daddy of a newborn Rafail is a fucking animal.

Well, he can get mad at us all he wants. The reality is, *he* is happily married while Semyon nurses his wounds and plans for option B, and I'm thinking of

No. I am thinking nothing.

I slip my phone in my pocket. I can't afford distractions,

least of all ones wrapped in unrealistic, staged internet fantasies. This is my job, my duty, and—

My phone buzzes.

With a growl of annoyance, I pull it out again. My heart flips over.

It's a notification. I follow exactly one person online, and here she is, and—oh my god. She's in her pajamas.

I swallow hard.

She's in *bed,* a bed with a sturdy headboard and a thick comforter while she playfully bites her lip while holding a paperback book.

She's so damn cute. If only she knew how far-removed real life was from her stories. Princes don't exist in our world—only wolves and their prey.

Still, my fingers hover over the screen. A stupid idea creeps into my mind, one that Rafail would probably punch me for.

What if I... I polish off my drink and look around. Dim lighting. It's perfect.

I open my camera, position the phone to catch the glint of my pistol holster under my suit jacket, and hit record.

The video's quick—just enough to show the weapon and a flash of stubble and a smirk. I add a caption:

Careful what you wish for @dreammafiaqueen.

It's a reckless, dangerous game. One that could unravel

everything. But as the video uploads, I feel like I've stepped off the edge, daring her to follow.

And yet, as I hit *post* and slide the phone away, I can't help the laugh that rumbles in my chest. Self-deprecating, bitter, but amused all the same. She likes Bratva? I'll call her bluff.

"I am going to regret that," I mutter.

I don't do distractions. Not when blood is on the line. But as I slip through the crowd, heading back to the hotel, my hand brushes the cold steel of the knife strapped to my hip, and I find myself wondering.

What would a woman like her taste like—innocence or fire?

And what would she do if she really met her fantasy man in real life?

My phone dings with a notification. I frown at the screen then click it as a slow, wicked grin spreads across my face.

Reply from @dreammafiaqueen.

WANT TO FIND OUT WHAT HAPPENS NEXT? ORDER YOUR COPY OF "UNTAMED: A DARK FORCED MARRIAGE BRATVA ROMANCE" BY SCANNING THE QR CODE BELOW. AVAILABLE ON JANUARY 24TH!

BRATVA
KINGS
UNTAMED
USA TODAY BESTSELLING AUTHOR
JANE HENRY

Jane HENRY

Romance for 'good girls' who love bad boys

Fueled by dark chocolate and even darker coffee, USA Today bestselling author Jane Henry writes what she loves to read – character-driven, unputdownable romance featuring dominant alpha males and the powerful heroines who bring them to their knees. She's believed in the power of love and romance since Belle won over the beast, and finally decided to write love stories of her own.

Scan the QR Code below to receive Jane's Newsletter & be notified of upcoming new releases & special offers!

Be sure to visit me at www.janehenryromance.com, too!

Printed in Great Britain
by Amazon

59528552R00218